Gideon looked too good to be true.

His brawny shoulders and arms made Carin wonder what he did for a living. Something that required strength on a daily basis, she would guess.

The blanket that was wrapped around him did little to cover his muscular chest. As he rubbed a towel on his clean hair, he looked at her, waiting for her to speak. His hazel eyes bore into hers.

Carin's heart thumped out warning signals. He was rugged and raw, and he filled her cabin like he belonged here.

Yet there was something odd about the tall, handsome stranger who had ridden in with the sunrise....

Dear Reader,

What could be more romantic *and* more mysterious than the man of your dreams traveling through time to meet up with you and share your life? We're especially delighted to bring you another book in the TIMELESS LOVE program, which showcases these much-loved time-travel stories. Stories you told us you want more of.

Here Patricia Werner returns to Intrigue with the story of Gideon Avarest—a wanted man for whom a twist of fate brings him face-to-face with the woman of his destiny. But has he outrun the bandits at his heels?

We hope you enjoy *Ride the Thunder* as much as you have loved the other exciting books in the TIMELESS LOVE promotion.

Happy reading!

Sincerely,

Debra Matteucci
Senior Editor And Editorial Coordinator
Harlequin Books
300 East 42nd Street.
New York, New York 10017

Ride the Thunder
Patricia Werner

Harlequin Books

TORONTO • NEW YORK • LONDON
AMSTERDAM • PARIS • SYDNEY • HAMBURG
STOCKHOLM • ATHENS • TOKYO • MILAN
MADRID • WARSAW • BUDAPEST • AUCKLAND

For Kay, Chris D., Chris J., Alice, Janet and the rest of the Monday-night critique group who helped. Also for the members of the Gothic round robin, who keep the flame burning for romantic suspense.
Thanks to Sharon, who knew when the rains come, to Laura and Barbara who pointed me in the right direction in Glenwood Springs, to Scott and Tina for research and wildflowers, and to Karen and Katrin who knew how to spot a thief.

ISBN 0-373-22431-1

RIDE THE THUNDER

Copyright © 1997 by Patricia Werner

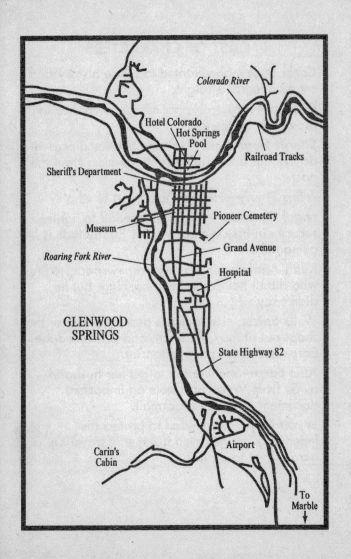

Colorado River

Hotel Colorado
Hot Springs
Pool

Railroad Tracks

Sheriff's Department

Pioneer Cemetery

Museum

Grand Avenue

Roaring Fork River

Hospital

GLENWOOD
SPRINGS

State Highway 82

Carin's
Cabin

Airport

To
Marble

CAST OF CHARACTERS

Carin Sage—She wanted to revise history and set the records straight.

Gideon Avarest—He got a second chance to prove his innocence.

Sheriff Hugh Cole—He searched for a present-day villain but couldn't fight travelers from the past.

Julius Eberly—He was guilty, but of what?

Nigel Henshaw—When he needed to tighten security in his ski resort, Julius Eberly took it personally.

Keith Armbruster—He was a newspaper editor who didn't believe in Earp bashing, but he didn't say why.

Wells Spicer—He took the depositions after the shoot-out at the OK corral, and prevented the Earps from ever coming to trial.

Allie Earp—She wanted to get her husband away from Wyatt and stole an important document to use as blackmail.

Wyatt Earp—He needed to protect his legendary image, even if it meant traveling across time to do it.

Chapter One

December 1881

Weather rolled in over Tombstone, but it hardly mattered to Gideon Avarest, curled up on his hard bunk in the city jail. Iron bars set in the little square window were all that shielded him from the gathering storm outside. Jagged lightning cut through the dark sky, but Gideon didn't bother to turn over when the rain started to come in. They could hang him just as well wet or dry in the morning.

An iron key scraped in the far door. Hinges squeaked.

"Visitor for you, Avarest," said the tinny voice of Deputy Billy Breakenridge. "You got ten minutes with your cousin. You sure you want to be alone up here, ma'am?"

"I'll be fine, thank you, deputy." It was a woman's voice, soft-spoken but firm.

Gideon turned his shaggy blond head to look into the shadow outside his jail cell. The row of six cells was lit by a single kerosene lantern swinging from a beam. The small woman stood with her back to the light, so he couldn't see her face. Gideon swung his booted feet off the bunk and onto the floor, squinting at the still shadowy woman, wrapped up in layers of clothing with a slat bonnet covering part of her face. He sighed, ran a hand through his hair. He didn't know any women in this town, and he didn't have any cousins.

"You just knock on this door when you want out, ma'am," said the deputy. "I gotta lock it shut."

"Thank you, I'll be all right."

Young Billy Breakenridge ambled back to the door. It scraped shut behind him, the key rattling in the lock again.

Gideon stood up as the woman's white hands reached through the bars motioning for him to come closer.

"Who—?"

"Hush," she interrupted in a low urgent voice. "We've little time. You don't know me. I'm Allie Earp, Virgil's wife. Here, take this and put it on."

She opened her voluminous cape and unbuckled a full leather cartridge belt. The butt of a revolver stuck out of the holster. She handed it to him through the bars. Then she lifted her careworn face, and for the first time looked him in the eye. He peered down at the sharp blue eyes in a face that had seen a lot of hard living. A straight, snub nose sat atop firm lips, and straight dark brows did nothing to soften her demeanor.

"It's got a full round and plenty more in the belt," she said.

He wasted no time buckling the weapon on. "Why're you doing this?"

She gave a grunt as she bent and pulled gray gingham skirts high enough to remove a short-barrel Peacemaker .45 from a holster tied to her calf. "I know when a man's been framed. Virgil don't allow me downtown, so I weren't in the courtroom. But I heard enough in my own parlor to know the judge's in the pay of that no-good Wyatt."

The fierce, determined set of her chin told him she knew what she was doing.

"Don't waste time askin' questions. That deputy'll be

back in a minute, and it'll be your only chance. I'll get him over here next to the cell. The rest'll be up to you."

"I thank you for your kindness, Missus Earp. You happen to know if Sheriff Behan's downstairs? I need to know if I gotta fight my way out."

"'Course, he ain't. He's over at the Crystal Palace with that actress he squires around. Quick now, don't miss your chance."

Gideon nodded, then stepped back against the wall, gun in hand. Allie knocked on the locked door, then stood where she'd be behind it when the deputy came. The key rattled, the door squeaked, and as Billy came through, she jabbed her gun into his skinny back.

"Up against the bars, mister, and quiet-like, this gun's loaded."

He grunted in surprise and raised his hands. "What the…?"

Gideon got to the bars before him, his six-shooter aimed at the deputy's chest as he reached through and grabbed the deputy's gun followed by the keys. In an instant, he had the cell open, shoved Billy inside, and then gagged him with his own bandanna. The puny deputy was no match for someone of Gideon's strength and size. The enterprising Allie handed a length of rope she'd brought to Gideon and held the gun while he tied Billy's hands behind his back. There was enough rope left to tie his feet.

After locking him in the cell, Allie put on her long cloak again. They made for the door, pausing to listen for sounds below.

"Deputy's horse is in front," she told Gideon. "You'd best put on the sheriff's duster, too, else you'll catch a chill in this storm. I saw it hanging on a peg downstairs."

"I'll be fine, ma'am. You sure you'll be all right?"

She gave a nod. "Deputy thinks I'm your cousin. No

one'll know better. I'll make my way home now. Virge'll never know I've gone out. He and the boys don't come home till late. You go on.''

He thanked the brave little lady again, and they went cautiously down the stairs. In the jail office, he took her advice and put on the long duster and his own felt hat, pulling the brim low over his wide brow. Allie went out the door before him, pausing to glance up and down the boardwalk. She gave a quick nod and walked on. Gideon knew he owed the woman his life.

He took the time to use one of the keys he'd lifted off the deputy to unlock a drawer and retrieve his personal belongings. There was money in coin and currency because he'd just gotten paid before the holdup and the trial. His rifle cartridges, a silver-cased pocket watch, all of which he dropped into the deep pockets of the duster. A bone-handled knife was sheathed in its leather scabbard. Then he lifted down his own Winchester .44 rifle from where they'd stowed it on pegs on the wall, and slid it into its buckskin scabbard.

A moment later, Gideon walked outside, stepped down to the muddy street, and spoke low to the deputy's saddled piebald gelding waiting there. The horse whickered, but Gideon rubbed its nose, reassuring it. Not wanting to draw attention, he took his time strapping the rifle scabbard to the saddle. Then he untied the reins and mounted up. Rain was coming down steady now and trickled off his felt hat brim. He turned the horse into the street and out of the way of folks making a dash across the wide street to get in out of the weather.

Still not drawing any attention, he rode slowly across Fourth Street. Piano music drifted out from the saloons and hotels that lined Allen Street. Just then boisterous laughter erupted from the Oriental Saloon and Gambling Palace, as a group of men staggered out onto the boardwalk. They wore high-peaked black Stetsons, long black frock coats, with string ties dangling down white shirt-fronts, and black trousers over black, high-heeled boots.

In a glance, he recognized the notorious Earp gang, the men who'd framed him for robbery and murder on the Kinnear and Company stage that had left Tombstone last month with eighty thousand dollars of silver bullion.

As Wells Fargo's most trusted agent, Gideon rode shot-gun on the stage. He would have been dead, shot by the gang that had held them up where they'd slowed for the grade, but for the fact that he'd switched places with Bud Philpot, the driver, to give the man a chance to warm his hands. The gang shot Philpot, who was riding shotgun, robbed the passengers and got the bullion.

And after Gideon had brought Philpot's body in, he was arrested and accused of changing places with Philpot pur-posely, so the gang could murder him and rob the stage. The bullion was never found and the gang's disguises had protected them, even though Gideon had recognized at least two of the Earp gang.

But there was no time to nurse his grudge or plot his revenge. He'd seen through the disguises of the men who got away, and they were carousing on the boardwalk in front of the Oriental Saloon now. He turned his face away and nudged the horse into a trot, mud splashing as he went.

He was almost to Fifth Street when behind him foot-steps pounded along the boardwalk from the direction of the jail and a voice yelled out, "Prisoner's loose. Avarest broke jail."

Gideon didn't wait for anything else but slammed his heels into the horse and bent into the rain to gallop out of town. Lightning lit up the road, and at the same time illuminated him for his pursuers. Thunder cracked over-head.

"There he goes," shouted another voice. "That's the deputy's piebald." Voices were raised and the men clambered down from the boardwalk to their horses.

Gideon rode for his life. Lightning and thunder were only split seconds apart, and he wished for his own horse instead of the deputy's.

Gunshots erupted behind him, and when another flash of lightning showed him where he was going, he left the road. The horse bolted, and Gideon held on. He was in as much danger of the horse stumbling in a hole as he was from his pursuers. A rock outcropping was just ahead, and the ground rose beneath him as the frightened horse slowed on the incline. Bullets whizzing past told him the posse had seen him leave the road and followed in hot pursuit.

"Whoa, boy," Gideon said as he halted the horse behind some rocks and dismounted.

He hastily wrapped the reins around a bush and dragged the rifle from its scabbard on the saddle. Then he took a position in a cleft of rocks. "Come on, you bastards, I'll pick you off one by one if that's what you want."

Gideon was no killer, but if it was that or a rope around his neck in the morning, he would aim for the heart. These con artists had pulled the wool over the eyes of the citizens of Tombstone one too many times, and he didn't take to their likes.

He cocked the rifle, rested it on the rock. In a second, lightning showed him four riders coming abreast across the sagebrush desert. Wyatt was on the far left, his younger brother Morgan next to him, then Virgil, who wore a silver star on his chest, and last, the skinny, half-dead Doc Holliday.

"There he is," shouted Wyatt. "Shoot to kill."

Doc Holliday's shotgun blasted in Gideon's direction, and he ducked as the shot sprayed over the rocks.

He waited for the next flash of lightning and got off a shot in the clap of thunder that followed. The four men fired as they galloped closer. Gideon cursed the darkness. It was no good shooting when he couldn't see. But the storm had followed them, and with the next round of lightning and thunder the ground shook. He couldn't hear their fire now, even when he saw the guns smoking.

Then a bolt of lightning split the air between them, and heaven and hell seemed to meet in a crash that moved the earth. Gideon staggered backward from the force of it, rain gushing in a sheet that blinded him to everything. But he grasped his rifle and crouched, ready. The posse would reach the rocks in seconds if they hadn't lost their footing.

"Come on, you bastards," he cursed as he stood up and moved to the side. If he had to die, he'd take as many of them with him as he could.

He aimed the rifle, and as the next glare of lightning lit up the desert, he saw them all. Wyatt and Morgan coming around the rocks on horseback to his left. Virgil and Doc Holliday, dismounted and leading their horses around the boulders on the other side. Their guns were drawn, and as soon as they saw him, they aimed. But the thunder crashed around their ears, throwing them all off balance.

Gideon clutched his rifle as he flew backward. His head hit something hard. An acute pain throbbed. Then he rolled downward across the ground. He clutched at the mesquite and sagebrush, but he kept on going, down, down, out over empty space, whirling, spinning, until everything went black, and he was lost in a void of time.

Chapter Two

"Get up now, slow, easy. I've got your guns. Don't try anything."

Carin Sage eased forward, her rifle aimed at the man sprawled on the ground by some rocks near the edge of her Glenwood Springs property. She'd seen him move, so she knew he wasn't unconscious. He was dressed like an old-time cowboy in a long duster, straight-cut jeans, and square-toed, scuffed boots. And there was a piebald horse a few feet away from him. The man was big and brawny with blond hair that came below his ears, hair now tangled from rain and dirt, which made her wonder how long he'd been out here.

Lying there with his eyes closed, he looked like he was waiting for a good-looking woman to kiss him awake. But his handsome face with its squarish jaw didn't fool her. She just bet he could handle those guns she'd taken off him and set a few yards out of reach. Carin had a right to be jumpy. Whoever he was, this man might be the one who broke into her cabin last night.

Gideon shook his head, his eyes still closed. His joints felt stiff, and his hand went to the painful lump on the back of his head.

"Ahhhhgh," he groaned as he tried to stir. He blinked once in the bright sunlight and closed his eyes again. Too much all at once, and his head ached something fierce.

"That's it, buster, get up nice and easy."

He realized it was a woman ordering him up and opened one eye to see the business end of a Winchester rifle aimed straight at him about six yards away. At that distance even a woman couldn't miss, so he held up his hands then rolled onto one elbow, the muddy duster twisting under him as he moved.

"Aahhh," he said, one hand going to his head again. He squinted up at the woman. Then it all came back.

He looked up at the sky, clear blue, with a few fleecy clouds drifting over the long green mountain ridge not far away. A whicker made him turn his head to see the deputy's piebald horse, pawing the ground, its reins tied around a low juniper branch.

"What the devil," he muttered as he staggered to his feet to stare down at a narrow mountain valley with a sprawling settlement below. "Where the hell…?"

"This way," snapped the woman, and she took a few steps in his direction, small rocks rolling from under her feet.

He straightened up again, arms wide open at his sides as he squinted at her. She was dressed like a boy, in tight denim pants and man's shirt, with a big silver buckle on her belt. But even with his head pounding, he could see rounded hips in the extra-tight jeans, and her long hair shone in the sun. What was she doin' dressed that way? They eyed each other long enough for him to see her green eyes flash. Her sandy-colored brows furrowed over the rifle sights.

"Where'd you come from?" He started to reach for his hat, which lay on the ground.

But the blast from her rifle made him jerk his hand

away as the hat skittered from the bullet, and the horse whinnied and reared.

He raised his hands again. "You part of the posse?"

"I said, don't move." She lifted the rifle another notch.

"Yes, ma'am."

His eyes found the Colt .45 that Allie had brought him and the rifle he'd fired at the Earps. Both guns were now on the ground some distance to his left. This time he used a gentler voice. "Look, miss, I ain't armed. You got my guns."

"What's your name?" She jutted her chin at him.

"Gideon Avarest." He winced at the pain when he moved his head. "Came from Tombstone last night. Don't know how I got here."

He glanced around warily to make sure, but the other men were nowhere in sight. He still felt as if a hammer were pounding behind his eyes, but he began to take in details. This was no desert. Red sandstone was everywhere. Junipers, pines, and some kind of white-barked tree he didn't know. He must've been knocked out long enough for someone to carry him up to the mountains. The horse's patched black-and-white coat was extra spotted from the mud splatter, and the duster Gideon wore dripped water onto the dirt at his feet. So where was the posse?

"Look, ma'am, all I want to know is what happened to the posse chasin' me and how I got here. Then I'll be on my way. I ain't meanin' any harm."

From her position a little way up the hill from him, the woman was staring warily at him. She kept the rifle aimed at his heart, its wooden stock braced against her shoulder.

"Did you break into my cabin last night, mister?"

"What cabin?" He glance up the hill behind her. "I didn't break into any cabin."

"Well, even if you didn't break in, you're trespassing,"

she said in a no-nonsense tone. "My name's Carin Sage, and you're on private property. Now unbuckle that cartridge belt and throw it to the ground. Slowly."

She stepped sideways on the rocky slope, keeping the gun steady as he shed the cartridge belt. "I'm gonna circle around. You walk straight up the slope with your hands high in the air."

Gideon did as he was told and started walking up the hill. "You homestead up here alone?" he asked over his shoulder.

"Go on up to the house," she ordered instead of answering his question. "How do you spell your last name?"

Gideon still didn't know how he'd come to land in the mountains, but the posse who'd chased him out of Tombstone seemed to have disappeared. He didn't see any immediate danger. He could disarm the woman if he really wanted to, but there was no sense in frightening her if she wasn't any part of this. If she was, and this was another setup by the Earp gang, he'd find out soon enough. Instinct told him to be careful.

Her new log cabin was surrounded by a split-rail fence. A big red barn sat off to the right, not far from the trees. He noticed there wasn't any smoke coming out of the chimney, and the log construction of her cabin was different from any he'd ever seen. The logs were all the same size, and they gleamed. He couldn't figure it out.

The gate stood open, so he went on through. He shook his head, trying to help clear it.

"I asked you how you spelled your name."

"Why do ya want to know?" He turned to look at her again.

She tossed her blond hair out of her eyes. "Well, somebody might be looking for you. We ought to give them some help."

That made him wary and he studied her. Just then a black-and-white spotted dog with long, floppy ears dashed around the corner and barked.

"Quiet, Shag," she said, moving the gun so the dog wasn't in range.

The dog gave a soft whine, then trotted up to Gideon and wagged his tail.

"Attaboy," said Gideon and started to squat down to pet the dog. Then he hesitated.

He turned to look at the puzzled young woman, who lowered the rifle just a notch. She made quite a sight standing there, nice figure shown off by those tight jeans and a man's denim shirt. Her face was prettier than any he'd seen lately, and her hair was wavy and shiny gold, kinda tangled. Those green eyes sure gave off a lot of fire, but there was something else in them too now, like curiosity.

Gideon held out his hand easy-like, as the dog came to lick him. He patted the dog and talked to it.

CARIN'S WARINESS eased. Shag was a good watchdog. He wouldn't act that friendly to a man who'd broken into the cabin and ransacked her office last night. The dog had been in the car with her when they'd come back and had nearly caught the intruders. Shag had picked up their scent and chased them up the mountain. She'd followed with the rifle. But she'd called Shag off when they got into the trees, rather than risk being jumped with no backup or having her dog shot.

Whoever had broken into her cabin had not only smashed her computer-hard drive and stolen articles she'd been writing for the weekly *Glenwood News*, but had also run off with her cellular phone. So she'd have to get her prisoner into the cabin before she could call her pal Hugh Cole, the Garfield County sheriff.

The rugged, broad-shouldered cowboy moved stiffly and seemed disoriented enough to have fallen off his horse. But he might be faking it. He was muddy, too, as if he'd been out in the rain last night.

Her cabin lay just outside Glenwood Springs city limits, so she'd called the sheriff's office, and Hugh had come around last night with Deputy Pete McGuire to check out the scene of the break-in. That's when they'd figured out there'd been more than one culprit. They'd lost the intruders' trail and hadn't been able to make casts of shoe prints because of the rain. There weren't any fingerprints in the cabin. Evidently the men had worn gloves.

Hugh and two deputies had spent time measuring, photographing, and sketching. They'd carefully collected shells left from some shots fired at her computer and some slugs that had lodged in the door frames. Outside they'd been unable to find any distinguishable vehicle tracks. Oddly enough, there had been some indentations in the earth that could only have been left by horses.

"Look, mister," she said, still trying to sound tough, although Shag's reaction and her own instincts were beginning to make her a little less wary. "I don't know if you had anything to do with my break-in, but I'm going to call the sheriff. Then we'll get you to the clinic in town so the doc can have a look at you. If you've got a concussion or something, they'll want to take X rays."

She crossed the yard to the tiny porch and watched the big stranger play with her dog. His mouth relaxed, and his hazel eyes softened. Hazel eyes with streaks of a darker brown, she'd noticed when she'd had him in the gun sights, and tiny lines at the edges of his eyes and at the corners of his mouth. She felt a slight dip in her pulse at his strong, appealing, slightly injured looks, but she ignored it.

The easy drawl in his voice and the way he staggered

a little as he got his bearings was real convincing, but
Carin wasn't ready to lower her guard any. Maybe she
was making a mistake. From his western dress, he might
be joining a rodeo or some show in town and had just
had an accident on the way. He did seem muddled. Maybe
the fall had shaken up his brains, and that was why he
didn't know where he was. But that didn't explain what
he was doing on her property. Well, she would call the
doctor after she called the sheriff.

The cowboy glanced up and saw her watching him. He
touched Shag's dog collar, and the dog tag flashed in the
sun. "You got a badge on your dog?"

Carin blinked, but didn't answer. Even though Shag
liked him, she still didn't know who he was. Maybe he
was playing with her mind. Or maybe something else was
wrong.

"You need to get out of those wet clothes," she finally
decided. "Hang your hat and coat out here to dry."

She lowered the rifle, keeping it handy in case she decided to shoot again. She watched him stand up slowly
as his gaze drifted over the log cabin and the barn.

He shrugged and came slowly toward the porch. Then
he hung his hat on the pair of antlers fixed beside the
door. The same for the duster.

He finally got around to spelling his name for her while
he was taking in the rest of the setting, as if he were trying
to figure out where he was.

Carin gave some thought to the gut reaction she was
having. If he were really injured, she shouldn't keep him
out here. She decided the best bet was to call her friend,
the sheriff, and then take him to the clinic in town. Before
she spoke again, she glanced around to make sure there
weren't any accomplices hiding nearby. But Shag would
know, and the dog sniffed the air and sat down, thumping
his tail.

"Okay, you can come on into the house and take off your wet clothes in the bathroom. But don't try anything foolish or you'll get a hole in you."

She nodded toward the door, and he went in ahead of her. Still holding the rifle, she opened a closet with one hand and brought out a folded brown blanket.

"Bathroom's through there. You'll have to wrap up in this until we can get you some dry clothes. Leave your wet things on that mat there."

Then she tilted her head up at him. "You really don't remember anything that just happened to you?"

"I was bein' chased in a big storm, that's all."

Carin studied his serious, rugged face and looked into his hazel eyes. She saw no meanness there. She noticed the little scars at his temple and chin, and the way his mouth was set in a firm, serious line. With the long coat off, she could see that he was dressed in old clothes, really authentic-looking. The jeans were cut a little loose, and the eggshell-colored linen shirt didn't have any buttons, just a slit at the neck so the wearer could pull it over his head.

She felt the attraction boom under her ribs, but backed away after handing him the blanket. He thanked her politely, and she nodded. She didn't need a dangerous, handsome stranger just now. She needed to know who broke into her cabin.

GIDEON TOOK the blanket and went where she pointed. To his left, he glimpsed a big brass bed with a quilt on it in a bedroom. But he turned into the fancy bathroom where she'd sent him.

A claw-footed tub sat against a wainscoted wall. He stared at the brass-handled faucets and pink-and-white-striped wall paper with little roses above the wainscoting.

Like something in a big-city hotel. What was plumbing like this doing way off in a cabin in the mountains?

There was something mighty strange about this. Maybe the thunder had addled his brains. Or maybe the fall had made him hallucinate and he'd wake up after all. He did feel a little dizzy.

The woman didn't seem to cotton to questions, so he hadn't asked her where her animals were. On a fine day like this, you'd think she'd have 'em out grazing. He scratched his head. From the little four-paned sash window at chin level in the bathroom, he could see there was a gravel road came right up to her closed barn doors, too.

He shrugged and sat down on the wooden toilet seat to pull his boots off, the pull chain above knocking into his head. He unbuckled his belt to drop his clothes and his long johns onto the small black and white square tiles of the floor. Before he set his clothes outside the door like she said to, he removed the money that was still on him and set it aside. Once in the porcelain tub, he approached the brass faucets warily.

How could she get running water clear up here? He didn't see any cistern outside. He burned his toe and then turned on the other faucet to make the water just right.

He scooted down in the tub, rested his head against the edge, and closed his eyes to remember. This was better. But he couldn't stay in here too long. Someone had brought him up to the mountains and left him here, and that left four men in a posse to account for. There'd been that lightning flash that hit the ground. Maybe it'd killed the others. It sure had knocked him out. But then who'd scooped him up to bring him up here? Unless somehow he'd gotten back on the horse and ridden for a while before he passed out again. Yep, maybe the horse brought him up here. But these mountains didn't look familiar.

He sat up and washed himself with the funny-smelling soap. He'd better find out what'd happened right quick. And then what? He'd been convicted of murder and robbery. Wells, Fargo and Company wouldn't be so anxious to hire him back unless he could prove the Earps had framed him for that stage robbery and paid a crooked judge. But if he ever wanted an honest job again, that's what he'd have to do.

As SOON AS the bathroom door closed, Carin reached for the phone in the kitchen and called Garfield County Sheriff Hugh Cole.

"I'll be right over," Hugh said on the other end of the line, after she'd told him about the man on her property.

"I can handle it," she said.

Something in her gut told her Gideon Avarest wasn't a bad man. A little strange maybe. But Shag had accepted him, and he hadn't made any move to take advantage of her. This reinforced her instinct.

"I'll be careful, Hugh, but I think he's just had an accident. You could help by finding out who he is." She spelled his name. "He doesn't remember anything else. I'll bring him down to the clinic soon as he's cleaned up. His fall from his horse might've caused a concussion."

There was a pause. "His horse?" asked Hugh.

"Yeah, he came here on horseback. You know if there's a rodeo or a live demo somewhere this weekend? He must be a cowboy or an actor in some show."

"Could be. Not in Glenwood. Maybe over in Aspen."

As assistant editor of the *News,* she was pretty familiar with the announcements that went into the paper herself, and she didn't remember any shows this weekend, either. The reenactment of the O.K. Corral shoot-out wasn't set for another week.

"Carin, we got a cast of the hoofprints we found on your property last night. I'd better send Pete over to check out this guy's horse. And give you some protection."

"I'm all right, Hugh. Shag's here to protect me."

She could hear Hugh's exasperated grunt. She knew he thought she put too much faith in her dog.

"Just the same, Carin, Pete will swing by while I run a check on this guy. And I'll meet you at the clinic when I get something."

"Thanks. Have Pete bring some dry clothes for the stranger. Extra large." They hung up.

Her strange guest would be in the bath for some time, so she took her rifle and went outside again, pausing to glance around. A soft gust ruffled the grass. Juniper and pine branches swayed with the whispering mountain breeze. Down in the valley, the town of Glenwood Springs sprawled beside the Roaring Fork and the Colorado rivers.

"Come on, Shag, let's go get his gear. Maybe we can figure out who he is."

She walked cautiously back down the hill to where she'd left the weapons. She didn't want to mess with them to see if they were loaded or not, because Deputy Pete would want to collect them and try to lift prints in the lab. She'd taken them gingerly from where they'd lain on the ground close to Gideon earlier and she'd moved them out of his reach. She squatted down now and stared at them. Both the Winchester .44 rifle and the Colt .45 looked like antiques. The lab would determine if they matched the shells and slugs from her cabin.

She clicked her tongue to the piebald gelding. "Come 'ere, boy."

The horse bobbed his head, but she soothed him. "Come on, boy, let's go up to the barn."

Shag trotted with them up the hill, and Carin lifted the wooden bar on the barn door. The place hadn't been used as a real barn in fifty years. Instead, her gray Isuzu Trooper was parked inside. The right half of the place was a garage. But there was still an old stall and some hay that her niece and nephew liked to play in when her sister's family visited from California. So she put the horse there. Then she pondered the saddle.

"I'm a newspaper editor, not a cowgirl," she said and patted the horse's neck.

The saddlebags might offer a clue as to who Gideon was and what his business was. She reasoned that they were too wet to be any good for fingerprints, so she lugged them off and spread them on the ground by the stall. Then she squatted on the balls of her feet, unfastened one of the buckles on the leather straps and shook the contents out onto dry hay. Pete could check for prints on this stuff. An oil cloth came unwrapped to expose what looked like a plug of chewing tobacco. A mean-looking hunting knife, some faded oversized playing cards on un-coated card stock, and some folded papers tumbled out. She grew more curious.

She read the old-fashioned block type on the wanted posters, staring at the printed engravings of various law-breakers as she carefully turned over the thick, stiff paper. Smaller notices offered a reward for horse thieves.

With hairs prickling on the back of her neck, she scattered out the contents from the other saddlebag. A pair of buckskin gloves, a tin box of long, wooden matches, a couple of really old boxes of cartridges with quaint old-fashioned labels, a pair of slightly rusted handcuffs with what looked like a nickel finish, and an old brass key all tumbled out.

She sat back on her bottom, her heels coming out from under her as her back landed against the wooden post.

"Jeez," she said.

Chapter Three

Carin left the contents of the saddlebags strewn where Pete could check them out when he got here. When she returned to the house, Gideon was still in the bathroom, so she went to the big oak dining-room table she used as a desk and fingered the cables of the computer hard drive, which Hugh had taken away to examine as evidence. Anger and frustration at the senseless destruction pricked at her.

Backups of the articles she'd been working on were on floppy disks at the office in town. But the culprits had taken some of her printouts and manila files as well as a few floppy disks she'd kept here. Oddly, some of the articles stolen had been based on her ancestor Allie Earp's diaries. Photocopies of old newspaper clippings and notes from the research she'd done to substantiate the diaries had also disappeared with the intruders.

She pondered the coincidence of the missing historical articles and the man in her bathroom. A little shiver of warning went through her. He'd said something about Tombstone. The old stuff in his saddlebags made her wonder if there might be more clues to his identity in the pockets of his clothing. She retrieved the wet garments piled on the bath mat in the little hall by the bathroom door and carried them through to the stainless steel sink in her sunny kitchen. She was invading his privacy, and she really ought to let Pete McGuire do this, but she needed to know.

The soaked denim jeans were of an unusual cut, with buttons on the fly. They showed signs of a lot of wear, with hems that were frayed in the back only. The material at knees and upper thighs was thinned from wear as well.

She picked up what passed for underwear. Quaint long johns, knitted with hand-sewn buttonholes and ivory buttons. It gave her a little flutter of embarrassment that she was holding the same material in her hands that had just been next to Gideon's skin. But she looked at them curiously until she heard the bathroom door open. Leaving the long johns in the sink, she stepped back into the dining room and rested one hand on the table.

Gideon emerged, the blanket wrapped around him under the arms, only partially covering his well-developed, muscular chest. His brawny shoulders and arms made her wonder what he did for a living. Something that required strength on a daily basis, she would guess. Where his shirt had covered him, his skin was a shade lighter than his tanned neck and face. He rubbed a towel on his clean hair and just looked at her, waiting for her to speak.

Her heart thumped out warning signals. He was rugged and raw, and the way he filled her cabin as if he belonged here caused a sinking feeling in her chest. Yet there was something weird about the tall, handsome stranger who had ridden in with the sunrise.

"Where'd you get those clothes?" she asked.

"Dry goods store in Prescott, near as I can remember. Why's that?"

"I...I thought maybe if they were antique clothing I'd better wash them by hand."

Gideon draped the towel around his neck and took a few steps into the room. Sure fancy for a log cabin, he thought. Smooth wood paneling, big oak table with a mess of papers covering it by the windows opposite, and upholstered furniture like in a fancy hotel. He wanted to ask some questions. But his head still hurt, and he was afraid she'd get nervous and point the rifle at him again if he talked too much.

He tried to work things out for himself. He recalled the big storm just before he was knocked out. Maybe he'd gotten into some kind of Indian curse and he was bein' messed with. He sure hoped he wasn't loco from the knock on the head. At least the girl didn't have the gun pointed at him anymore. But now that he looked close, there were things all around the room that were strange looking. Better figure out where he was and why right quick.

He walked over to a fringed lamp shade and squinted down into it. After a minute, he recognized what must be one of those newfangled electric lightbulbs they told of back east, even though it wasn't giving off any light right now. He narrowed his eyes at her. "I heard of these. You know Thomas A. Edison or something?"

"No," she said, coming into the room and looking at him strangely.

They stood a few feet apart, staring at each other.

"Have a seat over there," she said, but her tone seemed huskier than before, her words gentler. "I'd better take a look at that bump on your head."

He sat down in a tapestry-upholstered easy chair, knowing something was wrong, but damned if he could put his finger on it. She came back in a minute with gauze, cotton, and some funny-looking bottles. The print on the labels was so small you'd need a magnifying glass to read it. But he held still while she parted his hair with her fingers to examine him. He was wary, but it was nice having her take care of him. And she smelled good, too.

Carin's hand trembled as she touched his head, looking for any wounds. She saw that his cheek was cut, but it wasn't bleeding now. She was distracted by his big brawny shoulders, just beneath her hands, and took a breath to steady herself. He smelled freshly masculine after the shower.

"This'll hurt a little," she said as she applied medicine to the scrapes.

He barely winced.

Then she looked at the swelling of the lump on the back of his head and felt concern.

"Carin," he said.

"Yes?"

"Nothin'. I just wanted to say your name. Thought it might help me figure out where I am."

When he turned his head, she felt the same little dip in her pulse as she looked into his eyes again. She forgot about her nursing for a moment.

Finally she formulated her words, articulating carefully. "Gideon Avarest.... I don't know what's happened here. I think you have a case of amnesia. And I'm going to take you to the doctor. But I want to know..." She'd heard somewhere that, in situations like this one, snap answers sometimes helped the listener figure out where the confused person thought he was.

He was looking at her hair, her shirt, her throat.

"Gideon?"

Her voice brought his eyes up to hers again. "Yes, ma'am."

"What...uh...what year is it?"

He gave a bashful grin that weakened her knees slightly. "It's 1881...ain't it?"

She stared at him, trying to determine whether or not he was kidding. He simply returned her stare with those big, honey-colored eyes with spokes of brown that just seemed to make her want to drown in them. She couldn't find any words to deal with his answer, so she just swallowed as she put away the bandages and cotton. Finally, she pulled a straight-backed cane chair in front of him and sat in it.

"Gideon," she said again, leaning forward a little. "It's not 1881. It's July 1997."

She looked deep into the golden-brown eyes. She felt dangerously drawn into those depths, pulled into something where nothing was as it seemed. Somehow this strong hunk of a man had been cast into her care. She didn't know why, and she didn't have any reason to trust him. But she felt no fear, only some kind of urgency, like a threat that both of them had to elude. Crazy as it might seem, she felt a connection.

She reached out tentatively to examine what looked like a burn on his hand. But he wrapped his fingers around hers, and her heart leapt into her throat. Then he took her other hand as if it would steady him. Fear of the unknown swept over her, and she was afraid to put it into words. But he was gazing into her face with a question. She could almost see his mind working. She wondered whether his thoughts matched hers. Man from the past. Impossible notion.

She tried another question. "What do you…do for a living?"

"I'm an agent for Wells, Fargo and Company. Was, anyway, until my trial." He said it seriously, but she read the pride and regret in his words.

He seemed to be considering things. His sandy brows lowered. He concentrated his gaze on her fingers as if he too were making sure that she was flesh and not some figment of his imagination. Then a slow smile spread across his rugged face, making her heart hammer triple time, and he looked up at her with a twinkle in his eye.

"I think you're foolin'," he said. "Unless I went forward, magic-like, more than a hundred years into the future."

Then he released her hands, and she sat back. She shook her head. "Oh, heck. You probably just fell off that horse, and I need to get you to a doctor." She started to get up.

He grasped her hand and pulled her down again, shaking his head. "No doctor, not till I find out how I got here and where here is. The Earp gang is after me, and I don't reckon to go to town till I find out where they are."

She studied him, frowning. "You mean Wyatt Earp?"

"Yep. They were chasin' me out of Tombstone when the lightning hit."

There was a moment of silence. He was crazy, then. But she said slowly, "Tell me about it."

He related the story as he remembered it, from his crooked trial to the jailbreak and the shoot-out in the rainstorm with Wyatt, Morgan, Virgil and Doc. When he reached the end, he shrugged. "That's all I remember till I woke up here."

Her eyes were wide with wonder, her hands clasped tightly in her lap, and she moved her head slowly back and forth.

"Amazing." She thought about Allie Earp's diaries and her articles. "Maybe I've dreamed this all up myself."

But there was the break-in to consider. She started to feel wary again. Maybe he was perfectly sane but was part of some elaborate plot. She stood up, suddenly tense, and got behind her chair, where she could reach for the rifle if she needed it.

"You sure you're not playing some trick on me? Some practical joke at my expense? Besides, why should anyone care more than a hundred years later if I publish stories out of a dead woman's diary and do original research to back it up? What is it you want to hide?"

"I ain't tryin' to hide anything. What're you talking about?"

"Someone broke in here last night and stole some articles I was working on for the newspaper. Anecdotes about some famous characters." She explained her distant relationship to the Earp clan. "The Earps are known hereabouts because Doc Holliday spent his last days here. He's buried up in Pioneer Cemetery, but of course you probably know that."

Irony tinged her voice at the last words, and she edged toward her rifle, which she'd placed in its rack.

Gideon lifted his eyebrows in curiosity. "He died? Doc? Well, he was ailin', that's for sure." He shook his head. "I never did like the man."

She stopped by the table. If he was faking it, he was doing a good job. "They all died, sixty to ninety years ago. This is 1997."

"How would I know that? The four of them were chasing me just before the storm, like I said. They came around the rocks, then I..." He hesitated. "I rode the thunder." He lifted his hands for lack of better explanation.

She tilted her head and gazed at him for a long moment. Then she spoke more softly. "You rode the thunder?"

He eyed her with a trace of humor. "Well, it was unusual weather for December. Tombstone's mostly dry in December."

All she could do was stare. "December...1881."

"That's right."

She gave a little intake of breath. Since she'd been studying the Earps, she knew that December would be the month that Virgil had recovered from his leg wound from the O.K. Corral shoot-out. Morgan would have been up and around, too, after having been shot in the shoulder in the famous gunfight. Virgil had been seriously shot again December 28 and then Morgan had been murdered in March 1882. But in December 1881, they would have all been able to walk down the street in Tombstone and could possibly have ridden out of town.

She put her hand to her head. No, no, she must be hallucinating.

A car on the gravel drive interrupted her thoughts. Deputy Pete McGuire had arrived. She eased her rifle off the rack, so as not to spook Gideon into trying to stop her, and went outside to meet Pete.

Deputy Sheriff Pete McGuire was an easygoing soul of about five foot six, compact and wiry of frame. His schoolboy face and wire-rimmed glasses hid a bright intelligence. He was one of the most thorough officers Hugh had, and he'd proved it last night and this morning in the quiet way he'd gone over the crime scene. She doubted he'd had time for any more than a cat nap, but he looked fresh and ready to gather new evidence.

She stood between Pete's car and the cabin. When he got out of the car, he peered over her shoulder.

"You all right, Carin?"

"I'm fine, Pete. Gideon Avarest is in there wrapped up in a blanket. He needed a bath. I've got his clothes in my kitchen sink."

"I'd better question him," Pete said. He handed her a large box. "Clothes are in there."

"I'll give him these then while you look at the horse I put in the barn. The saddlebags have some very interesting stuff in them."

"You should have let me paw through things."

"I know. But I was careful not to touch anything. I had to take some weapons off him. They're down there." She pointed. "His old cowboy duster and hat are up there."

"Okay. I'll get the weapons first. But you shouldn't be inside with this man. He might be dangerous."

Humor tinged her expression. "Not dressed in a blanket, he's not. And he's disarmed. Anyway, you're here now. I think we need to get him to the doctor. He might have a concussion."

She nearly added that Gideon had been saying some awfully funny stuff, then decided to let the law enforcement officers make their own decision about that.

Pete went to collect the weapons while she took the clothes indoors. Gideon was standing at the edge of the window, peering out.

"Here," she said. "The deputy sheriff brought you some dry clothes."

"You got the law here?" He looked around warily, and she could see that he was searching for the back door.

"It's not anyone you know," she said somewhat impatiently. "Just put these clothes on. I told him I'd take you to the doc—"

Before she could finish, Gideon lunged for the rifle, and placed his hand over her mouth. The box of clothing dropped to the floor. He pinned her to him and set the rifle aside. Then he locked her right arm behind her with his free hand. Her squeal was muffled by the hand over her mouth, and in that position she was no match for his strength. He shoved her to the wall just next to the window and peered outside. She struggled. He let go of her wrist and brought his arm around her waist, pulling her against the blanket wrapped around his torso. He clutched her against him, bracing her mouth and chin with his hand.

"What the devil is that?" he said.

The only thing in their view was the deputy's car, a standard white Chevy Caprice with the gold star insignia of the county sheriff's department on the door. But when she tried to answer, her words were muffled. So Gideon dropped his hand to let her talk, his arm still pressed against her neck in case she tried anything. She wasn't going anywhere with him holding her so firmly.

"That's the deputy's car," she choked out. "He went down the hill to collect your weapons. Then he's going to examine your horse, and...uh, the stuff in your saddlebags. See, there he is."

Gideon's grip tightened as he watched the man come up the hill. There was no mistaking the silver star on his shirt. But he wasn't carrying any guns, just a big box.

"What kind of thing is that in the road?"

"That's an automobile. Oh, Lord."

If Gideon really did think he'd come from the past or if some weird memory thing had occurred from the knock on the head, she'd have a lot of explaining to do.

"The auto burns fuel. It's self-propelled. No horses."

They watched Pete put the boxes in the car. "He put your weapons in cardboard boxes so they can dust for fingerprints at the station. Do you know what fingerprints are?"

"I've seen fingerprints. What about it?"

At the moment Carin couldn't quite remember the history of fingerprinting, so she didn't argue. But she felt Gideon tense behind her.

"I think I gotta get out of here," he said.

Carin's heart pumped hard in her chest, but she realized she had to talk her way out of this. He couldn't go anywhere in the buff. If he let go of her to put on the clothes, she could reach for her rifle and yell for Pete. Gideon had outsmarted her, and it made her mad. But if Pete came in here and Gideon panicked, they could have a nasty accident.

She leaned her head back against his shoulder, relaxing

her body so it sank against his. She tried to speak in a soothing voice.

"Gideon, I want to help you. I swear to you that whatever's happened, Deputy Pete out there isn't one of the, um, posse that chased you. All he wants to know is if you had anything to do with the break-in here last night."

"I told you, I don't know anything about that."

"Okay, I believe you. Shag knows you weren't here. But you had a fall, a bump on the head. You need to see a doctor. You might have an internal injury."

"I'm feelin' better. Don't need any doctor. I just need to get away from here."

"To where?"

That stopped him, for she knew he didn't know where he was in the first place. She pressed the point. "You're in Glenwood Springs, Colorado, Gideon. In 1997. I can take you down to town to prove it. Please, let me help you."

She knew she ought to feel afraid, but his grip wasn't so tight as to hurt her, he was just panicked about the law being outside. When his grip eased further, she wriggled around to face him. Instantly, she realized her mistake. He looked down at her, still holding her in his arms, and a shiver of something that wasn't fear pulsed through her. Her whole body responded. Her lips parted, her heartbeat sped up, she stopped breathing for a minute. The same sensation that she was suddenly out of this world came over her, and the floor shifted beneath her feet. One thing was for sure, she wasn't frightened of being in his arms. Some part of her just wanted to stay there, with only a blanket between them. Desire lurched in her, and she had to command her hand not to caress the shoulder it had found.

But there were some logistics to consider. She moved her other hand up to his back and touched him gently.

"Please, let me go talk to Pete. He can follow us to town in his own vehicle. I'll be with you at the doctor's. No one, uh, the gang that chased you, we won't let them near you."

His eyes did have a slightly otherworldly quality, or was that just his sex appeal? She couldn't decide. She couldn't tear her gaze away. He kept the muscles in his face still, but she could sense that he was highly upset about something. Maybe he was on the run and was using this Wyatt Earp story as a cover. It was all very strange, and she had to think fast.

He glanced down at her and then looked out the window again. She watched him scan the landscape, and then he pulled her back out of view of the window as Pete moved in and out of the barn.

"Maybe I'll go with you to town, but I'll keep the rifle."

"You can't do that."

"Why not?"

"Because Pete thinks I'm bringing you in for questioning. You have to trust me." She tried to convey sincerity in her voice and keep it level so as not to startle him.

He grunted. "I'm a little low on trust right now."

"I understand." She did some quick thinking. "Let me take the rifle then. Pete's used to seeing me with it."

She met Gideon's gaze, her breathing still far from normal. "You just proved you can disarm me if you have to."

It was against her nature to admit to any kind of weakness, but she was doing some fast negotiating. And in his current mental state she had the feeling that she needed to reassure him or he might do something crazy. She held her breath while he seemed to consider his options.

"You say you're related to Allie Earp?"

She opened her green eyes wider. "That's right, why?"

"Well, then." He almost grinned at her as he lightened his hold and slid his hands up to her shoulders. "She let me out of jail. I guess if I have to take a chance, I have to take it with kin of hers."

Carin swallowed. Maybe the brawny hunk of man whose death grip had just turned into a near embrace *was* mad. Appealingly mad, but mad. But if she was careful and humored him, she'd get him downtown and into the right hands. And no one would get hurt. Then maybe she'd find out why he was trying to spook her about the Earps.

"All right. We've got a deal. You get dressed. You can use my bedroom. I'll go tell Pete what's up."

They eyed each other warily as he let go of her.

"Just the same," he said, bending over and picking up the rifle. "I'll keep this until we get outside."

Her jaw clenched as she backed away and then used her foot to shove the box of clothes in his direction. His eyelids drooped a little as if he too had been moved by holding her. His mouth turned up in a smile as he took the clothes.

"Thank you, ma'am."

He disappeared into the bedroom. She sank against the wall for a moment, just to get her breath, then she marched outside and met Pete at the car. She was about to let him know that their prisoner now possessed her weapon when she saw the puzzled expression on Pete's face. He shook his head.

"That isn't the same horse that left prints back there last night."

"How can you tell?"

"This one's hooves are an inch smaller."

She couldn't help feeling relieved that Gideon evidently hadn't been on the scene during the break-in.

"I got all the stuff from the saddlebags." He indicated

cartons full of individual paper and plastic bags now containing the items she'd seen with her own eyes.

"He says these things aren't his," she told Pete. She tried to laugh. "Says he made a jailbreak and fled town on somebody else's horse. In 1881."

Pete looked worried, scratched his head, glanced at the cabin. "Maybe I better question him before we take him to the clinic."

"I think his injury should be looked at first. Believe me, you won't make sense out of him right now."

She shook her head, her forehead creasing. "Something's wrong, I don't know what. He's scared, that's for sure. But I don't think he did this." She gestured toward her cabin indicating last night's intruders. "Anyway, he's agreed to cooperate. He's confused. I'll take him in my car. You can follow."

She didn't give Pete a chance to argue but went back to get Gideon.

The jeans and shirt were a close fit. Material stretched across his shoulders as he leaned over to tug on his own well-worn, low-heeled boots. Then he stood up and met her gaze and reached for the rifle to give it to her. A man of his word.

"Let's go," she said in a husky voice.

Outside, she made introductions. The two men nodded warily at each other. While Pete turned his car around, Carin led Gideon into the barn and opened her car door indicating that he should get in.

She saw him wait just inside the barn for his eyes to adjust to the light. Then he stepped sideways around her car, frowning at it. He reached out to touch it cautiously, and Carin shook her head again. He was really overdoing the reactions.

"Maybe I'd better take the horse instead," he said.

It took her a moment to realize he was serious. "Get

in, please. We don't ride horses for transportation anymore. I'll drive.''

He finally settled into the Trooper. She set the gun in
the back seat and got in. Seeing that he hadn't fastened
his seat belt, she showed him how. She tried *not* to show
how coming in close contact again with him affected her.

Then she started the car. Gideon almost bolted at the
sound of the motor, but his seat belt kept him in. He
gripped the dashboard with one hand. He flung his other
arm across the back of the seat and braced his feet on the
floor as if didn't know what to expect. The expression on
his face was one of stunned disbelief.

Pete idled the Caprice until he could follow her. She
backed out of the barn, swung the Trooper around, and
then barreled down the drive to the blacktop road leading
down to town.

The hairpin curves took them past a few bridges leading
across a stream to private property. Gideon glimpsed
dwellings with more of the horseless vehicles outside.
Carin's vehicle sped along the road. Most of the time
sunlight bathed them. Every so often, they entered patches
of shade from trees this side of the stream. He rode in
stunned silence, taking it all in, then squinted suspiciously
as they came to another road. Across that were more
buildings, and in the distance more roads with these
strange vehicles everywhere.

The panic inside him made him clutch the panel beneath the window where he held on even tighter. If this
was a dream, he wished he'd wake up. Or maybe he had
been hanged, and just didn't remember that part, and this
was the other place. He glanced at Carin and remembered
how real she'd felt in his arms, all soft and womanly. His
body had confirmed he wasn't dead.

But he knew for a fact that something strange had occurred. What had looked all right at first didn't look right

now. Then there was this woman. Holding her in his arms wasn't all that hard a thing to do. He liked her curves. He liked her voice, firm, but smooth. She was strong, too, just like a homesteader would be, though not worn and weathered from a hard life. He looked at the soft blond hair and the determined profile. She had lips he might have wanted to kiss at another time. But, just now, he needed a friend.

He hung on to his seat and watched as they came into the town. There was a lot to stare at, yet he didn't ask any more questions. Finally she pulled up in front of a long, square building with people coming and going, some of them wearing white coats. She stopped the vehicle and came around to let him out. The deputy sheriff pulled alongside, too, and Gideon glowered at the man as he got out of the low-slung carriage. But he allowed Carin to lead him inside.

While Carin stood at a tall counter talking to more people in white coats, Gideon stared at the metal contraptions in the room. He'd just about decided that he'd better not stay, when he turned to see the deputy sheriff and another armed officer outside. Gideon wasn't armed, and he was wary of starting a fight in the street when the territory was unfamiliar. Maybe there was a back way out. He took a step toward a hallway, but Carin grasped his arm.

"Come in here, Gideon. The nurse is going to take a look at you, then you can fill out the forms."

He'd better cooperate until he could figure out a plan. This didn't look like any doctor's room he'd ever seen. Carin told him where to sit, then the nurse in a white uniform came in. She gave him a smile and wrapped an armband around his arm, saying she was taking his blood pressure. Carin stood by while the nurse finished and then the doctor came in.

"What happened to you, young man?" said the middle-aged, portly doctor, wearing a stethoscope around his neck.

Carin lifted an inquiring eyebrow, and Gideon decided he wouldn't reveal too much.

Finally Carin spoke up. "I found him unconscious on my property, doctor. He'd fallen from a horse and doesn't remember how he got here. He doesn't seem to have broken anything."

"Hmm." The doctor examined Gideon's head and shone a tiny light in his eyes. Then he listened to Gideon's heart with his stethoscope.

"All right," he said to the nurse who was standing by. "Get him undressed. Heart's strong. Blood pressure's normal. I want X rays. We'll need to check for internal injuries."

While they all told Gideon what to do and where to go, he was cautious, ready to make an escape. But nobody threatened him, and they didn't try to give him any medicine that would put him under. After he sat in front of the machine that took the pictures of his head, he got dressed again and was sent toward a pair of swinging doors that led to the lobby.

"Just wait out there until the doctor is ready to talk to you again," said the nurse.

He peered through the little glass windows and saw Carin sitting on a leather couch across the room. She was reading a magazine. But he also looked out through the glass front of the building and saw that the deputy and a couple of other officers were still outside. Gideon decided he needed to get away and figure some things out.

He slipped through the swinging doors before Carin could look up and see him. He turned left and walked quickly down a long hallway. A few of the female nurses looked up at him and stared for a minute. Nobody stopped him and at the other end of the corridor, he saw a door marked Exit.

TWENTY MINUTES LATER, the doctor emerged, carrying a large envelope holding X rays. He glanced around. Not seeing Gideon, he spoke to Carin.

"Where's your friend?"

Carin was on her feet in an instant. "I thought he was still in there."

The doctor frowned. "He should have been waiting here. In any case, there's no sign of injury on these films."

She glanced around impatiently. But she tried to listen to what the doctor was saying. "You mean there's nothing wrong with him?"

"I haven't found anything wrong. It might be a good idea for him to check into the hospital for a day for more thorough tests than we can do here."

She cut off his suggestions. "Thanks, doc. I'll tell him that—when I find him."

Then she shot out the front door and plowed into Pete's conversation with the other deputy and two city policemen. "I have to talk to Hugh. The stranger's gone."

Chapter Four

Gideon crossed a park behind the clinic and came to a shady street. Frame houses with wide verandas sat on small lots. He felt some relief at seeing something more familiar, more like his own time, if what he'd actually done was travel forward in time to a different century. He turned the first corner and walked up the incline to another residential street that looked much like the first one. No one was following him, so he slowed down a little bit as he continued down this street.

People went about their business. A couple of children rode by on bicycles. He dodged out of the way of one of the horseless vehicles, but no one seemed to pay him any mind. No one seemed to think he looked as out of place as he surely felt. Cautiously, he made his way to the downtown area. Automobiles whizzed past, and he continued down the sidewalk until he came to a bridge that arched over a railroad and a wide river that curved around more of the town on the other side.

At the other side of the bridge he came to a big red-brick-and-sandstone structure with a red tiled roof, and he headed that way. He noticed gaslights planted by sidewalks and gardens in a central plaza between two wings of the building. Two towers jutted above the top story and a balcony terrace broke the facade. It was quieter here.

He went up the steps to the plaza then through double doors that took him inside.

Now, this was more like it. The big hotel lobby stretched from one end of the central wing to the other. Squat plush chairs and hassocks were grouped here and there on the beige carpet. Burgundy drapes framed big windows, and potted palms sat next to tall white pillars supporting the beamed ceiling. He crossed in front of a huge stone fireplace with moose heads mounted above it and approached the long oak-paneled desk with white marble countertop. A young desk clerk in shirt and vest stepped up to the counter.

"May I help you, sir?"

"I'll take a room."

"For how long?"

"Don't know for sure."

The clerk named the price, which Gideon thought exorbitant, but he didn't argue. Maybe this was a fancier hotel than he'd realized.

"Will you be using a credit card?"

"A what?"

Gideon pulled out some of the money he'd made sure to keep with him in the pockets of the new jeans and laid it on the marble counter. The clerk just smiled and lifted an eyebrow at the money. Gideon started to count out the amount needed. The clerk's eyes widened and his look changed to one of suspicion.

The hairs on the back of Gideon's neck prickled. There must be something wrong with the money. Having now seen some of the town, he was beginning to believe he had come forward in time like Carin said or he was in some foreign country. In either case, he didn't fit in. He had to watch for cues and do what people expected until he discovered if he was in any more danger.

He gave a reassuring smile to the puzzled clerk and fanned the money. "It's all I got on me."

The clerk studied the currency. "Is this real?"

"Sure is." Gideon reached in his pocket again and brought out some gold coins, laying them on the desk. "Are these any better?"

The desk clerk looked nervous, but he pushed the guest register toward Gideon. "Would you sign this, please?"

While Gideon was signing his name, the clerk stepped away from the desk. Gideon turned in time to see Carin Sage come barreling across the lobby toward him. He cast a glare in her direction then scanned the area to see if any lawmen were concealed behind palm fronds or pillars. But she appeared to be alone.

"Gideon," she said furiously when she reached him, though she kept her voice low. "Why did you run away?"

"You alone?"

"Why? Do you have something to hide from the law?"

The clerk came back with a man in a gray suit and horn-rimmed glasses. Carin knew Adam Little, the hotel's manager.

Recognition dawned in Adam's eyes, and he smiled. "Carin. I didn't know you were out here." He glanced at Gideon. "Is there a problem?"

"I want a room, that's all," said Gideon.

The manager nodded. "I'm sure we can accommodate. Is this gentleman a friend of yours, Carin?"

Rather than see Gideon bolt again, Carin hedged. "We are acquainted, yes."

The manager put the registration card on the desk in front of Gideon. "Then I'm sure it's all right. If you will sign here, please, sir. I understand you wish to pay cash?"

"Right."

Carin saw that Gideon looked troubled. She picked up

one of the old dollar bills on the desk. He must have tried to pay with the old currency.

"He, uh, doesn't have any ready cash on him, Adam. He's uh, here to do an Old West demonstration. I'm doing the story on it. Do you need a deposit for the room?"

"If he's a friend of yours, there's no need. From out of town?"

"He's from Arizona," Carin said when she didn't think Gideon was going to answer.

Arthur handed Gideon a key. "Second floor, east wing."

"Much obliged."

"I'll, uh, show him the way," Carin said. She touched Gideon's sleeve.

Carin led the way along the long, quiet corridor. The historic Hotel Colorado had been restored to its former glory and now appeared much as it had when originally built in 1893. They climbed the grand staircase and continued down the carpeted corridor to the east wing.

She saw Gideon peer in the open doorways leading to sitting rooms decorated in the Victorian style, and knew what he might be thinking. With the hotel staff in old-fashioned uniforms that fit with the setting, the hotel made a person feel like he'd stepped back in time. Carin watched Gideon out of the corner of her eye. Too much had happened too fast. But she knew that if she could get him settled into a room and keep him from getting spooked, then she could call Hugh.

The sheriff needed to question the man before he ran away again. If she went to a telephone now, Gideon would get suspicious. There was more to gain by trying to get the tall, brawny stranger to trust her. As they stopped before the door to his room, she was uncomfortably aware of other reactions simmering within her. If only he weren't so darned appealing.

She walked into the airy room and decided that Gideon certainly would be comfortable here. The marble-topped antique dresser, tall mirror stand, and chenille-covered double bed ought to make Gideon feel right at home, since he claimed that he lived in the nineteenth century. Lace curtains filtered direct sunlight coming in French doors leading to a small balcony overlooking the Hot Springs Lodge and pool.

He looked around and then stepped to the French doors to get his bearings.

She leaned against the floral gray wallpaper. "You going to be all right here?"

"I'll hole up and get some rest."

"The doctor said there wasn't anything wrong with you that he could see. But he wanted you to talk to some specialists."

"Told you nothin's wrong except that I was knocked out and ended up here, wherever this is."

He paused, still eyeing the town and the mountain ridge out the window. "You say this is Colorado?"

She sighed. Even if he wouldn't talk to any more doctors, he was still going to talk to the law, just in case. She'd make sure of that.

"Listen, I'll leave you here then," she said, standing up straight again.

He leaned down to poke at the bed. Carin felt a little flutter and backed toward the door. The memory of his strong arms around her was a little disquieting, and the thought of him stretching his long frame out on the bed made her suddenly embarrassed. She needed some rest, too, having been up most of the night while Hugh and Pete had gone over the crime scene in her cabin. She framed herself in the doorway, while Gideon stood up again to watch her.

"You going to bring the law here?"

He'd know she was lying if she denied it. "They just want to ask you some questions about my break-in. If you didn't have anything to do with that, you don't have anything to worry about."

"What about a certain hanging that was planned for me back in Tombstone?"

"They don't hang people anymore, Gideon. The crime the sheriff cares about took place here in Glenwood Springs. He won't send you back to Tombstone."

Gideon still frowned, but he sat on the bed and leaned back against the tall headboard. "Your friend, the sheriff. Has he got connections with Wyatt Earp?"

In spite of herself, Carin's mouth lifted in amusement. "He's heard of him, of course. Everybody has. But he's never met him."

The way Gideon eyed her made her want to both stay and leave at the same time. But she waited for his answer.

Gideon seemed to be thinking things over. "I have a few questions for your friend the sheriff, myself. I guess maybe we oughta talk. But he has to come unarmed. Can you guarantee that?"

She sighed. "I'll try."

"And he has to come alone."

She felt like she was in a bad Western, but she nodded solemnly. "Okay. Okay. You stay here."

She pulled the door shut behind her and then raced down the hall. The telephones were on the first floor, and she just prayed that Gideon wasn't bluffing, that he would stay put until Hugh could get here. She left a message as to Gideon's whereabouts with the dispatcher, who relayed it to Hugh. He was in his car and would be here within minutes.

After hanging up, she trotted up the stairs again to a small lounge at the end of Gideon's floor to wait for Hugh. She leaned against the back of an uncomfortable antique wing chair, trying to relax. Hugh was competent and would get to the bottom of the matter. If Gideon was cleared, then there was no more to it.

She frowned over the last thought. There was still the Earp gang connection. Maybe it was she who was mentally unsound. Why would someone who claimed to know the Fighting Earps show up out of nowhere in her yard at a time when she was researching them? And why had someone broken into the cabin and stolen papers relating to that research?

As COUNTY SHERIFF for the last five years, Hugh Cole had been a source of information for some of the articles Carin had done for the *Glenwood News,* the weekly that covered local events and carried advertising for town businesses.

She saw Hugh come up the stairs and spot her as she sat in the chair with her legs tucked under her. She untangled herself as he strode down the carpeted hallway, quiet as a cat, then sat on the edge of an adjacent chair and leaned forward, elbows on knees. He was compact and lithe with trimmed sandy-colored hair and blue eyes. He looked as if he hadn't had much sleep.

"Where's your friend?"

"Room 227. He says he'll talk to you as long as you're not a friend of Wyatt Earp's."

Hugh glanced at the door she was watching. "Crazy?"

She hugged her arms in a little shiver. "I don't know. He refused further treatment at the clinic. All I want to know is whether he's someone you're looking for or not. Any reports yet on who he says he is?"

Hugh's direct look met hers. "The name means nothing to any of the agencies we've contacted so far."

She relaxed her shoulders. "So Gideon Avarest is not a known criminal, or anyone's alias."

Hugh shook his head. "We're tracing him through data

banks now for his identity, but that'll take a while. I'll take him along to the department for questioning.''

Hugh gave her a curt nod and got up. She followed as he knocked on Gideon's door and announced himself.

Gideon's voice answered. "Come in."

He was still slouched against the headboard, his legs crossed on top of the bed, boots still on. His hair was tousled over his wide brow and his honey-colored eyes still made Carin's knees weaken. She hadn't felt so shivery about a man in a long time, and it broke her stride.

"Gideon, this is Sheriff Hugh Cole. He wants you to come with him to answer some questions."

Gideon spread his arms wide. "I can answer any questions right here."

Hugh made a quick survey of the room then returned his eyes to Gideon's. "We'd like you to come to the department so we can take your prints."

At Gideon's puzzled look, Carin intervened. "Fingerprints."

She spread the fingers of her right hand in an effort to remind Gideon that they'd talked about this before.

"Are you arresting me?"

"No, we just need to find out if you are who you say you are."

Gideon glowered, but swung his legs off the bed. The tension in her stomach eased when she saw that he was going to cooperate. They had no evidence on him yet connecting him to the break-in, and she knew Hugh couldn't hold him. But it did make sense to get the prints and take photos at the county sheriff's office. If he was a missing person with amnesia, the prints and photos could help them figure out his true identity.

Gideon rode in Hugh's car and Carin followed in the Trooper. The county sheriff's office was located on Seventh Street, one block off Grand Avenue. A one-story brick building tucked behind the county courthouse and next to the railroad track, it sat across from the big bend in the river.

Carin followed Hugh and Gideon in and waited in Hugh's office while they took fingerprints at the counter outside, then stood Gideon by the wall while they took his picture. As Hugh's office had glass partitions on two sides, she could see what went on. She watched Gideon glance suspiciously at the camera, but he did as he was told.

Then Hugh took him into the interrogation room, while Carin paced. Perspiration formed on her brow and palms as she waited it out.

Hugh came back after twenty minutes without Gideon. He didn't speak for a few seconds, but crossed to the window that looked out the side of the building, across the river to where West Glenwood stretched around the bend. He rested his hand on the window frame and frowned.

"Well?" Carin finally asked.

He shook his head. "He didn't say anything useful. I told him not to leave town. We might need him again."

There was a tap on the glass, and Henny Liverpool came in. The white-coated technician nodded to Carin and then spoke to Hugh. Her elegant brows and salmon-pink glossed lips formed a puzzled expression. Carin knew they had limited lab facilities in town. Most of their crime scene evidence would be sent to the state lab in Montrose. But ballistics could be checked out here.

"Sam Church took a look at those weapons Pete brought in this morning. I agree with him."

Sam Church was a weapons expert who lived in Glenwood and often consulted with the city police as well as the County Sheriff's Department.

Henny waved her manicured, dark pink nails as she

talked. "They're antiques, all right. The Winchester was made in 1873. It was a well-known model. The Colt in 1876. Funny thing is, they've both been fired recently."

Hugh rested one foot on his chair, looking more interested. The hairs on the back of Carin's neck prickled.

"What about the slugs we picked up last night?" asked Hugh.

Henny shook her dark head of perfectly shaped hair. "They don't match, not even close. Nor do the cartridges you collected." She tossed her report on the desk. "Funny thing is, those slugs and cartridges? They're at least a hundred years old."

Carin felt like someone had knocked the breath out of her. Hugh set his foot on the floor, sending his swivel chair turning by itself.

"You've got to be kidding," he said.

Henny shook her head. The heavily made-up face couldn't hide the fact that she was one of the best lab technicians in the state, as Carin well knew.

"Nope. Old guns, old ammo. Different calibers. Those bullets were fired by different makes and models than the firearms you brought in." She tapped the report. "It's all right here."

They both just stared at her. Finally Hugh spoke. "But you say the stranger's guns had been fired recently."

She shrugged. "Can't say exactly when. Definitely within hours of the time I saw them."

Henny waited, but after Hugh circled behind his desk and scratched his head, he just thanked her and let her go. Then he looked at Carin perched on the edge of his desk.

"I can't believe this. We've got a bunch of guys playing old-time outlaw, firing antique guns. The evidence matches Gideon Avarest's story. That the last thing he remembers was firing at the Earps outside of Tombstone.

But I can't hold him for the crime I'm investigating." He lifted his hands in the air. "Looney."

Carin was still rocking with the aftershock.

Hugh dropped his hands. "You sure you don't want to stay in town till this is cleaned up, Carin? You could stay with Henny. The perpetrators might come back to your cabin. We don't know for sure what they wanted."

"I'll think about it." She crossed to the glass to look out toward the interrogation room. "You're going to let him go?"

"Don't have a reason to keep him here. He says he doesn't know anything about the break-in. Nothing on him or that horse matches up with any of the evidence we got at the cabin so far. State lab will have to let·us know if they come up with anything else. Nope. He's free to go."

"Okay," she said. She turned around and gave him her thanks. "Let me know if I can help."

She went outside to her car and leaned on the hood. Intense, high-altitude sun blazed down, but the breeze from the river and the clear, dry air made the summer heat palatable. The hollow whir from the highway on the other side of the river echoed along the narrow valley.

In a few minutes, Gideon came out. He squinted into the sunlight and spotted her by the car. They just looked at each other for a moment. She didn't know where he'd come from or why, maybe some funny business having to do with her own research. But he was so darned appealing, it was hard to focus on the facts.

She opened her car door and gestured to the front seat. "I'll give you a lift downtown."

"Much obliged."

They didn't say much during the ride. She idled the car at the curb beside the Hotel Colorado. She could see that Gideon was contemplating the surroundings. A high fence opposite the hotel enclosed the grounds of the five-hundred-foot hot springs pool and bathhouse located down the slope. Visitors crossed the road with their bathing gear to go soak.

"Hugh told me he wanted you to stick around in case he has any more questions."

"Yes, ma'am."

"You really don't have any other cash on you?"

He drew his blond brows together, letting her know that he'd already shown the money he had in his pockets. She swallowed, then made a suggestion.

"If you want that stuff exchanged for money you can use in this town, I know a coin dealer who can handle it."

His face relaxed. "I'd appreciate that."

"Okay."

She drove around the block and then took Gideon to the coin dealer's place a few blocks away. "Let me do the talking."

The dealer looked at the old currency with interest and exchanged it for its antique value. He quoted a price for the coins that would keep Gideon nicely for some time. Gideon stuffed the wad of bills into his pocket.

When they were back outside, Carin considered. "You going to walk around with all that, or do you want to put some of it in a bank?"

His eyes darted along the street, looking at the stores and businesses. "Don't know how long I'll be stayin'. You have many bank robberies hereabouts?"

Carin couldn't help smiling at his manner. His sense of being out of place gave him a charm that set him apart from modern men.

She guided him into the glass door of a bank on the next block and helped him open an account. He gave as his address the Hotel Colorado, and Carin explained to the puzzled bank officer that he hadn't yet found a permanent residence. The deposit made, he kept plenty on him for immediate needs.

That done, there seemed nothing else to do but to drop him at the hotel. When he got out, he leaned down again to talk to her through the window. He looked very serious, and she gripped the steering wheel to try to steady the sudden fluttering in her chest.

"I owe you for your help. Would you be willin' to have dinner with me?"

Her heart did a little dance and she looked away, half embarrassed. A justification came into her head that she really needed to find out more about him, anyway. "All right. I'll come back here at seven o'clock."

He gave a quick nod that sent her pulse thrilling, pushed himself up from the car window, and stepped back onto the curb. Carin eased her grip on the steering wheel to steer into the street. Part of the tingling racing through her could be excused on the basis of the unusual happenings since last night. But she knew the adrenaline rush wasn't all just from being on the trail of culprits who'd broken into her place.

GIDEON TOOK his time walking through the hotel. Now, this was more like the places he was used to. But the people weren't dressed right. Women wore either short skirts that showed a lot of leg, or else they wore short pants like boys. Yup, he was startin' to believe he'd played some trick on time. That thunder had something to do with it. Problem was, how could he have come alone? It bothered him some that he was thought of as a criminal back in his own time, even if he'd gotten away at the last minute and saved his neck. Maybe Carin could tell him some more about that. She told him she'd been reading about the Earp doings.

He worked on that thought all the way up the stairs and while he got the key out. Maybe, just maybe, that had something to do with why he came here. Maybe he was supposed to meet the pretty blond lady. She was part of his fate.

He pushed the door inward. Too late, he sensed he was not alone. As he turned to defend himself, a punch to the jaw knocked him out cold.

AFTER A NAP, Carin straightened up the mess left by the intruders. The computer hard drive that Hugh had collected was no doubt beyond repair, which meant she'd have to shell out hard-earned cash to buy a new one. The destruction rankled, but the only way to handle the situation was to do something about it.

She tidied up the spilled files, concentrating on the research for her stories about the Earp gang. The small newspaper she worked for was the perfect place to publish items of interest about the Earps. Because Doc Holliday had died in Glenwood Springs, the town was Wyatt Earp crazy. The reenactment of the O.K. Corral shoot-out, or at least one version of it, was coming up next weekend at Doc Holliday Days.

Carin sat at the table facing the windows that looked out at the slope behind the cabin, rereading an old clipping about events in Tombstone, 1881. She glanced up to look out. A small woman dressed in an old-fashioned gingham dress and slat bonnet stood at the opposite end of Carin's property.

Carin rubbed her eyes, thinking it was her imagination. But when she opened them again, the woman was still there.

Carin stood up slowly, fingers pressed to the table, a shiver of suspicion creeping up her spine. Then she rushed out the back door, calling.

"Hello, wait. What do you want?"

But the woman only glanced her way for a moment, and then started walking up the hill into the trees.

"Wait!" Carin sprinted after her. Shag dashed out the back door and followed, barking.

She didn't slow even on the scrabbly incline. But as soon as she reached the stand of pines, she looked in every direction. The woman was gone.

Shag sniffed and whined but trotted back to Carin.

"Hello, hello," she called. She climbed higher on the hill to where only short scrub oak grew. The small-statured woman could not possibly have walked or run far enough in that amount of time to have crossed the ridge. Shag panted beside her.

"Where'd she go, boy?"

Carin hiked back down the hill, wandering for some time along the property. One way led to an impossible tangle of scrub oak, brush, rocks, and barbed wire fence that marked her neighbor's property. The other way sloped down to a bluff, and then formed a sharp drop-off to the road below. The woman was nowhere to be seen.

Carin stood on the bluff for a while, looking out over the town as the sun moved down behind the ridge that stretched all along the valley and the evening shadows took over, even though the sky was still light blue.

"That's fitting, I suppose," she muttered to herself. Twilight was when strange things sometimes happened, or so she'd read somewhere. For if the woman resembled anyone at all that she'd ever seen before, even in that one glimpse of the face half-hidden beneath the brim of the slat bonnet, she resembled Allie Earp, Virgil Earp's wife and Carin's ancestor. The woman Gideon claimed had let him out of jail.

Carin shivered and squeezed her arms. The phone rang just as she got back inside. It was Hugh.

"There's still some checking to do, Carin, but so far, Gideon Avarest has no social security number, no record of a driver's license in the states that are computerized and have gotten back to us. No bank accounts except the one he opened this morning. He's never filed taxes with the IRS. In a word, he doesn't exist."

"At least not in this time," she murmured, and sat down.

Chapter Five

When Carin met Gideon at seven o'clock in the Palm Court at the Hotel Colorado, she was mad. All the way down to town in her Trooper, she'd worked up questions to put to him. Standing on the bluff in the twilight, she'd been half ready to believe in the time-travel theory. But as she'd showered and gotten ready for dinner, her journalistic skepticism reasserted itself.

By the time she pulled up next to the hotel and went in, she was ready to interrogate him about what was going on. When she didn't find him in the dining room, she marched down the hall and up to his room, her calf-length flowered skirt swinging above canvas sandals. In a long-sleeved white cotton blouse with ruffled front, and with hair pulled back at the nape of her neck and held with a yellow ponytail holder, she probably looked like part of the Old West herself.

"Gideon," she called, rapping on the door.

She heard a moan from within. A moment later, the door opened and he let her in.

"What's the matter? You're not..."

But his hand on the back of his head and the pain that twisted his face stopped her accusations that he wasn't ready and had kept her waiting.

Still groaning, he slumped back into the room and into

a chair. Her heart jumped into her throat. New fear sprang
through her

"What's happened?"

He touched his jaw tenderly. "Someone was in here
waiting. Caught me by surprise." He grunted. "I was out
cold until a little while ago."

She knelt beside the chair to examine the new welt on
the back of his head where he'd either fallen or been hit.
At least he couldn't possibly be faking that. And the room
was a mess. Drawers open, the mattress twisted at an odd
angle, pillows on the floor. The French doors to the little
balcony were open.

"Was there a fight in here?"

"Not that I took part in." He sat up and moved his
head from side to side, trying to clear it.

Her heart pounded out danger. Attempting to remain
calm, she went into the bathroom to get a wet cloth to
have him hold against his head.

"Who did this?" she asked as she handed him the
washcloth.

He glanced up at her with a tinge of irony in his pained
expression, then just looked glumly at the disheveled bed.
She thought she knew the answer he would give.

"Well, don't touch anything. I'll have Hugh come
check things out."

Gideon's look told her that he didn't think the sheriff
would be able to catch whoever did this. "Like I said, I
came here for some reason. Maybe they did too."

She sat down in the other wing chair and leaned her
elbows on her knees. "You mean the Earp gang?"

"That's right."

Her heart turned over at the mention of this vulnera-
bility—imagined or not, and she felt drawn into his world
again, the way she had at the cabin. She restrained the

urge to reach out and comfort him, folding her hands under her chin instead.

"Something odd just happened," she finally murmured.

He lifted his gaze and looked at her. The hazel eyes conveyed his confusion and need for help, even if he wouldn't admit as much. She continued in a low voice, though they both knew there wasn't anyone in the room now listening to them.

"There was a woman in my backyard just a little while ago. A small woman, dressed in a gray gingham dress and a slat bonnet."

Still slightly distracted by the pain, he knitted his brows, but his face changed slowly as he speculated. "What did she look like?"

Carin described her. Gideon shut his eyes for a moment and then tried to sit up straighter. "That would be Allie Earp."

Of course Carin knew that was what he was going to say. So why did her heart hammer harder, the adrenaline rush through her?

"I can't believe this," she said more to herself than to him.

She called Hugh to come take a look. He agreed to meet them at the hotel in an hour. Gideon still refused to go back to the doctor, so after he cleaned up, she took him downstairs to get something to eat.

He followed her into the dining room, which was separated from the hotel lobby by a low partition topped by potted palms. The oval-backed chairs, white tablecloths, and antique sideboard were the same as they would have been in Gideon's time. If the crystal chandeliers were electric instead of gaslit, it made little difference.

They placed their order, then Carin pondered him, trying to gather her nerves. He took a sip of the wine the waiter had poured and then sat back, looking like he was feeling better. She sighed inwardly in relief. She had tried to steer him away from alcoholic beverages, in view of his recent head injury, but he'd just stared at her in disbelief and ordered the bottle of wine.

"So," said Carin. "Do you have an explanation for all this?"

"Maybe."

"Well, what?"

He hunched over the table, crossing his arms in front of him. "I think I came here to help you."

"Me?"

"That's right. You said you're writing these stories about the Earps. Allie was your ancestor. She let me out of jail and now she's sent me here to help you. Maybe she came, too." He paused, his broad, sexy face turning serious. "Maybe you're going to help me clear my name."

It was her turn for a look of disbelief. She dropped her hand to the table with a thump. "I beg your pardon."

"I was framed back in Tombstone. Couldn't get justice there, so I came forward in time, like you say."

"I didn't say all that."

"Same difference. Here I am and you told me it's now 1997. So I jumped forward in time. Maybe Allie knew some sort of magic, I don't know. Maybe it was the thunder. But you're writing about the Earps. Maybe you're supposed to prove I'm innocent, leastways, in the newspapers."

"But, Gideon, I don't have any evidence about you. How can I prove anything?"

He frowned and poured himself and Carin some more wine from the bottle the waiter had left on the table. "You say you got Allie's diaries?"

"Yes, and I've been doing research to substantiate

some of what she ways. It's rather interesting, really. You see, the Earps have become quite a legend in our time.''

"Don't know why that'd be. They're no different than anybody else.''

"I know that now. There's been a lot of confusion over what kind of men they really were and what they did. Allie says Wyatt was no more than a con artist.''

"Thought so myself. Always opportunin', always makin' friends that'd help him and his brothers get ahead.''

"Yes, but you see, he and his brothers have been painted as hero gunfighters who cleaned up Dodge City and then Tombstone of the cowboy rustlers who were thieves and murderers.''

"They weren't any good, themselves,'' said Gideon. "But if you'd been there, you'd know. It was a political feud, just two sides always trying to get each other.''

She warmed to the subject. "Yes. I've learned that much. There were the politicians who grabbed up all the town lots in Tombstone and sold them at outrageously high prices to the settlers who were already living on them. Sheriff Johnny Behan was their man. And they were in collusion with the cowboy element doing the rustling, is that right?''

He grinned, and she realized that she'd made her first indication that she believed his story and was asking him to verify events that had happened in Tombstone. She looked around suddenly as if to make sure that no one was listening. If she was going to carry on a crazy conversation with a man who said he was a time traveler, she didn't want anyone else to overhear her making a fool of herself. But her enthusiasm for the story she was so involved in carried her forward.

"Of course, Wyatt Earp and Johnny Behan were in love

with the same woman, that Josephine Marcus, the actress, but it was more than that, wasn't it?''

"You got it," he said. "The Earps were real clannish, always tryin' to get the upper hand in politics, always running for public office just to get badges on their chests. And then they took to robbin' stages."

His words piqued her interest. "How were they involved?"

He leaned back, evidently enjoying himself now. As he painted the picture, Carin inched forward, drinking it all in.

"Well, Morgan and Wyatt both spent some time as shotgun messengers for Wells Fargo. The stages were carryin' out bullion by the ton to Tucson, you see. From there, Wells, Fargo and Company sent it to the mint at San Francisco."

She gazed at him from under her bangs. "You said you worked for Wells Fargo yourself."

"Yup. That's how I got tricked by the Earps."

The air escaped her lungs in a slow sigh. "Tell me about it."

"They must have known the stage I was guardin' had the bullion. Not too hard to find out since they'd ridden shotgun themselves before they got appointed as officers of the law. And since I'd traded places with Philpot so he could warm his hands, we were caught off guard. He tried to shoot back, but they got him. I stopped the stage so as to keep the passengers out of danger. They'd have got shot up if we'd made a run for it. Then before I knew it, I was accused of tipping off the robbers about the bullion and trading places with Philpot on purpose. 'Course, that ain't true, but that's what the jury believed. Philpot was dead. He couldn't testify. You know the rest."

"And you want me to tell your story?"

"That's right. Leastways, I reckon that's the best we

can do. Might be right satisfying to see the true story in print.''

"Gideon, my readers may accept revisionist history when they're presented with convincing articles backed up by facts. But they will not believe that a witness traveled through time to offer testimony.''

He set down his glass and spoke in a more confidential tone. "I escaped a hanging, unless I'm still dreamin'. But I figure these bumps on my head would have wakened me up by now.''

"Yeah, maybe.''

She had to admit being charmed by his sincerity, moved by the man himself. She would look through her research materials, though. If she did find anything relating to his case, it might make for interesting reading.

Their dinner came, and they ate with gusto. When they were finished, Hugh met them in the lobby.

"We checked the room. Not much to see.'' He nodded at Gideon but gave him a frown. "Still don't want you to leave town, Avarest, just in case your amnesia clears up and we have to ask you more questions.''

Gideon eyed Carin. "I don't plan to go anywhere, not on my own accord, anyway.''

"Good enough.''

"What about my weapons?''

"What about them?''

"You going to give them back?''

Hugh's lip twitched, and Carin lifted an eyebrow. She knew that Gideon's weapons hadn't been used to fire the bullets at her cabin. Hugh had no reason to keep them unless they were illegal firearms. She knew all about the concealed weapons law. A concealed weapon required a permit to carry. But Gideon's weapons hadn't been concealed. She wondered how Hugh was going to handle this.

He frowned at Gideon for a moment, but he played it straight.

"You come to my office in the morning. You can have your guns back as long as you don't plan any bank robberies with them."

Hugh left them and Carin half felt she ought to take her leave. But Gideon was gazing with interest at the entrance to the hotel bar. Carin followed him as he wandered over to the entrance. Through the doorway they could see the polished mahogany bar that formed an island in the middle of a large and comfortable room. Old-fashioned tulip-shaped light fixtures on the walls cast a warm glow. A lattice-framed atrium space rose another story above the bar. The glasses were suspended from a brass frame like the brass foot rail, around which burgundy padded bar stools swiveled. The bartender wore a brocade vest and a white shirt, with a garter on her sleeve.

Carin shook her head, realizing that Gideon might be very comfortable in these surroundings, with hints of decor from the old days of the hotel.

"Join me for a drink?" he asked, as if reading her thoughts.

She was finding it hard to resist his special breed of charm and reasoned that maybe she needed to keep an eye on him. The only way she was going to find out who he really was would be to get to know him a little better.

"All right," she agreed.

They took a seat at a round table with claw-footed cast iron feet planted solidly on the dark blue carpet. The cherry wood armchairs offered comfortable seats.

While they waited for their drinks, Carin began to feel tongue-tied. His handsome face had an openness about it that made her think he wasn't lying. He looked a little bashful when he smiled at her, and she continued to battle her own wobbling pulse.

She clung to her coffee liqueur glass and looked down after catching his eye briefly. His hand rested on the table near hers. When he moved it as if he might want to touch her, she felt an electrifying pulse pound through her.

"What are you going to do tomorrow?" she asked, tossing her head and twisting her body sideways in a casual gesture as if she wanted to see the rest of the room better.

"Depends," Gideon replied.

She felt his slow, easy look on her and felt a warm blush touch her cheeks.

"On what?"

"On what I find out."

"You mean about the Earp gang."

He grunted assent. "If they're in town, they'll come after me again. I'll be ready this time."

"Because you'll have your guns back?"

"A man has a right to protect himself."

She smiled in amusement. "Gideon, in this century, you need a permit to carry a gun."

"A permit?" He looked at her in puzzlement for a moment. "Can you help me get one?"

"I suppose I can."

They listened to the muted clackety-clack of pool balls coming from tables separated from the main lounge by three arched openings in the stucco wall that divided the rooms. Carin reflected that she hadn't been out on a date in a very long time. If the situation weren't so bizarre, she might enjoy it. And who was she fooling? She enjoyed Gideon's company and wanted to be with him.

By the time they left the bar, her nerves were feeling pleasantly stimulated. She walked him slowly up to his room. He took his time getting out the key and unlocking the door. But he didn't invite her in. He stood there and gave her an almost melancholy smile.

"Much obliged for the evening," he said.

"Sure, it was nothing."

Then real slow, so that it seemed natural and didn't startle her, he placed his hand on her shoulder. His golden-hazel eyes drowned out any desire to step away.

"Carin Sage," he said real softly. "Can't help thinkin' we mighta met in another time."

Her heart knocked in her rib cage. She gave a weak laugh. "You mean in your time?"

He lifted his big shoulders and let them fall in a shrug. Carin was not a small woman. Her five-foot-seven-inch frame usually made her feel in command of any situation. But Gideon made her feel like a paper doll. She'd been in his arms once already when he'd had to pin her down in the cabin. She wondered whether, if she tried to run away, he'd do that again.

Now his head was bent and his face was coming toward her. She could only stand there, trying not to breathe too hard as his lips brushed hers in a polite, but ever so pleasant kiss.

"Thanks again," he said as he straightened up.

It was only a simple kiss, but she felt like she might sink against the door frame. Her feet managed to keep her upright, but her eyelids fluttered.

"Uh, sure." She could see that he looked real pleased, and he pulled his hands away from her carefully.

"Uh, you want a ride to the sheriff's tomorrow to get your guns?" She found that her voice was a little hoarse and shaky.

His brows moved upward and his eyes smiled. "That'd be right nice of you, if you don't mind."

She swallowed and rested her hand on the doorjamb to make sure she wouldn't stumble over her own feet when she stepped backward to turn around.

"I have some business on this side of town. We can

use some of your money to shop for some new clothes. You'll need them if you're going to stay awhile."

She realized the irony of her statement, but had no answer as to whether Gideon was here permanently or not.

"You can ride along with me while I make a stop at the Flat Top Ski Resort after we go to the sheriff's."

He seemed to be thinking. Finally, he crossed his arms. "I don't think I should stay at the hotel tonight."

Her heart gave a little bump in her rib cage. "What do you mean?"

"I know you can take care of yourself, but I don't like it. I'll be up here in this hotel room worryin' about you all night. Probably wouldn't sleep. Be better if I stayed on your couch with my rifle across my knees."

She couldn't help a self-conscious grin. "You think I need guarding."

"Well, you've had intruders. Allie Earp showed up in your backyard. It'd be better if we stuck together for a bit."

She thought about it, hesitated to agree. "Well, that might make sense. If these guys are after you, it would help me to get a better look at them next time they show up. Yes, I suppose you're right. Maybe we'd better keep close together from now on."

Then she pressed her lips together, embarrassed at how her words sounded. She hadn't meant to sound suggestive. But she knew it would be worse if she tried to explain herself.

Gideon relaxed and shifted his long legs. "That's more like it. I'll just get my gear."

While she waited for him, she began to wonder just what would happen between them if they were together in the cabin all night long. She couldn't help but speculate what it would feel like if he put his arms around her again and kissed her. The erotic fantasy of being half naked against his bare chest sent a thrill through her.

They said little on the drive to the cabin, but she felt the tension crackling between them. When she stole a glance in his direction, she could see the firm, determined chin outlined. The strong shoulders were relaxed, but ready to wrestle with his enemies should they show themselves.

All the way to the cabin she admonished herself. Maybe she was just being a sucker for a wounded hero.

Back at the house, Shag greeted them with his usual enthusiasm. But he wasn't at all agitated, which she took to mean that there had been no further disturbances. Gideon hefted his rifle and went to check out the property with Shag. Carin crossed the backyard, scanning the surroundings.

All around them the woods played its symphony. Crickets chirped, aspen leaves rustled. An owl hooted. The sounds of the evening were comforting and familiar. She knew that if human intruders were hidden in the woods, the sounds of nature would be different, as the beasts and birds were alerted to their presence.

Gideon and the dog returned. "Nothin' out here," he said.

The dog trotted back to the house with them, and she smiled to herself. Shag seemed to have found a new friend.

She fussed about the living room, making it cozy for Gideon. Then they managed not to touch each other again as they said good-night.

NEXT MORNING as promised, she took him to a Western store, where they purchased clothes. She thought he looked disturbingly good in a new pair of jeans and casual light blue denim shirt. He even picked out a new tan felt cowboy hat that made him look like the real thing indeed.

They drove across the bridge and turned back to Seventh Street and the sheriff's office. First, they arranged for the permit, then got the guns, which he started to strap on.

"You're not going to wear them, are you?" she said.

"Why not?"

"People in this county don't generally wear firearms. Only the lawmen do."

Gideon set his jaw, looking past her shoulder as if he had other concerns. "Can't be too careful."

"I understand. But the man I'm going to see will think we're both crazy if I bring an armed cowboy. Do me a favor and put the guns in the back seat." She held the Trooper's rear door open.

Gideon gave way grudgingly. Before he got in, he put the guns where he could reach them if need be.

He fastened his seat belt but sat hunched forward, his expression telling her that he disliked being strapped in.

"It's a safety precaution," she told him. "And it's the law." He glared at her last comment.

The Flat Top Ski Resort was a thirty-minute drive into the hills west of town. Behind them, green ridges reigned over a long, luscious green valley through which the Colorado River flowed. Roads forked off to folds in the mountains where hidden valleys and isolated settlements nestled. They took the next road and began a climb upward into the hills. Carin noticed Gideon studying the breathtaking scenery.

They came to a flat stretch with a high mountain meadow to their left. Indian paintbrush, purple asters, and blue and yellow lupines offered a riot of wildflower colors.

"Never been to Colorado before?" she asked.

"Not this part," he admitted. "Worked a stage from Santa Fe up to Fort Garland once. Never got further north."

She smiled. Fort Garland was once a prominent military fort, but all that was left now was a ruin at a sleepy town where two state highways crossed.

"I fly down to that part of the state once in a while."

She felt him staring at her and glanced over. Then she realized what she'd said. "I mean, I fly an airplane. A Citabria Explorer, one-sixty horsepower. I got my pilot's license two years ago."

She saw in a glance that she'd lost him. Okay, so if he was from the past he didn't know that flying had become a reality.

"You don't believe me," she said.

"I didn't say that. So you mean flying machines finally got off the ground. Never did see why anyone'd want to fly around like a bird."

"Air travel is part of the modern world, Gideon. A lot of people who live up here in the mountains have licenses. It's a faster way to get around than driving on mountain roads. I'll show you the airport in Glenwood when we get back."

She felt his skepticism, but didn't say anything else.

The road opened into the parking lot at the ski resort where she was to meet the owner, her father's old friend, Nigel Henshaw. She saw Gideon stare curiously at the chairlifts stretching up the mountain. She parked the car, then he followed her up the steps and into the lodge.

But as she and Gideon passed through the unlighted lobby to the seemingly only inhabited office in the building, she heard voices raised in an argument. She slowed her pace, a frown of concern on her face. She didn't want to embarrass Nigel if he was having a disagreement with someone.

"Gideon, would you mind waiting for me outside? It sounds like Mr. Henshaw is busy. I don't think I'll be long with him."

"Yes, ma'am." Gideon took himself off to examine the chairlift.

She'd already explained to Gideon earlier that morning that she was coming to interview Nigel about his plans for the opening of ski season this fall. She needed to put something in the paper about it.

Carin waited in the darkened lobby, out of earshot of the actual words being spoken. The emotion conveyed in the angry tones of voice of both men made her clutch at the strap of her leather handbag. She felt awkward. She was on time for her appointment, but she didn't want to interrupt. On the other hand, her insatiable curiosity, which made her a good journalist, made her want to edge closer to find out what was going on.

She stepped forward a few paces until she caught some of the words.

"I'm not accusing you of anything, Julius," said Nigel. "A 5 percent difference is nothing on a busy day. But the new locked bags will be added security. You and the new accounting manager will count the money in the counting room together."

"You didn't mention any discrepancies all season. Why now?"

"I'm not saying I was worried about it. I just want to increase my profitability this year. Pure and simple. I'm not saying you or anybody else is a thief."

"If you are, I want a lawyer. I won't have you watching me all season just to make sure I don't make any more mistakes."

"Julius, calm down. This is my business. If I decide to increase security and accuracy in accounting, that's my call, not yours."

Carin backed away a little, not wanting to make it appear she'd been eavesdropping. There were a few more words exchanged and then she straightened and walked toward the office as if she'd just arrived. The man Nigel had been speaking to came flying out of the room and down the hall. He paused and stared at her as they passed.

She'd met Julius Eberly last year shortly after Nigel had hired him as a supervisor, but she didn't really know the man.

Even so, the narrow gaze he gave her as he passed sent a steely jolt up her spine. His look seemed to accuse her of eavesdropping. Then he lifted his chin and strode through the dim lobby. He threw the outer door open, slamming it against the wall before it banged inward again making Carin jump. Nigel came into the hall just as Carin turned around, almost bumping into him.

"Carin," he said, extending an arm for a warm fatherly hug. "Sorry. I hope you haven't been waiting."

"Er, no."

He ushered her into his office and cleared some papers from a chair so she could sit down. Nigel Henshaw was a fit, attractive man in his early fifties with silver-blond hair and a permanent tan from so much time spent outdoors. His warm brown eyes were intelligent, and she could understand why her father had considered him his best friend. He always seemed glad to see Carin and asked how her father was doing in his new home in Palm Springs.

After catching up on a little family news, Carin asked about Julius's hasty exit. "What was he so upset about?"

Nigel made no effort to hide the truth from her. "Eberly supervised the cashiers last year. Had good recommendations from his previous employers, seemed to be doing a good job. But I've decided to tighten up on procedures. I lose too much money from carelessness, especially during busy times. Nobody's perfect. But I want to put in some double checks this year to make things run more smoothly.''

"Hmm. And Julius doesn't like it.''

"Oh, he'll come around. Just thinks I stepped on his toes. I suppose I might be offended if I were in his shoes.''

"You don't think there's any funny business going on, do you? People pocketing a few bills here and there?''

"I hope that's not the case.''

Nigel kept his face noncommittal. He gazed out the picture window at the ski slopes where Gideon was walking along slowly and admiring the scenery, his thumbs crooked in his pockets.

"He came with me,'' Carin explained.

"Friend of yours?''

"Uh, yeah. We just met.'' She felt a little embarrassed and quickly returned to the previous subject of conversation. "So you felt the need for greater security.''

He lifted a hand in a gesture of surrender. "We've grown a lot in the last year. It makes sense to tighten up the way we count our money. We'll use cash bags with locks on them instead of just relying on the number of tickets sold against the cash slips filled out by the cashiers. It would be foolish not to.''

"I see.''

"I tell you this in confidence, Carin. I don't want a word of this in the paper.''

"No, of course not. You were going to tell me about your new lift and plans for opening the season.'' She took out her notepad and pencil.

"Yes. We have an expanded capacity this year, and we're going to need it.''

He outlined the growth of the business and his new pricing structure, while Carin made notes. She got it all down, even though she was a little distracted by Gideon's movements on the slopes outside the window.

When they were finished, she shut her notebook and gave Nigel a look of concern. "I hope the season goes smoothly," she said.

The flicker in his eye told her that he did suspect there'd been some theft and was going to avoid it with his new security measures this year. But he wasn't ready to make any accusations yet.

She was curious about Julius Eberly's reaction, but now wasn't the time to push it. She wasn't here to do investigative journalism. Nigel was a friend of the family, and she didn't write sensational stories. She covered cultural events and attractions that made Glenwood Springs a good place to visit.

Nigel walked her outside, and she introduced Gideon. The two men shook hands and eyed each other. She could see Nigel's silent assessment of a man his best friend's daughter might choose to spend time with. She chatted about the ski season to avoid awkward conversation, and Gideon kept his mouth shut. He didn't offer any comments until they were back in her car.

"You get what you came for?"

"Yes," she murmured. "And a little more."

She speculated about Julius, but she didn't talk anymore as she pulled onto the road that curved through the mountains back toward town.

A slow-moving Toyota Cressida ahead of them kept them going slower than Carin was used to driving. She knew this road and was aware she could pass safely on the next stretch. When the road flattened beside the high mountain meadow, she moved out to pass on the left. The Toyota chose that moment to pick up speed.

"What the...?" Carin exclaimed.

The driver didn't even turn his head sideways, so Carin

tooted her horn. But his speed kept even with hers, not allowing her to pass. Ready to curse him, she eased up on the gas pedal to drop back. It wasn't worth an accident.

To her sudden horror, the other driver did the same. Both cars slowed, and Carin was still in the left-hand lane. Adrenaline pumped through her. Fear crawled into her throat.

She cursed under her breath. They were approaching a curve with a drop-off down the side of the mountain on the left. She braked. The Toyota swerved right and then left, grazing her car on the right side.

Gideon pitched toward her, but his seat belt held him in place. He reached into the back seat for his gun.

Fear shot through her, but she steadied the Trooper, terrified that at any moment another car would appear from around the curve ahead. The Toyota dropped back and swerved again, but as it came toward her, she slammed her foot down on the gas pedal, attempting to avoid a collision. But the Toyota slammed into them again.

Gideon aimed at the other car. The shot exploded in her ears, increasing the sudden threat of panic.

"Gideon," she yelled. But she didn't have time to tell him to put the gun down, she was too busy trying to avoid being hit again while keeping away from the drop-off as the two cars slammed together and then swerved apart.

Glass shattered in the back seat and she realized the other car was returning fire. In a moment they'd all be dead. She braked suddenly and the Toyota shot ahead. Gideon had his head and arm out the window, blasting away again as Carin fishtailed on the gravel shoulder.

Chapter Six

She shook like a leaf, her hands in a death grip on the steering wheel as the car finally came to a halt, inches from the drop-off, and she and Gideon bounced against their seats.

She was too shocked to speak, closing her eyes for a brief moment, an ugly taste in her mouth, the bolt of fear still in the pit of her stomach. Gideon had unstrapped himself and was out the door before she yelled at him again.

"Gideon, wait."

With shaking hands she unfastened her belt and tumbled out. She lurched around the hood toward him. "Don't shoot anymore."

But his gun arm was at his side and he was squinting at the curve around which the Toyota had disappeared. Then he laid the gun pointing away from them on the hood of the car and reached for her. He felt both her arms gently as if checking for injuries.

"You all right?"

"Yes, yes," she gasped. "You?"

"Yeah."

He pulled her toward him and held her against his chest and shoulder, his own chest rising and falling from the close call. She was still breathing hard, and her blood raced. She grasped his shoulders, not minding something to help hold her up until she could regain her wits. He cradled her and she nestled against him, drinking in the warm support.

"You sure you're all right?" he asked again, his voice at once comforting and gruff, as if he was ready to get on his horse and give chase to the threatening car.

"Hmm," she mumbled into his shirt. While her heart pounded and her pulse raced, she began at least to control her breathing and finally stepped back to look at the damage to her car.

Neither one spoke for minutes as she looked at the dents and scratches, shaking her head. However, the bent metal was nothing compared to the unmistakable threat they'd just received. Someone had wanted them dead.

She started to tremble again and leaned on the car, not wanting to appear so shaken in front of Gideon. She was a woman who had always taken care of herself, and she would do so now.

Anger began to replace the scare. "Why would someone do that?" she asked the air.

"Maybe they wanted me?" Gideon said in a low, serious tone.

She stared at him in disbelief. Was he going to claim that his enemies from the past had appeared here and learned to drive a car in order to follow him? She saw how easily he read her expression.

"It's possible," he said. "I'm not saying they drove the car. But the gunfire came from somebody in the back seat."

Ludicrous, and yet she had no other explanation. And he was right about one thing. The driver hadn't been firing. Someone else in the car had been. She drew a deep breath and sighed.

"Julius Eberly was mighty mad when he left Nigel

Henshaw. He saw me in the hall. But surely he wouldn't take his anger out on me."

"Who's Julius Eberly?"

"He works for Nigel," she explained. "Julius was in charge of the money last year. Nigel's decided to increase security and try to minimize cash losses. I heard part of the conversation. Julius took it as an accusation that it was his fault that money had gone missing, even though it wasn't meant to be."

But Gideon was still frowning into the distance. He got his holster from the back seat and strapped it on. This time, she didn't argue.

"Did you get the license number?"

"The what?"

She was beginning to feel irritated that he was so dense. Frustration welled up inside. "Gideon, if you're playing games with me, please stop. This is serious."

"I know that."

His words totally undid her and tears tightened her throat. She was caught up in something beyond her control and she didn't like it. But dammit, she wasn't going to cry in front of this big cowboy.

He didn't wait for her to regain control, but scooped her up in his arms again, smoothing her hair with his hand. He didn't say anything, just offered her his strength, while her shoulders shook and she clenched her fists against him, wiping moisture from her eyes with the backs of her wrists. Finally, she felt ready to stand on her own though she reluctantly stepped away from the comfort of his embrace.

"I didn't see the license plate, either, or the driver. I was too busy controlling the car. But we can report the make."

"Where do we go now?" he asked.

"Nowhere, until we report the accident and the sheriff comes to the scene."

She looked back the way they'd come. It was too far to walk back to the ski resort. So instead they flagged down the next car. The driver called Hugh's office on his cellular phone.

In fifteen minutes, they heard the sirens of Hugh's Chevy Blazer. He roared up the road, made a U-turn and pulled to a stop behind them.

"What happened?" he asked as he and Pete McGuire got out. Hugh glanced at Gideon, but didn't ask what he was doing there.

Carin reported what had occurred and gave the make of the car and best description she could while Hugh took notes.

"Sorry we didn't get the plate number. It wasn't out of state, but I don't remember anything else."

"You know what year the car was?" Hugh asked.

She shrugged. Hugh glanced at Gideon and frowned. "You?"

She answered for him. "Gideon hasn't recovered his memory yet."

Hugh looked disgusted that the man on the scene wasn't sharp enough to identify the model and year of the car. He snapped his notebook shut and went to assist Pete in measuring skid marks. When they were finished, she told Hugh about the argument between Nigel and Julius.

"I don't see how it could have anything to do with this," she said. "But Julius had a glare on his face when he passed me. His look gave me a bad feeling."

"Okay," said Hugh. "We'll check on his movements."

They assured Hugh that neither one of them was hurt.

"I'd better take the car to the garage." She glanced

sideways at Gideon as Hugh returned to Pete. "I'll have to rent something to drive while they fix this damage."

"I'll go along. You need protection."

In spite of the aftereffects of the accident, his words caused her a hesitant grin. He certainly was responding in true Western-heroic fashion.

"And what will you do? You can't draw that gun and shoot at everyone in town, Gideon. They may have done it that way in Tombstone, but people are not in the habit of shooting up the streets in Glenwood Springs."

His voice was deep, and he spoke in a determined tone. "All the same, if we're shot at, I shoot back. It's my job."

"So I've got a Wells Fargo agent protecting me?"

"You have until I find out what's going on. That sheriff of yours doesn't look like the type that can keep the town safe. I wouldn't trust him."

"Things just aren't done the way they used to be," she explained with a sigh. "They track criminals on computer now. They don't follow them on horseback through the mountains. They use scientific methods to examine evidence. Radios are used to notify law-enforcement officers any distance away to look for certain vehicles and individuals. Hugh might not look like a tough hombre, Gideon, but he's trained at what he does. Believe me, we're lucky to have him on our side."

She felt loyal to Hugh and respected his professionalism. It was important that Gideon see it that way.

Gideon looked unconvinced, folded his arms, and leaned against the hood of the car. Carin thought at that moment that he did look completely out of his element. The new shirt and jeans fit him well, but they did not hide a certain wariness, toughness, or a quick trigger finger.

Gideon squinted at the ground, walked onto the highway and stared at the asphalt and then into the distance.

He came back shaking his head. "No way to track them in these rigs."

"Not like you're used to. But there were some skid marks from the rubber tires. Hugh and Pete took pictures with a camera. That will help them find the vehicle and press charges if they catch up with the culprits."

They got in the car when Hugh said that they could go. Gideon took his time fastening his seat belt.

THE GLENWOOD NEWS was located in a two-story building on Grand Avenue and Twenty-second Street. The building sat back from the main thoroughfare on a small lot under a spreading oak, an elm, and weeping willows.

She introduced Gideon to Sallie Goodman, the young woman who answered the phones, and to her boss, Keith Armbruster, the editor-in-chief, who was just barreling out of the publisher's office. Neither colleague had time for much more than a quick handshake before taking the phone calls that hardly ever ceased during the busy work day. Keith hurried to his desk, the proverbial pencil stuck between ear and short dark brown hair.

Carin led Gideon between desks piled high with papers, photos, and page proofs to her own tiny office at the back. The window behind her desk looked out to an alley that stretched to the residential street one block over from Grand Avenue.

The office was so small, and so filled with stacks of papers, files, and correspondence, that when Gideon followed her in, it was a tight squeeze to get past him so that she could go behind her desk. He grasped her arm quite naturally as she slid between the edge of the desk and him. Carin felt the familiar temptation to stop and lean against him. But she continued to move past him, her pulse dancing at wrists and temples.

She was so distracted by Gideon filling the space in her

office that it was a moment before she noticed the note on her chair. The torn piece of white paper fluttered when she swiveled the gray padded chair around to sit down.

She thought it was just trash until she stared down at the thick black letters spelling out their warning: Mind Your Own Bizness, Or Else.

"What…" The warning unsettled her, and she felt its danger brush the back of her neck. She frowned at the open window behind her desk. Who had done this?

Gideon had been examining the room and now leaned over the desk to see what she was staring at. He frowned. "What's that?"

"Wait, don't touch it," she cautioned. "It might have fingerprints on it. Though I'd guess that whoever put this here was careful not to leave any of his own."

She rummaged for an empty clear plastic folder. Then she picked up the warning note at the very edge. Before she slid it into the protective sleeve, she stared at the awkward printing.

"It looks as though someone either used their left hand or tried to disguise their printing."

She attempted to ignore the queasiness in her stomach. Some strange things were happening, and if they were all perpetrated by the same person, that individual was dangerous and needed to be removed from society, pronto. But panic would not help.

Gideon studied the note then scratched his head. "Could be anyone's."

She glanced at him wondering about both his and her sanity for a second. Here she was in the company of a man who might be just as crazy as whoever was threatening her, and yet she was beginning to listen to what he had to say, as if it were truth.

"Come on," she said. "Your tracking skills might come in handy now."

Back in the outer office, she got Keith and Sallie's attention long enough to ask them if either had been in her office. Both had dropped things off there, but hadn't noticed anything on her chair. Neither had any of the other staff working diligently at computer terminals and at slanted art tables in the art department.

"There were people in here this morning," said Sallie between phone calls. She wrinkled her brow in concern. "The mailman, the UPS guy. John Ellis from the CPA office next door brought us cake from a birthday party. But none of them went back there. Unless they did it while I was in the rest room."

The phones rang and Carin questioned Keith, who stood with them at the front counter. He stared at the note she showed him, shock registering in his hawk-like face.

"Gosh, Carin. Some nut. I didn't see anyone go in there, but I was in and out a lot myself this morning. Meetings with Raylene." He referred to their publisher and owner, Raylene Sommer. "Could have been anyone. I can only vouch for the last hour." He shrugged his narrow shoulders. "Even then, I might not have noticed. I was on the phone a lot. Sorry."

"Okay." Back in her office, Carin slid the folder into her top desk drawer and locked it. Gideon replaced his hat on his head, and she led him out the front door and around the corner of the building. They halted at the edge of the gravel alley, where the shade spread from the weeping willow.

He didn't have to be told what to look for. He squatted down and examined the ground, working slowly along the edge of the building, leaving the comforting shade, until he was just beneath the window. There, he pointed at the impression left by the toe of a boot in the soft earth just beside the window.

"Someone was here, all right. They must have leaned forward to drop the note in."

With the sash window all the way up, it wasn't too far a reach to the chair. Someone with height could have reached in and with luck and the right air current, the note would have landed on the seat.

She pulled one corner of her mouth down. "So how tall is Wyatt Earp?"

Gideon answered the question seriously with no hesitation. "I'm six foot two. I've got two inches on him. He could have done it."

She shook her head. "It could have been Julius, or whoever was in that car. Or just some nut, I guess. But the coincidence in that case is a little hard to accept."

She crossed her arms and considered while the hot sun beamed down on them and warmth reflected off the brick wall. Gideon knelt down again and looked for tracks, then straightened up and followed whatever markings he saw to the end of the alley at the next street. He straightened up and came back.

"Can't track on those paved roads. But I'd like to ask around at those houses. Could be somebody saw what happened."

"Thanks, Gideon, but we'd better let Hugh and his deputies do it. It's their job."

Gideon stood with hands on hips and eyed the concrete-block building and garages that lined the alley. Once off the main street, Glenwood Springs was a quiet town. Tall oaks, maples and elms shaded yards that sloped upward to residences climbing the hill. And the homes on the next street were of an older vintage. It was a street that Gideon might find familiar.

"You going to stay here?" he asked her.

She nodded. "I'll phone this in to Hugh, so he can send someone over."

She started back toward the entrance to the offices and then stopped. Just because she was following the correct procedures for reporting these crimes, she didn't want Gideon to think she didn't appreciate him.

"Uh, thanks for what you did," she said, not quite looking him in the eye.

He turned from his scrutiny of the neighborhood. "Why, sure. Anytime."

She began to tremble and had to start moving toward the door in order to quell the yearning she seemed to feel every time he looked at her that way. Darn it! There'd been times when she would have appreciated a big, sexy cowboy in her life.

Carin was always careful choosing her dates. In a town like Glenwood Springs there were too many travelers, and one-night stands weren't to her taste. The rest of the men she met here had grown up in these parts and were already settled. The relationships she'd had in the past had been satisfactory for a while. But she'd always known, somehow, that they weren't for good.

He still watched her. "If you don't need me for a while, I'll just have a look around the town."

"That would be fine. I'll be here the rest of the afternoon."

He squared up his hat. When he walked off down the alley, she would swear he was headed for the main street of a town in another time. That man had a way of turning her head. But too much was happening too fast to even consider being with him. *Whoa, there!* she said to her emotions as she walked back inside and turned into her office.

After phoning the sheriff's office, she looked carefully around the room to see if anything else had been disturbed. The emotions churning in her stomach were not what she wanted to experience on a regular basis. Her space had been violated at home and now at work. There seemed to be nowhere to turn. And most frustrating of all was that she didn't know what they wanted.

She went to pour herself a cup of coffee from their automatic coffeemaker in the small kitchen on the other side of the humming workplace. With the din of computers, phones, and voices of people coming in and out the front door as background, Carin returned to her desk and pondered. The fresh coffee soothed her nerves.

What did the author of the note want her to mind her own business about? Before she got very far in her thinking, Hugh walked in the door. He crossed the room with a nod at Sallie and Keith and entered her office. When she handed him the envelope and explained where the note had been placed on the chair, he frowned and scratched his head. She noticed the lines of stress in his face. His blue eyes were alert, but the muscles of his face were tense.

"I don't like all this, Carin. Something weird is going on."

"You're telling me."

"I don't think you should stay in your cabin. Until we find out who's bothering you, I'd rather have you in a safe place."

"What do you suggest? Taking me into protective custody and offering me a cot in the jail?"

He gave an exasperated sigh, left the room and returned a moment later with a cup of coffee. "Be reasonable. Henny would take you in, or Nigel. He has a lot of extra space in his place."

"I don't like to impose. Having a guest is just too much work for busy people. Besides, I don't want to bring someone else into danger. I agree there may be some crazy person after me. They seem to want to scare me away from my normal routine. If you want to post a deputy outside my cabin to watch things, I'll agree to that. But I think the best plan is to just continue to follow up leads as to who might be doing all this.''

''What about your cowboy friend? You're not getting into something you can't handle are you, Carin?''

She gave him a wry grin. ''He is a little odd, I'll grant you that. From his amnesia, I guess.''

''What do the doctors say?''

She felt a flush of embarrassment. ''They don't say. He refuses further treatment.''

''Carin, he might be some con artist, and possibly dangerous.''

She met his gaze levelly. ''I understand what you're saying, and you may be right.'' Reason warred with her gut reaction to Gideon. ''But he tried to protect me when we were hit by that car on the road. And if the Trooper had gone over the edge, he might have been killed along with me. By the way, any leads on who that car belongs to?''

''Not yet, but we're working on it. Without the license plate number, there are only about seventy thousand Toyota Cressidas in the state to track down.''

''Sorry.''

''All right.'' He studied his coffee mug. ''What have you been doing that someone might want to scare you away from?''

''Aside from the usual news stories about harmless events like the local festivals and Nigel's expansion at Flat Top, my main research lately has centered on the controversy surrounding the Wyatt Earp gang. My takeoff point was the diaries my family inherited from my great-great-great-aunt Allie Earp.''

Hugh looked at her curiously. ''Well, maybe somebody has a reputation to protect. You know these old-timers take their ancestry pretty seriously. You stepping on any toes?''

"Wyatt Earp's toes. But the history associated with his and his brothers' actions has been interpreted and reinterpreted for years. I've just been looking for facts that would back up Allie's story."

"Okay. What else?"

"I already told you about overhearing Julius and Nigel arguing at the ski resort. I went to interview Nigel and he told me about his expansion plans. He's going to increase security this year. Julius saw me. Maybe he thinks I'm doing some investigative journalism, trying to implicate him in something unethical. But I didn't plan to."

Hugh paced toward the small window and looked out toward the alley.

"What were they arguing about?"

"You'll need to ask Nigel about that."

"All right. You don't have to tell me. But it sounds like Julius is nervous about something. Maybe Nigel's got some sort of problem. I'll have a talk with him. If we've inadvertently run into a crime Julius has committed, his guilt is going to make him react. In the meantime, I'll send Pete to dust for prints in here."

She preceded him out of the office and then turned to watch him stretch yellow tape across the door to prevent anyone from entering until Pete checked for prints and any fibers that might have been left around the windowsill.

She frowned, hands on hips. "How long will it take?" she asked. "I do have work to do, you know."

"I'll get him over here right away." He lifted a sandy eyebrow at her. "You should relax, Carin. You've had a rather harrowing couple of days."

"I have deadlines. The paper goes to press whether or not the editors have had a trying day."

She knew her nerves were showing, and she also knew she had a habit of responding to situations beyond her control by getting mad. She just needed a little time to simmer down.

"Where did the cowboy go?" asked Hugh.

"For a walk. But he didn't put the note there. He was with me."

"Okay, okay, relax. I'll stop telling you what to do with your personal life."

"Thank you."

She sat down at a nearby desk that wasn't used by anyone except as a place to store old issues. Hugh moved a stack over and sat on the edge to finish his coffee.

"Nigel should have told me last year if there was a problem."

She pinched her lips together, trying to decide how much confidentiality she owed Nigel and how much Hugh would need to know. But protecting Nigel was uppermost in her mind, so she decided Hugh should get the facts. She'd only promised Nigel not to publish her suspicions in the papers.

"He didn't suspect any theft, Hugh. He just wants to increase profitability, and it's easy to make mistakes when you're busy."

"Maybe Julius has something to hide. I'll check into his background, too."

She leaned back in the swivel chair and put her feet on the desk. "Tell me what you find."

He shrugged, and then he gave her a wink. "Only if it's relevant to the break-in, the car that tried to run you off the road, or to this."

She folded her arms across her stomach. Maybe Hugh was right. She was too agitated to work right now.

"I might as well go down to the computer store and

replace my hard drive. I need a computer at home to work on now.''

Hugh nodded absently. ''Carin, I'd like you to give me copies of everything you're working on. There may be a reason someone is threatening you that you don't see. An outside point of view might help pinpoint it.''

''Fine. I agree. I'm too close to my work to tell. But I'm warning you, you'll see more historical research than you've been used to reading in a long time.''

He removed his glasses and rubbed the bridge of his nose. ''Might be a nice change from reading dull lab reports and lists of traffic violations.''

GIDEON WALKED the back streets of Glenwood parallel to Grand Avenue. Gusty wind ruffled his hair, and he clamped his hat more solidly on his head. He was still a little spooked by the notion that he had traveled in time, and he kept on guard just in case he had to deal with the unexpected.

He worked his way closer to downtown, took his time crossing the busy bridge again and stopped to overlook the big outdoor pool stretched in front of a sandstone bathhouse that looked like it had been built in his own time. Massive walls of two-foot-thick red sandstone rose three stories in the center section of the lodge. The two-story eastern and western wings were capped with ornate cupolas. It made him feel better to see things he recognized from his own century.

People thronged the pool to bathe in the sulfur hot springs. Up a rise of green lawn and shade trees above the pool was the hotel. The red brick and sandstone walls enclosed a courtyard on three sides and seemed to shoulder the mountain ridges behind it, topped off with bright blue sky.

He'd read some about the old structures that were still

here from his own time. At the hotel, he'd seen pictures of what Glenwood Springs had looked like in the 1890s shortly after it had sprung up and after the spa had been built by the silver kings to entertain the wealthy who came out from the East. Natural sulfur springs and good rail connections made this an ideal place for the rich from both coasts and abroad to vacation and do business deals in the grand hotel.

And many had come here for their health, to take the healing waters. Such as Doc Holliday, who had apparently become part of the local lore. He had treated himself in vain in the Yampa hot springs, so the stories said. He died in bed.

Gideon left the bridge and turned west onto the shady streets again. He worked his way to a brick house with a clapboard second story that housed the small historical museum. He paid the two-dollar entrance fee and decided to look around.

The women who took his money and showed him how the old house was laid out were dressed like women he knew in his own time. When they explained their clothing to him, he refrained from telling them that their manner of dress was familiar to him already.

In the parlor, he read an old newspaper clipping that said Virgil Earp had come here, too. He meant to treat his bad arm, which had never healed properly after he took a load of buckshot in the left side on December 28, 1881. Virgil's elbow was badly chewed up in Tombstone. Gideon found that the little museum had preserved this and many other accounts of the early days of Glenwood and now had them on display.

Gideon reread the news article that was displayed in a glass case on the second floor of the museum. He stayed there for an hour, reading stories about what happened to the Earps in Tombstone after he was supposed to have been hanged.

The museum was so quiet, Gideon was lost in time and had the feeling that while he stood there everything might have reverted to the past again.

Gradually, he came out of his reverie, having read all about the Earps and Doc Holliday and what Doc had done hereabouts before he'd died. When Gideon stepped into the little hallway, the floorboards creaked. The only other sound on the upper level was the ticking of the tall grandfather clock. Muted voices drifted up from downstairs.

He sensed another presence in the house, and went slowly down the stairs. The voices broke off and when he stepped onto the blue floral carpet of the main room, the woman who'd taken his money was back on her stool by the door, and the other one was in a little nook to the side where she had some books and trinkets for sale. He moved into the next parlor. The edge of a gray gingham skirt disappeared through the doorway into the kitchen and he followed.

Allie Earp stood in the sunny kitchen. At the same time, a gust of wind blew the door open. She turned to face him where he framed himself in the doorway.

He blinked and took off his hat. "Missus Earp," he said. "I need to talk to you."

Her face was half-hidden under the bonnet and the wind blew particles of dust into the room, making him rub his eyes. When he looked again, he thought for a moment he'd imagined seeing her, for she'd retreated into the shadow of a corner.

"Missus Earp? Allie?"

Another gust of wind blew her whisper to him. "Find the transcript…"

He was distracted by some tourists who had just come into the next room, and he moved farther into the kitchen.

"Allie, wait. Do you know why we've come here? How'd we ride the thunder?"

She lifted her face just briefly, and he remembered those sharp eyes from when she'd let him out of jail. She spoke in a low voice, or at least he thought she did. "Watch your back."

He glanced to the side, interrupted by the newcomers pointing at things in the parlor. When he turned back, Allie had moved toward the back door that opened to a little porch.

"Allie, wait."

"Excuse me, sir," said an intruding voice. One of the tourists stepped into the kitchen. "Howdy do? You work here?"

"No, I don't, sorry," he answered.

In the split second it took him to answer the distracting question, Allie had gone. Gideon moved outside to the porch and down the back steps. But it was too late. He went across the tiny backyard and through a gate in the high chain-link fence to the street. But Allie Earp was nowhere in sight.

Chapter Seven

Gideon returned to Carin's office around five o'clock. He found her at her own desk rummaging through the bottom drawer. He couldn't help admiring the way her open shirt collar exposed her throat and some of that peachy skin. She returned his glance as he leaned against the door frame. Then she broke off from what she was doing and stood up slowly.

He had time to look her over again and couldn't deny the warm feelings he had about her. Her hair was mussed, some of it loosened from the band at the nape of her neck, but it flattered her attractive face. There was just a tinge of pink on her slightly tanned cheeks. And those emerald eyes sparkled. Her lips were slightly pursed in curiosity.

He felt the urge to take her chin in his fingers and tilt her face up toward his for a kiss. But he folded his arms and stood still, trying to quiet the signals his body wanted to give. He'd already kissed her once, all too briefly, at the hotel. And a kiss was a promise. It wasn't right to make any overtures or promises he might not be able to keep.

He remembered the way she'd trembled in his arms and clung to him on the road. 'Course, she'd been scared. But he sensed that in another time and place she might not mind his courting her. He had to force his mind away from such notions before his imagination conjured up things he'd like to do but couldn't.

"Did you discover anything on your walk?" she asked, her voice a little shaky.

"Matter of fact, I did." He unwound his arms, moved farther into the tiny office, and told her about his experience. She listened with awe as she took in what he said.

"What about here?" he asked. "That sheriff find anything?"

She pushed the straggling hair back over her ear. "They dusted for fingerprints, but probably all they got were my own. There were some threads on the windowsill. The laboratory might be able to tell us something."

He didn't ask what a laboratory had to do with threads from clothing. He could tell she got a little irritated when he couldn't put two and two together and understand how things worked in this century. He'd best play along, picking up as much as he could until it all began to make sense.

"Are you hungry?" she asked.

"Sure will be soon. Would you like to have some dinner with me again, seein' as how I don't know anyone else in town? I'd like the company."

He saw the little smile, even though she was putting things away on her desk. "I'd like that."

He looked down at a copy of her newspaper spread out on the desk and read the advertisements while she tidied up. He pointed to a notice about Doc Holliday Days.

"What's this all about?"

She saw where his finger was pointing. "One of the annual festivals. I already told you about Earp and Holliday lore hereabouts. People dress up in Old West clothing for the festival, and actors reenact the shoot-out of the O.K. Corral."

"Why would they do that?"

She paused and looked at him, a serious expression on her face. "Were you, um...in Tombstone when the shoot-out occurred?" Her voice was a little hesitant.

He met her gaze evenly. "I was close by. Not on Allen Street, but nearby. I heard the guns roar and went to join the crowd like everybody else, but by then it was all over."

She slung the strap of her handbag over her shoulder. Then she frowned, wrinkling her brows. "You must have heard all about what people said."

"You mean after the fight? 'Course, folks talked it over."

"What about the hearing? Did you listen to any of the testimony."

"I was workin' the stages at the time. But I read about it in the *Daily Nugget*."

"'Justice of the Peace Wells Spicer heard preliminary evidence for the purpose of determining if there was sufficient evidence to hold the Earps and Doc Holliday to answer before a grand jury on a charge of murder.' Do you suppose that was what Allie was talking about?"

He nodded slowly. "Could be. She whispered something about a transcript. Least, that's what I think she said."

Carin seemed to look inward, thinking hard. "Yes, that would make sense. The transcript is a very important piece of this puzzle."

Then her eyes cleared and she looked at him. "Did, um, people agree about what happened that day?"

"Depends on who you talked to. Both factions had their friends. That's all it was, you know. Politics. If you were on the wrong side of a discussion at the wrong time, you might end up in jail. I had that misfortune, myself."

Carin put her hand on the top of the computer terminal to anchor herself against something solid. Wasn't it every researcher's dream to have someone step out of the past and tell what happened during certain key events? The fabric of history was so difficult to flesh out when all one had to go on was the printed word. And the fact that she was attracted to Gideon didn't help. She couldn't help believing in the honesty she read in those hazel eyes.

She nudged her desk drawer shut with her thigh. "Come on. Let's go get something to eat."

He smiled. "That's beginning to sound good to me."

CARIN CHOSE THE GRILL in the Hotel Denver across from the railroad station. It was quiet and comfortable with varnished oak booths. And they could talk against a soft background of jazz music without being disturbed. It gave her a chance to question her companion more closely.

After explaining the menu to Gideon, who found some of the food puzzling, she settled back to listen to him.

He spun a tale of growing up in Illinois. He'd been fourteen when the Civil War broke out. But he finally got to serve two years later. He'd seen things he didn't want to talk about and had been much happier when he'd migrated west with some of the wagon trains.

Fascinated, Carin simply listened. The men and women he described were just as she'd imagined. People always on the move, tolerating incredible hardships for the sake of a dream they'd had. It drew her in, whisked her away from the present. And made her feel closer to Gideon.

They finished their hamburgers and sipped on mugs of coffee. There was no hurry to leave. The restaurant was not crowded. Darkness gathered outside, and the soothing jazz rhythms were relaxing. She felt as if she could have stayed there all night. At the same time she was incredibly aware of the pull between them. Each time his hand brushed hers, she felt her fingers want to coil around his of their own accord. But each time, she withdrew.

They both hunched forward, leaning on their elbows, the flat table keeping their bodies apart. But it didn't matter. There were moments when she almost lost track of what he was saying. If they'd been alone, she might've cuddled up in the crook of his arm, nestled her head against his chin as he crooned on with his story. Just as if they were out on the prairie before a campfire at night.

"I—" she hesitated. He had just described the moment he rode the thunder to the present.

"How do you think it happened?" she asked. "And why?"

He shifted in his seat, his broad shoulders and muscular chest moving in a way that sent a shiver of desire running through her. Lucky they were here in a public place. If he reached for an embrace tonight, she really wasn't sure at the moment what she would do. She thought Gideon had been feeling the spark between them just as she had. But talking had to come first.

Before he could speak, she blurted, "Tell me more about seeing Allie Earp today."

His expression changed. "Well, over at the museum, I'd been readin' about things. Then the wind just seemed to blow her in."

Carin leaned a little closer. "What was she wearing?"

"Gray dress, slat bonnet. Same as when she let me out of jail. I saw her eyes, just for a second."

When Carin spoke, her words were hushed. "Then it must have been her in back of my cabin before. At least that's who it looked like. I couldn't believe it."

Gideon lifted a shoulder and let it drop. "If I came through time, why not Allie, too?"

Gideon glanced around as if to make sure nobody new had entered the room. Then he leaned closer, a conspiratorial tone in his lowered voice.

"If Allie came and I came, then you can bet the rest of them came, too."

Chills iced her nerves, and she had to hold on to the edge of the table to keep herself steady.

In the distance the sound of thunder suddenly announced the coming of the storm. A few drops of rain spattered against the glass front of the restaurant. She was reminded of the other storm that he said had brought him here. She watched him stir his spoon slowly in his coffee mug. What would happen if lightning came nearby again?

Carin exhaled a long breath. How or why he came here, she still didn't understand, but she wanted to know what the woman he thought was Allie had to say. She pressed the question again.

He frowned, "Just 'Find the transcript.' Then she said, 'Watch your back.' I can understand why. The Earps don't like to be proved wrong. The newspapers wrote about the killings. 'Course, they just mostly quoted the court hearing. Maybe she's tryin' to tell us to find Judge Wells Spicer's court transcript before they do."

She felt as if the breath had been knocked out of her. "Then she thinks they're here." She looked at Gideon quickly. "That might explain why they came, wouldn't it? To find the transcript before we do?"

Carin felt excited as some of the pieces started to fit. "The hearing was reported verbatim in the *Daily Nugget*. You read it yourself. The original testimony was all taken down by a court stenographer in shorthand. But the transcript was lost, stolen or destroyed. All historians have had to go by are the issues of the *Daily Nugget* that reported the hearing. But a lot of details seem to be missing."

"Allie must have known about it at the time," he speculated.

"Exactly. She's referring to the testimony, surely. And

she says we have to find it. Oh, Gideon, you don't know
what it would mean if we could locate that original court
transcript. Historians have been hunting for it for the last
sixty years. Maybe Allie knows where it is.''

"I think I do know what it would mean," Gideon said.
His somber voice made her shiver.

"I'm sorry. You're right."

"It might mean my life. There was a lot said at the
hearing about those stage robberies the Earps were allegedly involved in. Maybe they stole the court records themselves to make it harder for somebody to press charges
against them. They framed me and got away with it because the witnesses who said at the O.K. Corral hearing
that they knew about the Earps tipping off the robbers
were dead. And at my trial their testimony was missing.
Convenient for the Earps.''

Carin gazed at the pensive lines of Gideon's face. Her
heart knocked against her rib cage as she realized that he
was serious. If it was true that he'd been framed for tipping off robbers about a shipment of money out of Tombstone, he hadn't deserved to hang. The fact that evidence
of the Earps' involvement with the robberies might be in
the original hearing transcript made it imperative that they
find it. Such a coup would be hailed as important in the
historical journalistic community and would top off her
articles with just the facts she needed. And it might help
clear Gideon's name.

What if Allie Earp was trying to reach both Gideon and
herself? The fact that Carin's ancestor might have somehow managed to jump ahead in time to reach her made
goose bumps rise on her skin. She'd never heard of such
a thing really happening, but a quick glance at Gideon's
solidness and strength made her convinced that it had. The
best course of action would be to follow up on any leads.
In the end, the facts would speak for themselves.

Her heart told her that Gideon Avarest, who was charming her almost more than she was ready for, was a real time traveler. And he needed her help. Was it too wild a thought to believe that maybe he had jumped forward in time because only *she* could help him?

They paid the bill and went out to the car. She was aware of the crackling heat between them. It had been a while since she'd had time to date anyone, and her timing wasn't exactly great now. A man who came from the past? Great choice, she chided herself in silent sarcasm. Whatever quirk of fate had brought them together might just as easily split them apart. It would not be wise to encourage any attention from Gideon.

She idled the motor for a moment to let it warm up. She wondered if she was going to get any sleep with Gideon stretched out in the easy chair in her living room with a rifle across his knees.

The rain started to come down more heavily now, and in the darkness, she could just make out Gideon's silhouette in the seat beside her. The car provided a warm cocoon.

"Thanks for the company for dinner," he said.

"Sure."

She felt the chemistry between them begin to stir. Suddenly a flash of lightning illuminated the scene, and she saw his rugged face clearly. In another second, thunder boomed above them and she jumped. She realized her heart was beating triple time. He leaned toward her across the seat, and then she was in his arms. It felt so good to be enclosed in them. His clean, masculine scent exuded from him, and he cradled her head between his shoulder and chin. Moments later, they were holding each other, pressing, searching. Their lips came together naturally, and she sighed at the kiss. It seemed so right.

She wanted more, but felt alarm bells go off, telling her

now wasn't the time. She pulled away. In gentlemanly fashion, he let her go. The space allowed her to gather her wits. She needed to be clearheaded to drive home.

Her windshield wipers swiped away the downpour all the way up the blacktop road. The driving conditions didn't bother her, but the storm only added to her agitation about other matters. Gideon satisfied himself that the cabin was secure, the horse fed and watered. Then he parked on the sofa for the night.

Images tossed in her mind as she lay in bed. She tried to fight off the thoughts of Gideon's strong arms warming her and scratched Shag's ears to expend some of her pent-up energy. She accepted the dog's wet nose and rough tongue licking her face, and then finally rolled over and managed to sleep.

The next morning, Carin dressed for Doc Holliday Days in fitted jeans, wide leather belt with silver buckle, cowgirl boots and a white cotton shirt with green and crimson embroidery on the bodice. She took the time to weave her hair into a French braid.

Gideon's new plaid Western shirt, yellow bandanna, vest, belt and fresh jeans made him look like he was part of the festival. She thought he seemed pleased at the bright, sunny morning after last night's rain. They ought to feel relieved that the night had been uneventful.

She was already beginning to feel a sense of anticipation about the festival. She didn't know what she expected, but her nerves were certainly charged up. Sometimes her senses came alive like this when she was covering an event for the paper, but the festival wasn't her assignment now. She'd written a preview article weeks ago and listed the event in the upcoming events column. Keith planned to write the follow-up article today himself.

In the living room, Gideon strapped on his six-shooters.

Half the town would be decked out in 1800s clothes to-day. He wouldn't look out of place. But before they left, he filled the belt with cartridges and checked to make sure his gun was loaded. A little tingle went up her spine, but she didn't say anything.

Last night's rain had left the streets fresh, and a warm sun complemented crisp, fresh air. In Gideon's mind, Grand Avenue, now lined with booths selling refreshments and crafts, hardly resembled Tombstone in 1881. The corral they'd built on the corner of Ninth and Grand was too small. A low brick wall planted with pansies separated the corral yard from a concrete sidewalk, the likes of which had never been in Tombstone.

Cowboys in long dusters and ten-gallon hats lounged and talked in groups. Weapons were much in evidence. Carin said in a hushed voice, "They're just replicas." He wasn't so sure.

They walked slowly along the sidewalk, not saying anything. His eyes scanned the crowd. They stopped to greet some of her friends and then crossed Ninth Street to wander along the booths.

When Carin touched Gideon's sleeve, his attention was drawn toward a man portraying Sheriff Johnny Behan. He was dressed in a gray checked everyday suit with white shirt and bow tie. His sheriff's badge glinted on his vest, and his short-brimmed, low-crowned hat was perched on his head the way a gentleman Easterner would wear it. He strutted along, greeting townspeople in a voice that projected, in his role as the sheriff of Tombstone. Then, with no ado, a cowboy, wearing a fancy woolen shirt and tight-fitting doeskin trousers tucked into half boots, led a horse into the mock O.K. Corral, and Gideon could tell that the action was about to begin. He and Carin stopped beside an old chuck wagon to watch.

Gideon spotted three more cowboys sauntering up, set

apart by their wide-brimmed sombreros and long, gaudy silk neckerchiefs and vests. They stood in the street just outside the corral. Carin whispered in his ear. "They must be the actors portraying Billy and Ike Clanton and Tom McLaury."

Of course Gideon knew the gang who had been threatening the Earps for complicated reasons having to do with stages carrying bullion that some of the cowboy gang had allegedly robbed. Gideon pointed to the one with the horse. The resemblance was close enough. "That would be Frank McLaury. The one with the Winchester rifle in the scabbard on the saddle."

It had been a day much like this, Gideon reasoned. Bright warm sun, people congregating to talk in the streets. And no one seemed to pay much attention to the fact that the cowboys were gathered at the corral. But then Sheriff Behan's voice rang out as he hurried toward the McLaury brothers and the Clantons.

"Hello, boys," he said. "I'm afraid I need to disarm you. You'll have to give up your weapons. I don't want any trouble in town."

"I don't have any arms," protested Ike Clanton.

The sheriff put his arms around Ike's waist to check that he was telling the truth.

"I don't want to fight," said Billy, in a loud, high voice.

Tom McLaury pulled his coat open to show he wasn't armed, either. The sheriff seemed to ignore the rifle in the saddle.

The spectators had been focused on the action at the corral. Like the rest of them, Gideon and Carin didn't turn to look in the other direction until now. What he saw there made the hairs on the back of his neck stand on end.

They stood four abreast in the street at the end of the block. Their faces weren't quite visible from this distance, and their black Stetsons shielded their brows. But Gideon knew who they were. The tallest man, standing a little ahead of the others, stood with feet a little apart, his coat thrown back to reveal his gun. The polished city marshal's badge on his gray vest reflected the sun. His long string tie draped over a white shirt and the scooped vest that fit his long, lean body. It was Virgil Earp, the man in charge of keeping the peace in the town.

Next to him was the emaciated Doc Holliday, covered in a long, square-cut coat. The barrel of a shotgun stuck out from under the skirt of the coat. To Doc's right was the young Morgan Earp, with fairer coloring than his older brothers, but with the same cocky presence of a clan convinced of their destiny to come out on top in any feud. On the far right was the infamous Wyatt Earp, recognizable no doubt to this crowd by the drooping mustache on his hawklike face. But it was his eyes that told Gideon the truth.

Gideon's hand went reflexively to his gun. The Earps hadn't seen him yet, but they would, if he remained where he was.

A murmur went through the crowd as the Earps and Doc Holliday began to move forward. This wasn't Tombstone, Gideon reminded himself. The spectators thought they were going to see a performance. But he grew wary. Beside him, Carin placed her hand gently on his arm.

"Gideon, relax. This is just an act."

He barely heard her. All of his concentration was focused on the men in black coats, armed to the teeth, coming down the street toward the cowboys. Sheriff Johnny Behan broke off and rushed up the street toward the Earps, looking back over his shoulder as he apprehended danger.

"Wait up," cried Behan. Then when he reached them, he said, "For God's sake, don't go down there. You'll get murdered."

Virgil Earp spoke in a clear, determined voice. "I am going to disarm them."

Gideon braced himself. The words had fused past and present in Gideon's mind. For a moment, he believed they had all been thrown back to the past. He sensed the uneasiness of the watching crowd, tried to be ready for anything and to be prepared to protect the woman beside him.

"I have disarmed them," said Behan. "I'm the sheriff of this county, and I'm not going to allow any trouble."

Wyatt drew his pistol from his belt and put it in his overcoat pocket. Holliday's shotgun came into full view. None of them paused. They passed right by the sheriff, who followed them for a few steps, expostulating. They strode toward the four cowboys, who'd lined themselves up.

"You sons of bitches," Wyatt snarled at the Clantons and McLaurys in a voice that carried to the crowd. "You've been looking for a fight and now you can have it."

Billy Clanton and Frank McLaury had six-shooters in plain sight now. Ike Clanton was standing a little farther off, toward the granite building at the edge of the lot. Holliday produced a nickel-plated pistol and pointed it at Billy Clanton.

"Throw up your hands," called Virgil Earp. "I have come to disarm you."

Billy and Frank grabbed their six-shooters, and Tom McLaury reached for the Winchester and jumped behind the horse. Virgil's shout to disarm was drowned in the blasts that flared. Gideon pushed Carin behind him as the watching crowd squealed. Frank McLaury staggered and grabbed his belly, but he got off a shot at Wyatt. Holliday fired at the man behind the horse. Virgil fired at Billy Clanton, two shots in quick succession. Ike Clanton darted up to grab Wyatt's arm, but Wyatt shouted at him.

"Either fight or get out of the way."

Ike ran behind the Earps, leapt over the low brick wall, and came across the street in Carin and Gideon's direction.

Wyatt turned and fired as he fled, and the bullet zinged by Gideon's left ear. Gideon pushed Carin behind the wagon and drew his gun. Ike Clanton ran for the sidewalk, and Morgan broke off from his firing and chased Ike, jumping the planter like Ike had done. Wyatt's next shot was aimed straight for Gideon, who ducked behind the wagon next to Carin and returned fire.

"Stay down," he shouted to her.

Beyond, a semblance of the O.K. Corral fight still blasted on. Virgil Earp had been hit in the leg and limped forward, still firing. Tom McLaury was on the ground. From his back, he rose up and fired at Wyatt.

Morgan Earp grabbed Ike and rolled with him into the street. Gideon took a shot at Wyatt. Morgan tried to grab the gun out of Gideon's hand, but Gideon grabbed his other wrist and twisted his arm downward. Morgan butted his head into Gideon's stomach, sending him sprawling.

The excited crowd was drawn into the variation on the brawl and cheered the fighters on.

"Gideon, stop," he heard Carin scream, as he and Morgan rolled into the street.

Chapter Eight

Dread and horror numbed Carin as she dug her fingernails into the wood of the wagon. For, unlike the rest of the crowd, she realized that what was happening was real.

She hadn't brought a weapon. This was supposed to be an entertaining event. It took less than a second to realize no one was going to help Gideon. Everyone thought this was part of the act, a variation on the shoot-out in the O.K. Corral to surprise those who had seen the same thing being reenacted year after year.

Another bullet grazed the wagon and Carin ducked. She looked around in desperation and saw that one of the spectators in Western dress was carrying a Henry rifle with gold engraving. In one bound she reached him and grasped the rifle with both hands.

"Give me that."

He was so startled, he let go. She swung it to aim at Wyatt Earp. She had no idea if it was loaded, but neither would he. Before he could get off another shot, she took two steps left and pointed the muzzle at his head.

"Drop that gun," she yelled.

She succeeded in distracting him, and he turned to stare at her. The steely eyes held hers for a split second, and she knew she was looking at none other than the real Wyatt Earp.

"Drop the gun, I said," she yelled again. She held the rifle steady.

From her right a gun exploded, and the bullet ricocheted across the pavement. She didn't dare take her gaze from Wyatt to see who had the upper hand in the tussle between Morgan and Gideon. But Morgan would hardly shoot at his own brother unless the shot went wild.

She paid no attention to Billy Clanton, lying dead on the ground, and Doc Holliday, who bent over as a bullet supposedly whacked his pistol scabbard. Out of the corner of her eye, she saw Gideon lunge for the gun that had skittered away from Morgan and him. Morgan groaned and rolled, and got to his knees unarmed. Gideon had the gun and aimed at Wyatt.

"Drop the gun, Wyatt," she said again.

Wyatt's eyes flickered in Gideon's direction, and she saw the irritation on the legendary face. She willed Gideon to lower the revolver before blood was shed. She didn't know if Wyatt was a phantom or not, but she didn't want to get either herself or Gideon put away for murder.

Gideon took a pace closer, so that she could see the anger on his face. *Please, Gideon, don't shoot,* she prayed silently. But she didn't betray any sign of weakness to the man in her sights.

She was dimly aware of the hooting and hollering as the crowd around them enjoyed what they supposed was an act. The firing had stopped, and now the rest of the players came on stage. Sheriff Johnny Behan pushed his way through the crowd to examine the bodies of Billy Clanton, Frank and Tom McLaury, who had been slaughtered. But he looked at the four of them who had rewritten the script. Some of the other actors seemed to be having trouble knowing what to do. Morgan, who was supposed to have been shot through the shoulder blades and seriously wounded, was getting up and dusting off his pants.

The actors around them improvised, but only Carin and Gideon were aware that the performance was not as it should be.

The spectators were so carried away that many of them joined in what they thought was the fun. Several came to look over the dead men, who for a horrifying moment Carin feared were truly dead. *Oh, my God,* she thought. *What if they don't get up?*

Wyatt holstered his gun, and then the spectators flooded the street, allowing the Earp brothers and Doc Holliday to melt into the crowd. She lowered the rifle.

"Gideon." Then he appeared beside her. She took a deep breath.

"You all right?" he asked with great concern in his voice.

"Yeah, fine."

"Hey," a voice boomed as the rifle owner shouldered his way through. "Give me back my rifle. You can get hurt aiming guns at people, even if they aren't loaded."

She stared down at the rifle in her hands. Not loaded. Well, she had bluffed Wyatt Earp.

"Sorry." She gave it back and then tugged on Gideon's sleeve, hoping to escape before they were asked for an explanation. "Let's get out of here."

Gideon eyed the crowd. She couldn't see where the Earps had gone, but he was taller.

"This way," he said, and took her hand to pull her up the street. She glanced back and with relief saw the actors who had portrayed the McLaurys and Billy Clanton get to their feet. Not dead, only actors after all.

The Earps? But Gideon didn't give her a chance to ask questions yet.

When they reached the outskirts of the crowd, her heart was still hammering and the blood pounding in her ears.

She caught the comments of a few passersby, referring to the show.

"Sure didn't adhere to the script this year..."

"Who were those other two?"

Carin saw men in black coats disappear around the corner of the next block. Gideon's gun hand jerked up. She caught it just in time.

"Not now, Gideon. You'll get arrested."

"Come on," he said, and they lit out at a run.

The Earps weren't shooting anymore, but by the time she and Gideon turned the corner, they had disappeared. She and Gideon moved down the middle of the residential street, keeping their eyes open, but they saw no sign of the gang. She scanned the frame houses, set back on green lawns. It wasn't that much of an anachronism to think that the Earps and Holliday had simply walked into one of the Victorian homes on the quiet street.

Her breathing was still coming in gasps from the sprint. Now she and Gideon walked silently, their bodies taut, ready to spring at the onset of new danger. Hairs prickled along the back of her neck. Those Earps had to be somewhere. Could they be watching from the windows of one of the houses?

A car turned the corner in front of them, breaking the intensity of the mood. Still, Carin didn't breathe easily until Gideon shook his head.

"No telling where they went. I guess they're not going to draw attention to themselves by firing in broad daylight again. That playacting was the perfect cover."

Carin's mind spun. Those bullets were real.

"Oh, my gosh," she exclaimed. She stopped dead in her tracks and clamped her fingers over Gideon's arm.

"What?" His gaze flew beyond her as he must have thought she'd perceived another threat.

"No, not that. But we've got to get back. We've got

to find those bullets and give them to Hugh. The lab can prove they came from the same guns..."

"Let's go."

They hurried along Tenth Street. Might as well not risk going back the way they'd come in case the Earps were holed up somewhere with a lookout posted.

The crowd from the shoot-out had broken up and now tourists and townspeople milled up and down Grand Avenue, some with refreshments in their hands. She found where the bullets had splintered wood on the wagon, but it was nearly impossible to search the area for the actual slugs with so many people around for the festival. She and Gideon knew the bullets were real, but no one else seemed to realize it. They were forced to give up their search.

It was well past lunch, and Carin realized her feelings of frustration were not being helped by an empty stomach.

"Let's go get something to eat," she finally said. "Maybe we'll have some luck later."

She guided Gideon into a café with Western decor and red checkered tablecloths. Many of the customers wore the Western dress of festival participants. As she and Gideon took seats at a table near the wainscoted wall, she peered into the corners of the restaurant. It would be bizarre to find that their recent assailants had come to the same restaurant for a meal, but she couldn't help the eerie feeling that hadn't left her since the shoot-out.

Nourishment would help clear her head and she gratefully swallowed hot coffee from the mug the waitress put on the table. After she and Gideon had scanned the crowd carefully enough to feel satisfied they weren't being watched by mysterious strangers, she hunched forward, her hands folded in front of her.

"You sure you're all right?" Gideon asked.

The concern in his voice and the slight frown on his

face moved her. She realized that danger brought people together and warned herself not to get carried away. She might be losing her head over Gideon, but there was no reason to believe he felt anything for her but the old-fashioned chivalry a man showed a woman that was part of the code of the West.

"I'm fine," she said, meeting his gaze and trying to smile.

She took a deep breath. They were both overwrought and might say things they would later regret. When she did speak, she kept her voice low to avoid anyone over-hearing their conversation.

"Gideon, I can understand why the Earps and Holliday followed you here if they were chasing you out of Tombstone. I guess they're mad that you missed your hanging."

She paused to swallow uncomfortably. She was facing a man who barely escaped his appointment with death. Her heart wobbled anew and she was tempted to take his hand and squeeze it. But she commanded herself not to get sentimental. They had a job to do and a lot to figure out. She continued thinking out loud.

"And if we can find those slugs it will prove to Hugh that someone was shooting real bullets." She paused, considering. Hugh was already suspicious of Gideon's involvement with the events at Carin's cabin. If he thought Gideon was being shot at, it might only increase Hugh's suspicions that Gideon had something to hide.

"But we don't yet know if the warning we found at my office or the car that tried to run me off the road had anything to do with your pursuers, do we?"

He drummed his fingers on the tablecloth. His face darkened. "Who else do you think might be threatening you?"

She shrugged. "It does seem farfetched to me. But I think it's possible that I have a more immediate enemy."

"Who would that be?"

He hunched forward in a defensive posture that charmed her. He'd drawn his gun in her car when they'd been threatened on the road. He seemed to be ready to protect her when danger was near. Trying to keep her voice even, she continued her speculations after the waitress refilled their coffee cups.

"I think Julius Eberly has something to hide from his employer at the ski resort."

"Why would he blame you for that?"

"His boss, Nigel Henshaw, is a close friend of my family's. Julius saw me going to talk to Nigel and probably reasoned that Nigel told me he suspected Julius of making off with some of the funds last year."

"But you'd said Henshaw never made any accusations."

"Right. Nigel's being generous in saying that he thinks the errors are just that. When you take in that much cash from that many customers, it's easy to make a mistake. He may have seen a pattern developing, but he isn't accusing anyone. But if Julius has something to hide, he might not want publicity drawn to the ski resort. With my job at the paper, he might have panicked and thought I'd write something about the missing money."

"You think Eberly tried to run us off the road and left the threatening note?"

"He could have. I don't know. I'm just saying we can't ignore that possibility even while we try to solve your dilemma." She wanted to help Gideon, but it beat her if she knew how.

She lowered her voice even further and asked in a somber tone, "What are we going to do about the Earps?"

Gideon thrust his jaw forward and set his mouth in a grim line. "It's me they want, not you."

Her heart lurched at the possibility that Gideon might

have escaped a hanging only to travel through time and be shot on her doorstep. She grasped his hand impulsively, and he closed his fingers around hers. "I'm not so sure it's only you they want."

"What do you mean?"

"I'm writing about them, aren't I? It sounds fantastic to me, but it's just possible that they want to stop me from further clouding their reputation. Maybe they know somehow that I'm Allie Earp's great-great-grandniece. Maybe they know I have her diary, or that she's trying to speak to me, and they want to get to me first. They could kill two birds with one stone if they not only get you out of the way, but prevent me from coming up with whatever evidence would corroborate your innocence. Don't you see? We're both in danger."

Her own words worked her into a heightened state, and Gideon's expression showed her that he felt her involvement. His grip on her hand tightened, and he looked deeply into her eyes in such a way that without words he seemed to be conveying both apology and empathy.

But there was more. When he looked at her that way, her body tingled with desire. She'd heard the expression soul mate, but had never met anyone who made her believe in the concept. Until now. When she was with Gideon and saw the way he responded to action, she felt so akin to him that she began to wonder if he hadn't come through time just to find her.

"Oh, Gideon." The words slipped from her mouth.

He inched closer, and she thought that if the table hadn't been between them, he would have enfolded her in an embrace. As it was, his lips brushed her temple, and she released a long, shaky breath.

Trembling, she inched backward, not wanting to make a spectacle in the restaurant. But the kiss had done something to her insides and heated what had been percolating ever since she'd met him.

The waitress brought their bill. Still, neither she nor Gideon spoke as she dug out money. "My turn to pay."

He gave her a sly grin. "Is that how it's done these days?"

She curved her lips in relief, as the tension of a moment ago was dissipated. "I like to pay my own way."

After they left the hotel, Carin located Hugh, who agreed to meet them at the scene of the shoot-out. By this time the crowds had dispersed enough that they could make a more thorough search. They located several slugs on the sidewalk and street, which had been deflected from the solid masonry of the post office building behind the booths and chuck wagons on Ninth Street. If Hugh was surprised, he didn't show it.

"When we find the owners of these guns, they'll be fined for using loaded firearms."

"What about arresting them on a charge of shooting with intent to kill?" asked Carin. "They fired directly at us."

Hugh's face was stony. "You can't be sure of that, Carin. Witnesses say Wyatt Earp was firing at Ike Clanton as he dove into the crowd. You just happened to be in the way."

She knew different, but wasn't sure it would pay to press her point. The Earps had disappeared. Hugh was under the impression that the actors were the ones he was looking for. And this raised the question of what had happened to the men who were supposed to play the roles. A small doubt worked its way into her mind and she gave Gideon a questioning look. But she didn't speak to him until Hugh walked away.

"Gideon, are you sure those were the Earps? Actors were hired to impersonate them. Maybe Hugh is right."

"If you don't believe me, then find your actors. They can speak for themselves."

"True."

She didn't know how to tell Hugh that they suspected the real Earps and Doc Holliday had taken part in the performance. But if that was true, then the actors were missing and needed to be found. She took Hugh aside.

"Hugh, I need to talk to you alone."

"What about?"

"It's a little hard to explain. I think you need to search for the actors who were hired to play the roles of the Earp party this morning."

"I'll have to do that in order to nail them for shooting real bullets."

"Good. Would you let me know when you find them?"

"Sure. You plan to file charges?"

"If they were the men who shot at us, of course we will."

He looked at her a little strangely then went back to supervising the search for any more slugs. She and Gideon walked slowly back to where she'd parked the rented car, a green Subaru station wagon. When they got in, she sat staring out the windshield.

"We oughta be tracking the Earps," said Gideon.

"I believe you, but I need to think. We're not officers of the law. We can't just barge through the houses and yards where we saw them go. You need warrants to do that nowadays. We'll have to think of another way." She thought a moment, then said, "If what you say is true, Allie Earp came with them."

She shook her head. "I don't know anything about time travel and I don't know anyone who does. Are these people here permanently? Or do they go back and forth?"

"I ain't gone anywhere since the thunder threw me in

your yard. If they came along, too, I don't see how they could get back.''

"Then if they're here, we have to discover what they want,'' she said.

"They want my hide.''

She shivered, in spite of the heat beating down on the car. "Then we'll have to outsmart them.''

"How?''

"I don't know yet. We need to go over all the details again. It's just too much of a coincidence that I was trying to locate records about them when you all showed up here. If I'm not really dreaming, then there must be a reason for all this.''

She started the car. "There's a quiet park near here where we can talk without being interrupted.'' She gave him a quick glance. "And we'll be able to see anyone who might be trying to ambush us.''

"If you say so.''

They pulled up at Eleventh and Cooper Avenue and got out. Ash, weeping willows, poplars and Colorado blue spruce shaded the green park that was just behind the Chamber of Commerce. Two children laughed and played in swings next to a sandbox. Traffic buzzed by on Grand Avenue, but at this end of the park, the street was quiet.

Gideon reached for her hand, and Carin felt the warmth wash over her. She couldn't sort out her feelings about what was to happen to them. All she knew was that they needed to depend on each other right now if they were to survive the present situation.

They sat on the grass next to the wide trunk of a giant elm tree. Together they went over everything that had happened, and Carin made Gideon repeat what Allie had said while he was in the museum. She knew it might seem ridiculous to try to apply logic to spectres from the past. But Gideon was no spectre, he was flesh and blood. That he was here seemed to indicate that these time travelers arrived body, mind, and spirit, not just the latter.

She finally leaned back against the tree, twisting a blade of grass between her fingers. "I flew to Tucson a few months ago to search through the files of the Tombstone newspapers."

"Did you find what you wanted?"

She shook her head pensively. "I spent several days there, but it was curious. Most of the materials relating to the Earp-Clanton feud and the stage robberies that seemed to lead up to the shoot-out at the O.K. Corral were missing."

He had stretched out on the grass, leaning on his elbows and chewing on a reed. He lifted a curious eyebrow, but let her continue.

"The original court record of the hearing before Justice Wells Spicer is missing. Seems like a vast amount of material about the Earps is either in someone's possession or has been destroyed. Other authors who've written about them have come up against the same hole in the research. I wonder why?"

He shifted the reed to the other side of his mouth. "They always were awful jealous of their reputation. Always trying to get the upper hand in Tombstone. Always bragging about their feats keeping law and order back in Dodge City. I doubt if half of it is true. One or the other of them was always running for the office of county sheriff or city marshal until finally Virgil Earp got appointed when the regular marshal left town and never came back. Virgil was a deputy U.S. marshal, too. Then when he was injured, Wyatt got that appointment. Men like that might go a ways to make sure people thought the right thing about them."

"Hmm. Either that or others who wanted to make sure their story was told in the best light. Curious." Something niggled at the back of her mind, but she couldn't quite reach it. Some connection she had overlooked.

Gideon looked around the park again and scanned the houses and yards across the street. It gave Carin a chill to think that no matter where they went, they might be being watched. She hadn't yet decided if she wanted the Earps to show themselves so she could demand to know what they'd come here for, or whether she wanted them to disappear again into their own time and just leave Gideon alone.

But she needed to take one piece of the puzzle at a time. His gaze came to rest on her again and she dropped hers. She was too aware of the way her heart flopped around in her chest when those hazel eyes looked at her. She was beginning to think she would have enjoyed living in the Old West if the heroes of the day all treated a woman the way this man treated her. It made her feel more like a lady.

Gideon noticed her little smile and the way she brushed the hair out of her face. Her hair had gotten disheveled and had long ago come out of her fancy braid, but he hadn't said anything to her because of their predicament. He felt the embarrassed grin on his face probably making him look like a fool and looked down to pull on the grass. Out of the corner of his eye he saw her pull her booted ankles closer to her. Those long, limber legs of hers were fast and strong. He could tell from the way she'd lit after the Earps beside him. He liked feeling like she was his equal in some things. He was surprised at the way women showed so much leg these days, but he sure hadn't missed the opportunity to admire Carin's when he'd had the chance.

He gazed into the distance. What could you say to a woman you might be separated from for all eternity? Especially when you didn't know how you got here in the first place? She must have been thinking something along the same lines, for she broke softly into his reverie.

"Gideon?"

"Hmm?"

"What's it like in the 1880s?"

He straightened up and scooted to the tree to sit beside her, leaning his back against the scratchy bark so their shoulders just touched.

"Well, it ain't like this."

"I know there weren't any cars, or telephones. But that's not what I mean."

"I know. You mean, what's life like, livin' in those times?"

"Yeah." She tilted her head sideways. "I guess every history buff wants to know. What does it feel like in the towns? What does it sound and smell like? What are the people really like?"

"Well, I haven't been here long enough to say, but I don't know that people were any different. They just have a different way of expressing themselves."

She didn't say anything for a while. "I think you're different."

"How?"

"You're...a gentleman."

"I try to be."

Her voice sounded a little hesitant, like she was feeling shy. "And you stand up for what you believe in."

What she said pleased him. "Now, how do you know that from just knowing me for three days?"

She moved a little, and he liked the way her shoulder nudged his. "I guess with some people you just know."

Her voice sounded a little husky, and it made him feel emotional. It made him want to take a hold of her and pull her over so she rested against him. He didn't say anything for a minute. Then he took her hand, kissed her knuckles and laced the fingers on his right hand through hers.

"You think you know about me?"

She turned her head, her face close to his. "Maybe."

"Wish I could…" He didn't know how to say what he felt, so he trailed off and frowned at the park.

"Wish you could what?"

"Well, darn it." He couldn't face her. Instead, he stuck his jaw forward. "If you lived in my time, I might ask if I could see you."

She smiled, and he caught the tinge of pink that crept into her cheeks.

"That's a nice way of putting it," she said. "And you are seeing me, sort of."

He dropped his chin. "Well, in my day, a man pays court to a woman. Coming to see her and sitting on the front porch. Walking in the woods. Going to church socials. 'Course, that's when a man's in town. In my job, I was on the road guardin' the ironbound boxes of payrolls and bullion over the lonely roads of the frontier."

"It sounds exciting, though."

"Just a job."

"A dangerous one."

Gideon decided that he wasn't going to waste the moment and snaked his arm around her waist, pulling her nearer so her back was against him. Her hair tickled his face, and he smiled at her clean, soapy scent. Might not be right to be expressing so much affection to this woman, but he couldn't help it. He knew he'd see if she would have him if things were more normal. But with the way things were, what promises could he make her?

She rested against him as if she liked it, and she clasped his arms in her hands, leaning the side of her head against his chin. The feel of her in his arms started to undo him.

Being in a public place, he wasn't going to do any more than maybe kiss her ear.

But her little moan of pleasure awakened the possibilities of nightly pleasure in his mind. She was a no-nonsense woman, not to be trifled with unless she said so. He could tell that from the way she took charge.

She was a lady, and he knew he'd darn well better treat her like one. But as he kissed her ear and moved his arms upward so that he could feel the supple underside of her bosom, he realized suddenly that he had absolutely no experience with any lady of these times.

Chapter Nine

Euphoria settled on Carin. The feeling of Gideon's strong arms around her sent her mind spinning in cartwheels. She tightened her hold on the arms encircling her and thrilled when he nudged her breasts from underneath. She let out a soft sound of pleasure and nuzzled his head with the side of hers. Then she took a deep breath and sat still, overwhelmed by her next thought.

How could she get involved with a man not from her own time who might disappear at any moment? It would be crazy. She searched for some humor to lighten up the moment.

"I've never been held by a hundred-and-fifty-one-year-old man before."

He loosened his hold, but he grunted. "Very funny, miss."

The joke gave her time to dampen the fire that was building inside her. But they needed to talk seriously. She couldn't afford to lose her head over this man until they had some answers. She decided to ask for a serious one right now. Scooting sideways so she could see his face, she placed a hand on the stiff blue jeans covering his muscled thigh.

"If you had the choice between going back and staying here, what would you do?"

He gave her a crooked grin and ran a hand through his hair. "You mean if I could choose between going back to that jail cell and being hung or staying here to keep you company, which would I like better?"

A laugh erupted from her throat. "That's not exactly what I meant."

He erased the smile and looked into her eyes, as if looking for a way to frame his thoughts. "I had a good life until I got tangled up with the Earps. I'm not sure I fit into these times."

She looked down. She'd been afraid his answer would be something like that. "I guess there isn't that much to stay here for."

"I didn't say that. I was beginning to hope there might be. But I don't know if I can stay here. On the other hand, I don't exactly know how to get back to my time, either. I may not have a choice until we find out how I got here."

"I know. The thunder. None of us knows about that. I was just asking."

He reached around her shoulders and pulled her toward him again, his eyes on her lips. "I'm kind of glad you asked. If I did stay, what would I do here?"

"You could be a lawman."

Then he kissed her, gently. Just enough to give her a taste and let her know she wanted more. Did he?

They broke apart and she felt the heat spread through her entire body. She'd been forward enough. He was probably used to women who were more ladylike and not so brassy unless they were whores. It made her want to ask him about what women were like in the 1880s, whether they matched her idea of them. But she'd asked enough questions for now. She was pushing him, and she knew no man wanted to be pushed, especially one who had no control over his fate. She made a move to get up.

"We'd better go see what else we can find out. I want

to talk to Hugh and see if they've located the men who were supposed to play the parts of the Earp gang this morning.''

She didn't say that she hoped they could be found at all. It gave her a chill to think that the Earps might have blown them away. Or sent them back to the past in their stead.

As they walked back toward the rented Subaru, Carin noticed two sheriff's department cars and an ambulance parked outside a white frame house on the block beyond. Two deputies stood talking outside on the porch.

''Come on. Let's go see,'' she said. And they set off down the street.

They found Hugh inside the house with four rumpled-looking men, three of them with cuts and bruises that were being examined by a paramedic. They were all about thirty years of age and in good lean physical shape. The type who busted broncos at local rodeos. One of them had a small but wiry frame and curly brown hair. Another one was dark-headed with a squarish jaw. Blood had dried from a cut on the mouth of a blond young man. At the moment they were all glaring about the room, trying to keep from interrupting each other so that Hugh could get the story from each one of them at a time.

''There were four of them,'' said the blond man.

Then she saw the racks of old-fashioned suits in the dining room and makeup kits on the table. This was where the actors had been going to change into their costumes.

''We didn't know what they were doing here,'' the blond actor continued.

The medic turned away from him to examine the actor with longish sandy hair beside him, who was slumped back on an easy chair holding his head.

The talkative blond continued. ''They had costumes on

so we thought they had something to do with the festival. They just came in here and looked around.''

The small wiry one took up the story. "Yeah, Harry said, 'What can we do for you?' That was before the trouble broke out.''

"You're Harry?" Hugh clarified, looking at the blond actor, who nodded.

"Harry Cartwright."

The wiry one spoke up. "I'm Jimmy Johnson."

"All right, Cartwright. What happened next?" asked Hugh. Carin came to stand in the middle of the room to listen while Gideon had a look around.

The sandy-haired actor was moaning slightly as the medic examined his head. Harry continued the story.

"One of them came over to where I was putting on my makeup. He put that big red handkerchief over my mouth. Well, naturally I got up out of my chair real fast, but he kicked my feet out from under me and I went down. Must've hit my head on the floor. When I woke up I was tied up and so were these guys.''

Jimmy rubbed his wrists tenderly. "The skinny one pulled a gun on me while his friend tied me up. ''They didn't say much. One of them found the bedroom and said, 'In here.' They dragged us all to the bedroom and just left us there. We were completely stunned. Had no idea what they wanted.''

"Did any of them say anything else?" Hugh asked.

Jimmy shrugged. "That's about all. I tried to get out of my ropes. I was worried about Harry and Coop. They were out cold. I was afraid they wouldn't wake up.''

Carin felt the steely grip of fear clutch her heart and shivered. She continued to listen to Hugh's questioning but turned to watch Gideon going over the room. She was afraid she knew what had happened. The Earps had incapacitated their doubles for the festival so they could take part instead. Unbelievable, but it fit.

"How did they know?" she murmured to herself.

"How did they know what?" Gideon asked, getting up from where he'd squatted to look at the floor.

"Well, how did they know about the shoot-out and where to find the actors who were going to play the roles?"

"The newspaper. You did a story about it, remember? I saw it myself."

"Okay, but how did they locate this house?"

She turned and waited impatiently until Hugh took a break from his questioning. Then she posed a question of her own.

"What about the other actors? The ones who portrayed the Clantons and McLaurys?"

"They dressed earlier," volunteered Jimmy. "Went on down to get the horses they were using in the act. They had to take up positions at the other end of the street. All we had to do was go out of here and stand at the end of the block."

She shook her head. It made sense except for how the Earps knew where to find these actors.

The medic had looked them all over and told Hugh he didn't find any broken bones. "Better take 'em in to make sure though. The doctors will want to look at those contusions."

"All right," said Hugh. "You'd better all go down to the hospital. We'll find you four later if we have any more questions. You may be needed to identify your assailants when we catch up with them. Just make sure the deputy has your addresses and telephone numbers."

The four actors were well enough to walk to the ambulance.

Carin and Gideon waited while the deputies searched

the house for evidence. She saw Gideon scan the scene for any more signs that his pursuers had been here. There was blood matted on the bedspread from the scuffles. The lab would tell if it matched that of any of the actors. While the men were finishing up, Carin waited on the porch. She leaned against the corner post, gazing at the neighborhood. People had come out of their houses, of course, to watch the commotion from their porches across the street.

Gideon joined her and placed a hand on her shoulder. "They're after me, not you," he said.

"Maybe."

"I need to draw them out, force a showdown. Nothing's going to handle this but a standoff where nobody else gets hurt."

"You mean go somewhere in the open and summon them to a shoot-out. Gideon, you can't do that. Either they'll kill you or somehow the forces of nature will take you away again."

His face was stoic as he looked straight ahead. "I don't know how I got here, but it's my own fate, Carin. I can't let you get hurt because of it. You've got your job to do here."

"And you don't?"

"Hard to say."

She interpreted another meaning that was hard to put into words. If they all went back to the past, she would be left to do her research without interference. She could write whatever she wanted to about the Earps. And if she found proof that corroborated Gideon's story that, as a Wells Fargo agent, he'd been framed, he would be avenged in print. But he wouldn't be here to enjoy it.

She bit her lip to keep the tug of grief down inside. But Gideon slid his arm across her shoulders, and she reluctantly leaned against his side.

"You care a lot about your good name, don't you?" she managed to get out.

"'Course I do. I wouldn't be a man if I didn't."

He cared more about it than he cared about her, but she couldn't say that. It would sound like whining. Since they didn't know how it worked, the thunder that brought him here could easily take him away again, or something else might. Or he would face the Earps to right the wrong done him. But now that his fate had become intermingled with hers, she wasn't ready to see him carried off just like that.

"It's not fair," she whispered.

"Hmm?" He tightened his hold on her, but she just shook her head.

In a more audible voice she said, "There must be another way."

Hugh came out of the house and told them Pete and the deputies would finish up here. His glance at Gideon was speculative, but he didn't say anything. Carin walked him to his car.

"I'd like to know if you hear any more from the lab," she said.

He gave her a frown. "We still don't have any ID on your friend."

"You don't have to worry about him."

"Carin..." But her look stopped him and he shook his head. "You'd never take advice from me, I know that. So I won't waste my breath."

"Don't worry, Hugh. I'll be fine."

"You always are."

He got in and drove away, and Gideon came down the sidewalk to join her. "What's next?"

She thought for a moment. The sound of car doors opening and closing and kids yelling in the neighborhood helped bring her back to earth.

"We need to apply logic even if these things aren't

logical. The Earps are human whether they live in the past or present. Logic applies to what they want. What about Allie?''

"What about her?"

"It seems she's going to some effort to tell us what to do. Maybe if we can talk to her again, she can help us.''

"She just comes and goes as she pleases, it seems to me.''

"Maybe she's being careful. She doesn't want anyone to question her except us. Maybe she doesn't even want the Earps to know she's here. But we can let her know we want to see her.''

"How's that?"

"There's one place she might be likely to visit. Come on, I think I know where to go next.''

The Pioneer Cemetery was located above town in a shady grove of trees. It was reached by way of a steep half-mile trail up the hill. By the time they got there, perspiration moistened their brows, and Carin was thankful for the gentle breeze through the juniper and scrub oak to help cool them off. They sat on a wooden retaining wall in the shaded, hilly cemetery to catch their breath.

Old marble markers, weathered now, marked the graves of pioneers and citizens from the last century. Many family plots were crowded within wrought-iron enclosures. The graves were scattered over a rolling, rocky terrain, clearly from a time when land was not graded and plots laid out in rows.

"Doc Holliday's memorial grave is over there," she said, pointing in the direction of a tall flagpole rising above the trees.

They got up and walked over the hilly ground to stand before a large headstone, marked off with an iron railing. "Doc Holliday, 1852–1887," the gravestone read. "He died in bed." Five playing cards were engraved on the

left, fanned out in a poker hand. Two six-shooters were
cut in the stone on the other side.

"They don't know exactly where he was buried up
here. Just that it's somewhere in the cemetery," said
Carin. "But if he's lying dead up here, then he can't be
in town at the same time."

"We don't know that," said Gideon.

A tremor passed through Carin as if someone had just
walked over her own grave, and she grasped the metal
railing. A breeze danced in the trees, and she imagined
for a moment the whisper of voices. It was fantastic to
believe that they were being threatened by beings from
the past.

Gideon covered her hand with his and squeezed it. Then
they saw the figure wandering among the graves beneath
the trees on the rocky path. Carin sucked in a breath and
held it. The woman wore a gray dress with long sleeves
and a skirt to her ankles. On her head was a slat bonnet,
tied under her chin.

She gripped Gideon's hand, afraid to speak. Neither did
they move for a moment, as if afraid that the woman
might run away. Finally Carin hissed out her words.

"Is that her?"

"Looks like," he replied. "Your hunch that she might
be here was right."

"Will she talk to us?"

"Don't know. But try not to spook her."

Carin started to move forward slowly, but Gideon held
her back. "Wait. Maybe she'll see us and come up here.
She knows darn well we want to talk to her. If she starts
to leave, we can head her off."

Carin stared at the woman, wondering if they were
dealing with a ghost. But the woman who pondered the
gravestones looked like flesh and blood, even though her
face was shaded by the bonnet.

They stayed where they were, under the branches of the big oak tree as the woman they thought was Allie worked her way around the graves. Carin realized her pulse was racing nervously and she fought the impulse to hurry forward and grab the other woman's arm to plead that she tell them what was going on.

But in her own time Allie took a few more steps down the slope, glancing this way and that. When she finally settled her gaze on the couple waiting for her, she appeared unruffled. Before Carin could open her mouth, Allie spoke from a little way off.

"I took the transcript with me," she said.

"What transcript?" asked Carin, looking at the face that she could barely see under the bonnet.

The sharp blue eyes and straight dark brows brooked no argument. "From the court hearing, a' course," she answered. "I was tryin' to make the men behave. There was stuff said in that courthouse that they wouldn't like spread around. Things about them stage robberies. I knew they'd see to it the records disappeared. So I got to 'em first."

"Where did you take the transcript?" asked Carin. She held Allie's gaze, willing her not to disappear the way she had last time.

"I brought it here," she told them. "When Virgil came here to try to heal his arm in the hot springs. That was in 1893."

The air went out of Carin's lungs. "Then it's here? Where?"

"Don't know, that's the thing. When we unpacked in the hotel, the transcript was gone. Someone took it."

Wind rustled the leaves, and Allie turned her head as if she were expecting someone to join them. Carin moved forward, determined to keep her there until they had all their questions answered.

"Allie, I don't understand. If you came from the yea
1881, how do you know about events that happened i
1893?"

Allie gave a shrug, looked away. "Maybe I been her
and back a few times."

Carin got more excited. "You're a real time traveler
How do you do it?"

From the trail below the cemetery, the voices of chil
dren could be heard. A family appeared around the bend
and the children raced to the opening in the fence.

Allie turned around and started to move off down th
hill. Carin followed, reaching for her arm. "Aunt Allie
wait. We want to talk to you some more. Please. It's im
portant."

Allie turned and looked at Carin once more. "It's u
to you, now. You gotta find it, if you want to save you
man. I finally got Virgil away from Wyatt. It's Wyatt'
the bad influence."

Then she stepped off the path and circled a tall scru
oak with dense growth low to the ground. Carin snatche
at the material of her dress, but just missed. She lurche
forward, the branches of the tree slapping her face, mak
ing her shut her eyes to protect them.

"Allie," Carin called. But Allie wasn't there.

She went all the way around the oak and the grave
next to it. No Allie.

She hurried to the edge of the bluff and looked ove
the fence, down into the cut in the hill below the ceme
tery. Erosion, boulders, roots and trees offered a choic
of places to hide, but it seemed unrealistic that Allie coul
have scrambled down there in the few seconds she'd bee
out of Carin's sight.

When Gideon caught up to Carin, she panted. "That'
impossible. Where could she have gone? She couldn'
have got down there so fast."

She looked upward. Dense brush and prickly bushes would make passage up the mountain slow and labored. "I don't get it."

Gideon shook his head, not venturing a guess. "She doesn't like strangers, that's for sure. Only seems to want to talk to people when she chooses. I don't think we'll see her again today."

"But she did give us a lead."

"The transcript. It came here, to Glenwood Springs."

Carin nodded. Things were beginning to fall into place. "She actually brought it here. At least she says she did. What do you suppose could have happened to it?"

"We have to find it. Don't you see? If Allie knows it's here, then so does her husband, Virgil. Wyatt probably found out. They're looking for it. Or if they know where it is, they're waiting for an opportunity to get it. And they want me out of the way."

His last words sent a tremor of uncertainty through her. "Those bullets were real. I suppose they mean business."

Gideon's mouth set in a grim line. "They mean business, and you need to stay out of it. You'll just get yourself hurt."

"I'm already in it. Besides, you need me to help you find out whatever she did with the transcript. I'm the one who lives here, remember. Nobody's going to let you poke your nose around by yourself. You're a stranger in these parts."

Then she bit her lower lip and looked away. She didn't mean to snap at him, and she hated for her feelings to show. Maybe Gideon was just trying to protect her, but she interpreted another meaning as well. His feud with the Earps was more important than she was to him. But she was angry with herself for caring about that.

Gideon put his booted foot on the lower rung of a railing around a family plot and crossed his arms. "I just don't want to bother you with my problems," he said. "In my day, a man protected womenfolk. It ain't your fight."

"You landed on my property," she retorted, hands on hips. "It *is* my fight. I'm the one researching the past. Maybe somebody doesn't like that. Maybe fate threw us together because of it. I need that transcript as much as you do. Maybe there's something in it that will clear your name. And I need it in order to put together a critically acclaimed story. This could make my career. I say you can't do this alone." She kicked the dirt. "If you and the Earps blast each other away, I guess I'll be free to write what I want. But I guess I don't want that to happen."

"You don't?"

She tipped her head sideways and shrugged quickly. She wasn't going to admit she cared about him. He'd already said he cared about her. Let him prove it. That he was trying to prove it, but in his own way, was dimly apparent to Carin. But she was a modern woman with modern emotions. She wanted him to stay here and help her, not lock her up in her cabin while he stalked the mountains looking for his enemies.

Gideon strode over to her and settled his hands on her shoulders. As she'd expected, he didn't waste words. He just turned her around and dropped a kiss on her forehead and then held her against him in a comforting embrace. She conceded to resting her head against his cheek. But what might have been meant as a comforting embrace only succeeded in igniting a slow burn of desire.

They were alone in the cemetery again. The family had only made a cursory tour and then followed their children, who ran ahead, down the trail. Nothing disturbed them now except the twittering of birds in the branches of the trees.

If Allie Earp was somewhere watching, Carin felt

somehow that she would approve. Allie had adored her husband, had done her best to support him and fought to get him away from Wyatt Earp. She would know what it was like to be drawn into the life of a man who came up against those who would plot against him for gain.

Maybe it was Gideon's rough edges that attracted Carin. He was honorable and he was tough. That he wasn't particularly used to the way they did things these days didn't stop him from wanting to take on his enemies. He was a good man in a fight, as Carin had seen for herself.

But right now other notions were distracting. He was holding her tighter and bent his head to kiss her. She clung to him helplessly as his sensual mouth met hers. She returned the kiss and felt a thrill run through her as he pressed her to him. An erotic tingle began where his body pressed against her thighs.

"Gideon," she said breathlessly, when he released her mouth to kiss the base of her throat. Her breathing was coming in gasps, and he made a soft sound of desire, deep in his throat.

Then, slowly, he let her go, as if he realized he couldn't finish what he was leading up to. He raised his arm to encircle her shoulders again and pressed his forehead against hers.

"Can't help it," he murmured. "Guess I never met any woman like you."

"Well, how could you," she said, her heart still lurching toward her throat. "You've never been here before."

Her breasts still ached to be touched, but she made her legs move her as she slipped her arm around his waist. Together they walked toward the gate, and then separated to head back down the path single file. Still, a feeling of exhilaration filled Carin, lifting her down the rocky path, so that she felt almost giddy when they reached the street again. He took her hand, and she felt the strength flow into her.

But this was no time to lose her head. They had a job to do and several puzzles to solve. They walked back through the neighborhood and she got the flood of emotions back under control.

"Allie said Virgil came here to soak in the sulfur springs," Carin said thoughtfully. "They took a room in one of the hotels. Some of them are gone, but the Hotel Colorado, the one you stayed in, was built in 1893. They might have records. We can ask."

Now a new burst of energy filled Carin, that of being on the research trail. Every new piece of information was a piece of the puzzle. That it might help clear Gideon's name was important. She would just have to put off thinking about what would happen after that.

Back at the Hotel Colorado, they met with Adam Little in his office. Carin explained her research on Allie Earp's movements.

"I recently learned that Allie and Virgil Earp came here to take the sulfur waters for Virgil's injured arm. I was wondering if they stayed here."

"Could be," acknowledged Adam. "I believe those old ledgers were given to the museum for their archives. You could check there."

"We will, thanks. I have another question though. Does the hotel keep any old relics that might have been left here by guests by accident? You know, people sometimes forget things in their rooms when they leave. It would have been the same in those days."

"I know what you're getting at. And yes, things have turned up from time to time that were left from the old days. But the hotel was renovated in 1942 and 1992. Many things were stored in the 1940s, and some of them used again in the nineties as the restoration began. If they aren't on display here, then any historical artifacts most likely found their way to the museum. Liz Sheppard, their archivist, would know.''

"Thanks, Adam. We'll check there.''

"I hope you find what you're looking for.''

It was getting near dinnertime, and Carin felt a gnawing in her stomach. The idea of cooking something for the two of them appealed to her. And then maybe they could look at some of her research files and see if any of the old clippings had anything to do with Gideon's stage robbery.

"The museum archives will be closed now,'' she told him. "But we can look there tomorrow. How about I rustle up something for dinner at the house? I'm starved.''

"Sounds fine to me,'' he agreed.

She glanced at her watch. "I have to pick up a press pack back at the hotel later this evening.'' At his quizzical look, she explained. "A press pack is a folder with press...that is, printed articles and typed notices and photographs for publicity.''

"Oh, I see.''

"This is for a story on the community theater. The director is meeting someone at the hotel, so he planned to drop the press pack there later this evening.''

"Well then, why don't we get a bite to eat, like you said, and then I'll buy you a drink at the hotel later?''

She smiled. "Now, I like that idea.''

They made the drive through town and left traffic behind when they crossed the bridge over the Roaring Fork River. She pointed out the landing strip and the planes in the hangar at the airport as they passed.

"Maybe I'll get a chance to show you which ones I fly,'' she said.

Gideon glanced at her with some skepticism. "Is it safe?''

"It is, if you use good sense."

At the cabin, Carin checked her answering machine for messages while Gideon had a look around the property. There was a message from Hugh, so she returned his call. What he said made a sizzle of uneasiness run down her spine.

"I just wanted you to know," Hugh said, "that I checked into Julius Eberly's bank accounts via the computer. In addition to his paychecks last year, he was depositing large lump sums every month or so. It's obvious that he had a second source of income."

"That doesn't mean his other source of income was illegal, does it?"

"No, but we also checked his tax returns. He didn't claim any other income than his job. He can legally accept gifts from family up to ten thousand dollars without reporting it, of course. We're still checking on that."

"So you think Julius might be guilty of embezzling?"

"I can't say yet. I just want to check out the leads. I'd be careful if I were you, Carin."

She squeezed the phone, thinking hard. "Even if he has embezzled, it doesn't explain why he would threaten me. I would think Nigel would be the one in danger."

"I'm going to give him a call as well. Both of you should watch your back until this is straightened out."

She thanked him for the warning. *Watch your back.* It was the same thing Allie had told Gideon to do.

As Carin put the phone down, she pondered. Julius Eberly might be a criminal, and if so, they would find out and he would be prosecuted for it. But did that mean he was threatening her? He would have to go to some lengths in order to hire thugs to engage in the elaborate scheme of tying up the festival actors just so the thugs could shoot at Carin and Gideon. But until she knew for sure, they would have to be alert.

Chapter Ten

When he was satisfied that the property was secure, Gideon came inside and took off his gun belt. Carin started dinner in the kitchen while he read some of the articles she'd copied from various archives during her research. But he was distracted from his concentration by watching her come out of the kitchen to set the table. When she finally indicated that he should take a seat, he was hungry for more than the food on the table.

"You say some of the files are missing?" Gideon asked after he'd taken care of about half of his plate of spaghetti.

"Yes, it's odd. Whoever broke in here took a lot of the articles I was working on. There doesn't seem to be much reason to it. Some had to do with the ski resort, some were the historical articles, and some were just notices about festivals and events taking place in town. I'm in charge of the cultural events column. Hardly anything threatening. But my new hard drive will be ready tomorrow. I'll print out whatever I have on the disks they left behind, then try to determine what else is missing."

"After we visit the museum and talk to them?"

"Yes, after that. But there's still the possibility that the threats, or some of them, are coming from someone else." She told him about Hugh's phone call.

"I never met this Julius Eberly," Gideon said.

"Let's hope you don't have to." She gave him a cock-eyed grin. "If he's stealing the company's money, then he's just the sort of rat you fought as a Wells Fargo shot-gun messenger, when you protected those shipments of silver and payrolls."

"Yes, ma'am. And nobody ever robbed a stage I guarded until the Earp setup. I had five years of service to show for it."

Her face clouded into an apologetic frown. "I'm sorry, Gideon. I didn't mean to bring it up. I know you were good at your job."

"Do you?"

She glanced away, but he saw the tinge of pink on her cheeks.

"Yes, I think so. You have the intrepid qualities that Wells Fargo must have looked for in its men. Utter fear-lessness and a strong sense of honor."

They finished their dinner and she made coffee. When the evening turned to shadows outside, she busied herself cleaning up. Gideon helped carry the dishes to the kitchen.

"This is women's work," she said, when he offered to help her with the dishes.

"Then you do a woman's work and a man's work as well."

She smiled, but he could see her embarrassment.

"I guess that's the way it is now," he conjectured, brushing her cheek with his finger and gazing at her for a thoughtful moment. He wanted to kiss her again, but he knew she was anxious to go pick up that package at the hotel. So he put on his guns, just in case, and they went on out to the automobile.

"I love the way the daylight lingers in summer," Carin commented. "It's not truly dark until after nine o'clock."

Gideon took a long breath, inhaling the fresh mountain scent of juniper, pine, sage and all the wildflowers and trees that cleansed the air up here. It was the kind of place a person could live long and peacefully. He might like to end his days in such a place. If he had a choice.

As Carin said she would pick up the package after their drink, they went directly to the lounge. People were still in Western dress from the festival, so no one seemed to think it odd that Gideon wore a gun belt in the hotel.

They sat companionably in the quiet bar at one of the round tables, and she told him about her life. "It was my father who encouraged me to learn to fly a plane," she said. "He paid for the lessons. He was a pilot himself and I must have gotten my love for flying from him."

Gideon shook his head. "I don't know if humans were meant to fly in the air like birds. A lot's happened in a hundred years, I guess."

"Why don't you come up with me?" she asked. "I have to cover the air show for the paper. They want all the local planes up."

"Well, I don't know. Flyin' is one thing I never planned on doing."

"You'll be safe, but of course you don't have to if you don't care to. Some people don't like to fly."

"I'll let you know after I take a look at your aircraft."

"Fair enough."

He felt peaceful sitting in the relaxing lounge. A few other groups of people talked quietly. The ambience seemed to be one of restful gentility.

He didn't know what to make of the strangeness of being here, but it seemed as if Carin knew what he was thinking. There was a potential for joy between them. If only the evil surrounding them could be banished, and if only he knew what to do about being from a different time.

He stared hard at some movement on the other side of the bar and Carin turned to see what he was looking at.

A couple of youngsters played billiards at the tables on the other side of the arched openings that separated the other room from the lounge.

"What is it?" she asked him.

He leaned forward, narrowing his eyes. Then he was out of his seat. "There."

He didn't need to explain what he meant. He dashed between the tables and around the bar, heading toward the archway where he'd seen two men lounging a moment ago. Carin was on his heels.

"Excuse us," she managed to say as they flew between some surprised men holding their beer glasses and standing near the bar.

When they reached the pool room, only the two teenagers remained. No exits led out of the building. Gideon darted toward the door to the kitchen. Not stopping to ask, he sped past a busboy, who yelled, "Hey!"

"We're following some men who went out this way," said Carin as she ran to catch up with Gideon.

The old tiled floor was slick, and she almost lost her footing. Gideon had paused before a large steam table holding a huge vat of soup. They had to make a choice between the aisle that led past utensils hanging from a rack above, and the narrow passage toward the back door.

They plunged toward the screen door that opened to a darkened alley. There they stopped, and Carin caught her breath. She wasn't sure who they were looking for. She'd only vaguely seen two figures behind the customers at the bar before Gideon lit out, but she knew he must have thought he'd seen the Earps.

It was eerie to stand on the concrete drive that ran behind the kitchens. At the moment, it didn't exactly feel like the safest place in the world. To their left a large Dumpster blocked the way to a garage. To the right was a stone building that housed a workshop. Opposite that a corrugated tin building stood in darkness. No one seemed to be about. Behind them came the clanging and the light from the kitchen, but no one followed to ask what their business was.

She was afraid to speak. Gideon took a step, and the scrape of his boot broke the silence of the night. Finally, she tugged on his sleeve.

"Gideon, let's go back inside. There's no one here."

And they'd be safer inside the hotel with other people around. But a glance at him showed her that he was angry. He wasn't a man to sit and wait for his pursuers to choose their time. He drew his gun, turned, and walked in the direction of the workshop. Carin followed warily. Only one street lamp illuminated the alley at the other end. No windows offered friendly light.

They came out of nowhere. She saw a figure jump out of the shadows and grab Gideon from behind, hitting him on the side of the head and knocking the gun from his hand. She opened her mouth to scream, but a hand clapped over it.

Her scream was lost in her throat as she struggled, but the man who grabbed her was stronger than she was and he twisted an arm painfully behind her as he stuffed a rag in her mouth. Still, she kicked out, but he outmaneuvered her. She saw Gideon recover and turn, swinging his right fist. She heard knuckles and jawbone crack. Her feet were knocked out from under her and she was forced to her knees. Her wrists were tied behind her. She heard the fight going on and saw the legs and torso of another man waiting to take on Gideon, should his colleague fail.

Then she was blindfolded and dragged against a concrete-block wall and dumped unceremoniously. She wriggled and grunted, and her captor cursed. But the words were soft and almost indistinguishable. Just beyond, she heard only grunts and thuds. What was happening to Gideon?

Then a gunshot exploded in her ears and she croaked a terrified scream.

"Damn!"

"Don't kill him," came a deep voice.

"Gun went off," a younger-sounding voice proclaimed.

Carin wriggled closer. Was Gideon dead? Had they killed him? Her bonds made her dumb and blind. The only things she had to go by were her ears. *Oh, Gideon,* she cried silently. *Don't be dead.*

Then a siren erupted in the night, and she prayed that a patrol car was near by. *Hurry!* she groaned, though no one would know what she was struggling to say.

"Let's get out of here." Footsteps pounded past going up the alley.

The siren got louder and Carin made garbled sounds of desperation. What if they couldn't find them? What if they chased the attackers instead of coming to Gideon's aid? *Oh, my God,* she prayed. *Let them come around that corner.*

Her prayer was answered as the siren's wail grew louder and the headlights from the car shone on her face. She renewed her wriggles. Then car doors opened, and familiar voices were raised.

"There they are. This one's hurt."

She heard a grunt that gave her hope.

"Carin, are you all right?" Pete McGuire's fingers worked quickly to undo the gag.

"Gideon's hurt," she said even before the blindfold came off.

"He'll be okay. Hugh's calling the medics now."

She feasted her eyes on Gideon, sitting up, but with a trickle of blood on his temple. As soon as her ropes were undone, she got unsteadily to her feet and then collapsed beside him again, afraid to touch him in case he'd been injured.

"I couldn't see," she gasped. "What happened?"

He shook his head as if he'd been stunned. "You all right?" he asked.

"I'm fine, but what about you?"

"Jumped me from behind. Two of them." He winced. "I was doing fine till one of their guns went off."

"You could have been killed." Her nerves were still taut with the fright.

Pete walked back, his flashlight swinging along the concrete drive. "Some blood over here."

"All right," said Hugh. "Which way did they go?" he asked Gideon.

He gestured with his head, then took the handkerchief Hugh handed him. Another siren roared from a few blocks away, and in seconds the ambulance pulled up behind the sheriff's vehicles. But when the medics rushed up, Gideon waved them away.

"I'm not hurt. Got to catch the attackers." He swayed to his feet and retrieved his gun, which had been kicked to the side.

"Sir, I need to examine you," said a young medic.

"I said, I ain't hurt. A scratch, see?" Gideon turned his head so the medic could at least get a look at the gash.

"It should be cleaned."

"Later. I got things to do. Which way does that blood lead?" he asked, refusing any medical treatment and striding along the alley to where Pete was checking to see how far the blood trail went.

Looking closely with the flashlight, they could see drops every few feet going in the direction the attackers ran. Carin peered at the ground under a street light. Gideon came in her direction.

"Is the blood from the gunshot?" she asked as they followed the drops around the corner, using Pete's flashlight.

"Can't say," said Gideon. "It didn't get me. But I threw Wyatt against the corner of that tin building when he came at me," said Gideon. "We both got a little bloody."

Blood had run down Gideon's cheek, but she didn't think the wound was deep. The fact that she wasn't completely sure about who they were chasing made her feel ill at ease. She hadn't seen their faces, so she couldn't swear they were chasing the Earps.

It seemed they'd lost the trail when Gideon spotted a few drops on the pavement a dozen feet away. The next sign of them looked heavier. Carin scanned the houses on this block. If the Earps really had come forward in time, where were they staying? It would make sense that they had money on them, as Gideon had, which they could exchange for modern currency to use to rent a place to stay. And that gave Carin an idea.

They were on the next block when Hugh bent closer to the red drops on the pavement they were following.

"Wait a second," he said. He crouched down and sniffed. Finally, he shook his head, put his little finger in the red stain and raised his hand to his nose, sniffing the scent again. Then he held his hand out to them.

"Some blood," he said. "Smell this."

Carin came closer and took in the oily scent. She looked at Hugh quizzically.

"Brake fluid. Hardly a blood trail."

Gideon glowered. Fortunately he didn't ask for an explanation of brake fluid right then.

"Brake fluid," repeated Carin. "I guess we lost the trail."

She squeezed Gideon's arm meaningfully. She knew

his frown of anger was the exasperation of losing his assailants again. Like Allie Earp, they seemed to appear and disappear at will. Though why they should have the ability to slide in and out of visibility any differently than Gideon, Carin didn't understand.

"Let's go, Gideon. We still have to clean and bandage your cut."

Back at the scene of the fight, the officer going over the ground had found a few traces of blood, but not the trail they thought they'd been following.

"Keep looking for that bullet," Hugh told him. "It could be in the trees for all we know. But if it's here, I want it."

Gideon still didn't trust the white-coated medics, so inside the hotel, Carin picked up a bandage and antiseptic from the hotel desk. The clerk loaned them a small office where she could clean his wound. He sat in an upholstered wing chair while she did her work. She couldn't help being reminded of when she'd first found him in her yard.

"Seems like all I do is fix your wounds," she said once she was satisfied he wasn't badly hurt.

He gave her a slow smile. "It's nice of you to do it."

She allowed herself to enjoy the comfortable intimacy that had grown between them, but she was too smart to stay close by once the job was done. For once, she worried that he was the one who needed a bodyguard. She wished suddenly that whatever was going on was over. Would life ever be normal again? But then she pushed away that thought. Normal meant that Gideon hadn't traveled forward in time. She realized suddenly how mundane her life had been before he'd come.

True, she had a challenging job and lived in a mountain paradise. She and her parents and siblings, all of whom lived in other states, were well and had no immediate financial problems. But she'd been traveling her path alone, isolated in a sea of other people. As she placed the bandages and antiseptic spray on the desk beside them, she realized how empty that was. She'd kept herself busy with work to avoid the loneliness. But when she was with Gideon, she didn't feel lonely.

He stood up when she was finished, and she turned and put her hands on his chest when he came close to grasp her elbows.

"It's late. I'll pick up my package at the front desk, and then we'd better be going."

"I know," he said. "I just wanted to say thanks."

"It's okay."

She snuggled her head against his shoulder for a brief moment, her heart pounding hard. She looked up at him. "The only way out of this is to find the answers. Tomorrow."

He nodded, the serious look on his face telling her he understood. There was a look of yearning in his eyes. But she understood that he couldn't make any promises until he resolved his fate.

She was still on edge as they drove back through the streets, crossed the bridge and wound up to her cabin. Shag came to meet them and danced in the yard. Gideon cared for the horse, made sure the doors and windows were secure, and stowed the guns within easy reach, should they need them again. Then she and Shag settled down in the bed. She hugged the dog for comfort, knowing that her sexy protector was just on the other side of the door. Her mind spun with questions and plans, but Shag distracted her with wet licks on her face until finally she pushed him away and managed to sleep.

MONDAY MORNING, the coin dealer was open before the museum, so they went there first.

"Has anyone besides Gideon here changed money from

about 1880 recently?'' she asked after the amenities had been exchanged.

''As a matter of fact, yes. Two men were in here the day after you came in. I thought it odd myself, but I purchased a lot of old coins from them. They got a fair price.''

Gideon kept his face neutral as the man began describing his customers. But when they got outside again, he nodded. ''That's them.''

''It does sound like them,'' acknowledged Carin. ''Then they've no doubt taken rooms someplace. But surely they're not using their real names. It will be impossible to find them that way. Well, let's go to the museum and ask about stuff donated when the hotel did its renovations.''

The hunt for the court transcript held double meaning for Carin. Not only might it force a showdown with the Earps if they were truly chasing them, but for the first time she would be able to lay her eyes on the original document of the hearing following the famous shoot-out at the O.K. Corral. The newspaper accounts showed that there was conflicting testimony, and the disputed points had been argued by historians for more than a century. Of course eyewitness accounts of anything were bound to conflict. People did not see the same event in the same way.

But, more important, there might be evidence in the hearing transcript that would help Gideon clear his name. Carin was no longer writing historical accounts merely for the public's enlightenment and entertainment. What she wrote in her section of the *Glenwood News* made a difference to Gideon.

As she parked the car on the street beside the little museum and got out, she realized just how much that mattered. She believed in her heart that Gideon was innocent of the crime for which he'd been jailed. She couldn't go back in time to set the record straight. But she could publish what she found out through research and let today's public see in print what could be gleaned from the hearing transcript.

If Judge Wells Spicer had been bribed or pressured by the Earps to keep the evidence from going to a trial by jury, Carin could perhaps publish enough of the story to let today's reading public make up their own minds. If she could build a case that implicated the Earps in framing Gideon, it might make all the difference. Then what? Would they give up and go back to their own time? She couldn't know, but she had to try.

The archivist at the museum was a slim, attractive woman in her forties named Liz Sheppard. In the small basement of the tiny museum, she looked in her index for them and then located the old wooden filing cabinet stuck behind other desks and boxes in a corner.

"These should be the files you want," said Liz. "Maybe if we move some of the boxes, it will be easier for you to go through them. I haven't consulted those files for some time, but if I remember correctly, they're not in very good order. The best we could do was place everything the hotel gave us in the same cabinet until an ambitious volunteer or researcher had the time to put everything in date order."

"That's fine," said Carin. "I'm sure we'll be able to identify what we're looking for if it's here."

Liz helped them rearrange the tight corner so that they had room to maneuver. A wooden chair was placed behind an old desk so that Carin could work, and Gideon rested one foot on a three-legged stool while he fingered through the files in a long file drawer. A second chair was placed on the opposite side of the desk for their use.

"Be careful," cautioned Carin, after Liz had left them

to their task. "These papers are very old and fragile. They might crumble or tear easily."

Then Carin gave a self-conscious grin. The pages were Gideon's age, but they hadn't leapt forward in time the way he had.

She opened the ledger for 1893, the year the Hotel Colorado had opened and Allie had said she and Virgil had come to the springs. The brown ink of the scrawling signatures had soaked into the pages, and Carin scanned them with a tingle of excitement. She couldn't travel back in time, but looking at original handwriting in a ledger that had been used a hundred years ago made her feel almost as if she could.

She found the signatures she was looking for under the week of September 14th. "Mr. and Mrs. Virgil Earp." It wasn't Allie's handwriting, but of course Virgil must have signed the register. A little tingle went up her spine.

"Here it is," she said. "She wasn't lying. They were here."

She remembered the elongated strokes and thickened curve of the *V* and the top of the *E* that she'd seen in other documents Virgil Earp had signed. Gideon leaned over her to study the page.

"Looks like you're right."

"So at least we know they were here. But Allie said her precious transcript was missing. Either someone stole it or she misplaced it. I suppose the odds aren't very high that we'll find it in these files. But we have to look."

Carin lifted out a thick folder and set it on the desk. Gideon took another and sat across from her, leaning forward in the second wooden chair. They paged through old papers slowly, and Carin had to resist getting caught up in reading documents that had nothing to do with their case. The stories these old papers could tell would be fascinating to anyone with a love of the past. But she pressed on. The transcript would be identified as a court document. It shouldn't be hard to spot.

They worked through one file after another and on to the second drawer. They took special care with documents still in their original cardboard folders tied with frayed fastenings. Carin's shoulders started to ache, and more than once she had to stop and rub her eyes.

"Do you want to rest?" asked Gideon.

"No," she said leaning back in the chair. "I'm all right."

He dropped his work and climbed around the desk to massage her shoulders. His strong hands pressed into her strained muscles. The relief was instant.

"Mmm," she murmured. "I could use about an hour of that."

"That'd be my pleasure."

She wanted to let him continue, but she forced her mind back to the job.

"I'm starting to doubt the transcript is here," she said. "But we have to finish every file."

"Then what?"

"I don't know," she admitted. "But I've searched for documents like this before. One clue leads to another. I haven't given up hope."

"That's good."

At the end of the day, the files had failed to reveal the missing court transcript. But Liz did have one bonus for them. She provided Carin with copies of some articles from the *Tombstone Epitaph* and the *Tombstone Daily Nugget* to replace those that had been stolen from the cabin.

"We'll need more time to look for the transcript if it's here," she told Gideon. "And tomorrow I need to go to the office and at least pretend I have a job."

"No problem. I can still work on these files."

She was envious that Gideon had time to do the research while she would be tied up for the next few days. But that was life.

They adjusted their schedules for the next three days. Carin and Gideon had breakfast and she dropped him at the museum. She got her new hard drive installed at the cabin, picked up the Trooper when the body work was done, and spent time working at the office as well. The Earps, if they were around, seemed to be lying low.

On the third day, when all the files had been searched, they sought out Liz to ask her advice. They didn't have to explain that they were trying to clear Gideon's name.

"I'm trying to substantiate my great-great-great-aunt Allie's diaries," Carin said. "I have reason to believe that Judge Wells Spicer's hearing transcript made its way to the Hotel Colorado, based on something Allie said in her diaries."

"I know how it is," Liz said. "At least you found out that Allie and her husband were here. You just need to figure out who might have got their hands on the documents. Adam was right when he said that anything of historical value found at the hotel was either used in the hotel's own display cases in the lobby, or was stored here. If you didn't find what you were looking for, then perhaps someone not associated with the hotel took the transcript."

Liz gave Carin a sympathetic smile. "I guess you have to figure out who that someone might have been."

Chapter Eleven

It was confusing. She couldn't understand what was going on in the present, much less figure out someone's motives who lived a century ago. Carin's mind felt fuzzy and tired. She thanked Liz for her help and then went outside with Gideon.

It was past closing time, but Liz had let them stay to do their work into the evening. Now shadows claimed the valley from the west side under the steep ridge that guarded the town, though summer light would last for two more hours. Food would revive them. And then they needed a bright idea.

"Let's walk somewhere and get something to eat," she suggested.

"A steak sounds mighty good to me right now."

"And I'd better phone Hugh to find out if he's come up with anything else."

They chose the café on Seventh Street across from the railroad tracks where they'd eaten before. The tall booth against the wainscoted wall enclosed them comfortably. And by looking out the glass storefront windows over the river at the sheer rise of the mountain behind, Carin was able to give her eyes a rest.

Gideon surveyed the other customers before he leaned into his corner of the booth and gave her hand a squeeze.

Carin felt tired. "I hope we can eat in peace. I don't feel like chasing anyone out of here this evening."

"Looks all clear," he said. His understanding smile told her he knew how she felt. But how much worse it must be for him. A man uncertain of his past and uncertain of his future.

Gideon was reflecting much on the same thing. He glanced over his shoulder at the dark green shadow blanketing the slope on the other side of the Colorado River. The town sprawled westward along the bend in the river and out toward the valley beyond. But the main part of the town had grown up to the south along the Roaring Fork. It must have bustled a century ago with the discovery of coal. The hot springs made it a place to relax for the rich silver kings of Aspen.

It seemed to him that the town bustled now. It had its own airport for the flying machines, and automobiles roared up and down Grand Avenue. Across the river it was quieter. And Carin's cabin was located a good distance up the mountain.

He watched the woman opposite him after they ordered steaks and coffee. He'd had long enough now to know how he felt about her. If he'd known her in his own time, he'd have courted her once he felt he could provide for her. In this time, she didn't seem to need any providing for. But her tendency to action combined with her womanly features was a strong draw. He wanted to kiss her again. Wanted to hold her in his arms.

His jaw clenched as he felt a flash of resentment that what had thrown them together might just as easily take them apart. It would be wrong for him to speak to Carin about a future together when he didn't yet know what that future held. If fate had brought him here, perhaps fate had something in store. These were things he'd never spent much time questioning before.

He was a Wells Fargo man. He'd spent five years riding the stages and guarding the green wooden express boxes and occasionally facing robber gangs. He was proud of his job and up until the Earps had framed him, Wells Fargo had been proud of him. He was one of the best. Only that last stage robbery had pulled the wool over their eyes. If there was one thing he had to do, it was to salvage his reputation. And the only way to do that was to get a confession out of the Earps that they'd set him up for the benefit of their friends.

It made him angry to think about it and angrier that luck hadn't yet turned in his favor. Looking for the court transcript that Allie talked about was well and good, but Gideon hankered to face the Earps once and for all and resolve matters. He didn't want to get himself killed. And no small part of that now had to do with the woman he was with. A man thought differently about his own skin knowing that someone cared about it. But this was his fight and he had to see it to the end.

The steaks came and Gideon tried not to speculate anymore. The present was more compelling and he wanted to savor being with Carin. There might not be any tomorrow. It started his thoughts turning in a certain direction.

But those thoughts were interrupted. The door to the café opened and the now familiar figure of Sheriff Hugh Cole entered. Gideon saw him glance around and spot them, then head their way.

"Here comes your friend," Gideon said.

Carin glanced up as Hugh swiped a chair from a nearby table and sat on it backward, his arms folded over the chair back.

"Sorry to interrupt, but I thought you'd want to know, I've been talking to your friend Nigel Henshaw."

"And?" asked Carin.

"I told him that his employee Julius Eberly was getting large sums of money from somewhere. He's decided to have an audit done."

Carin leaned against the hard, straight back of the booth. "Well, I'm glad. I'll talk to him, as a friend. I know it'll be unpleasant for him to do that." She glanced at Gideon, including him in the conversation. "Nigel's always taken such pride in his business. It'll be an embarrassment if he discovers someone's been stealing from him."

"He's agreed to file charges if there's enough evidence," said Hugh.

Gideon watched Carin grow more intent. "Do you know something else?" she asked.

"We traced the Toyota Cressida that collided with you. Found the body shop that did the repairs. The car belongs to a Martin Sampson."

"Never heard of him."

"To make a long story short, he worked at the same place Julius Eberly did on his last job."

"Oh?"

"Sampson wasn't there long. Had some disciplinary problems and was let go. But the two kept in contact."

Gideon was certain that they were being followed everywhere by his enemies. The fact that Sheriff Cole had tracked down the automobile owner made no difference to him.

Carin gave Hugh a disturbed look. "So you think Julius may be threatening me?"

He shrugged. "Not enough proof yet, but I say he's up to something. That's why I'm warning you to be careful."

"But the bullets? They seem to be coming from antique guns," she pointed out.

"Who knows? Maybe Eberly is an antique collector."

"But why? Just because he suspects Nigel may have

said something to me about the missing funds? Surely if he wants to draw my attention away from him, he's doing just the opposite.''

Hugh lifted himself off the chair, signaled the waitress and ordered a cup of coffee to take with him. Then he put the chair back where it belonged. "Hard to say what a desperate man will do.''

Carin glanced at Gideon. "I think it's time we go talk to Nigel,'' she said with worry in her voice. "He is an old friend, after all.''

"I'm not sure that's a good idea," said Hugh, frowning thoughtfully. "It might send the wrong signal to Julius.''

"Do you think Julius is actually watching our every move?''

Hugh shrugged. "You can't be too careful, that's all. I can't arrest him just because he used to work with a man who owns a Toyota that seems to have collided with you. But I don't want to see you hurt.''

For the first time Hugh looked at Gideon with something like empathy in his face. It was as if Hugh finally acknowledged him as being there when Carin needed someone. Something passed between the two men that pleased Gideon. Take care of her, Hugh's look seemed to say. Gideon responded with a gesture of acknowledgement.

It was still a pleasant late summer evening by the time they left the café. They got in the Trooper and headed along the highway beside the big curve in the Colorado River. He gazed with the same sense of wary amazement at homes that seemed to sprawl across their pieces of the mountain. They sure had a breathtaking view of a snow-capped peak dominating the valley from the south.

They parked at the top where the road ended. The summer hush filled the mountainside, and the hustle of town was left below. Nigel came out to the porch to welcome

them into his home. Carin made the introductions. Nigel
Henshaw had a fit and debonair look about him, and from
the lines in his face and his silvery hair, Gideon put him
at about fifty years old. He looked comfortable in denim
shirt and jeans. And the concern in the friendly eyes gave
Gideon to believe the man had troubles of his own.

The house was a sprawling structure with high ceilings.
Gideon stared at the living room with its big glass window
as their host offered drinks. Some Indian artifacts hung
on the paneled walls, and a long sofa and oversized padded leather chairs offered comfort.

Carin sipped at some sherry, while Gideon clinked
whiskey glasses with his host and then admired the view
while Carin talked to her friend. The other two took seats
on the sofa across from the stone fireplace.

"I don't mean to pry," began Carin, "but I'm worried.
What have you found out?"

Nigel took another sip and then leaned back, stretching
his arm along the sofa back. "I might as well tell you, I
looked into all our former procedures and I was shocked
myself at the possibility that I had allowed for someone
to embezzle if they wanted to."

"But you've changed those procedures now?"

He nodded, setting the glass down on the small round
table in front of him. "There are always a certain amount
of voided tickets due to a small percentage of the visitors
asking for their money back. Personal emergencies, parties not showing up to meet their friends, things like that.
We had a pretty lenient policy about refunding tickets as
long as the person didn't actually use the ski lifts and get
up the slope."

"And you'll still maintain that procedure?"

He gave her a nod. "There's nothing wrong with the
policy. It maintains good public relations. But it also of-

fers the ticket sellers a chance to mess with the records if they want to.''

''How's that?''

''If the ticket seller pocketed the money, all he would have to do is void that ticket on the computer printout. But he'd have to be in collusion with the ticket taker. The ticket taker would have to know which ticket to give back to the cashier, so the cashier could mark it void. The skier would never know. He buys his lift ticket and hands in the portion that he tears off at the gate. He's paid, and he skis. But the gatekeeper and the ticket seller both mark that ticket void. On the computer it looks like the money was returned and that person didn't ski that day.''

''I see,'' she said, frowning in concentration. ''Then the two who worked out the plan split what they pocketed. But Nigel, that's hardly a lot of money. They couldn't have done it terribly often. Don't you have a feel for how many tickets are voided each day?''

He nodded. ''I'm ashamed to admit it, but I didn't keep a very close eye on that last year. We were expanding. Most of my time was taken up making sure the new lifts were working and I had enough personnel to fill all the jobs. But there's more. The money was counted by the cashier and a deposit slip made. Another chance for the cashier to pocket money and deposit less than he'd taken in.

''Julius was a cashier, but I also had his check deposits and should have verified them against the number of tickets printed and sold. I didn't have time to do that myself. My mistake. I'll do it from now on.''

''I can see how quick growth could provide an opening for an opportunist with the boss busy elsewhere. It makes me angry, Nigel.''

His mouth tightened into a firm line as a muscle in his jaw flinched. ''Me too. It's not a lot of money per day, but multiplied times all the months we were open.'' He shook his head. ''A tidy sum. Hugh told me what he discovered about Julius's bank account. Still, that's no proof. He could have gotten money from family.''

His mouth twisted into an expression of distaste. ''And like I said, I wasn't double-checking, myself, and I should have been. In any case, I've corrected the way we do things this year. The voided ticket buyers have to sign a sheet and give their license plate number, verifying that they got their money back, so we can match them up with the number of voided tickets at the end of the day.''

She declined the offer of a refill, while Nigel poured one for himself. ''But what will you do about the money you believe was stolen last year?''

''I'm letting the sheriff's department quietly investigate. I want to keep the newspaper out of it, though, Carin.''

''I promise to keep my mouth shut. I wouldn't do anything you don't want.''

''Good. If there's real proof, I'll file charges.''

Nigel glanced up at Gideon as if not wanting to appear rude by not including him in their conversation. Gideon joined them and took a seat in one of the big comfortable chairs, still pondering the twentieth-century house.

Carin felt awkward. She wanted to share some of Gideon's background with Nigel, but couldn't tell her older friend what he would consider impossible. She settled on a compromise.

''Gideon is familiar with the Wyatt Earp lore. He's been helping me with my research.''

''Ah, yes. Your famous ancestor, Allie Earp. The historical articles have been very interesting, Carin. I suppose we all take those Earp legends for granted. One doesn't stop to think that it might have happened somewhat differently than legend has it. When are you going to publish more?''

She and Gideon exchanged quick glances. ''Soon, I hope. Uh, it turns out that Gideon has ancestors who also knew the Earps in Tombstone.''

''Oh, really? Then you two have a lot in common.''

She nodded, inspired by a way to expand on her theme. ''Gideon had an ancestor with the same name. He was implicated in a stage robbery the family believes is a setup. We may be able to set the historical record straight and clear the earlier Gideon Avarest's name.''

''Is that so?'' Nigel raised his glass in a salute. ''Good for you.''

She made a face at her sherry glass. ''Unfortunately, someone seems to be trying to stop us.''

Nigel shook his head, a look of concern on his face. ''Do you think that's why someone broke into your cabin?''

''I don't know for sure. It could also be the same person you're about to accuse of stealing from you. People know that we're friends. They might have panicked and thought I would draw too much attention to the case in the paper.''

''Hmm, possibly. I don't like to think that my affairs place you in any danger, Carin.''

''That's not your fault. I work for the press. And I guess when you say things in print, it's easy to annoy folks.''

''Is Hugh providing you any protection?''

She didn't look at him directly. ''I feel safe enough.''

''Hmm.''

Nigel was a perceptive man and had known her since she'd moved here with her parents at the age of twelve. She thought from his expression that he could perceive that there was more than met the eye between Gideon and herself. But he was a gentleman and he would never ask. As the three of them sipped their drinks, the air crackled with speculation, and she knew that in his quiet way, Nigel was sizing Gideon up.

"If someone is trying to stop Carin from speaking out in the paper about your ancestor, Gideon, that person must not be a friend of yours."

"Exactly." Gideon lifted his chin and met the other man's scrutiny. "I don't want Carin to get in any trouble either. I'm anxious to settle whatever is going on."

"Well, we have a good sheriff's department. Let's hope they catch whoever broke into the cabin." Nigel grimaced. "If Julius Eberly is at the bottom of all this, we'll find out soon enough. He'll be punished."

They watched the breathtaking scenery out the window as darkness claimed the valley and lights twinkled below.

"I've always loved coming up here," said Carin. "My cabin doesn't have a direct view. You have to walk to the end of the property at the top of the bluff to see any of the town, and then it's not at this angle."

"I've been happy here." Then the worry lines returned to Nigel's face. "I just hope this ugliness is settled so I can enjoy what I've got. And share it with my friends, of course."

"Of course." Carin reached across and patted his arm in a warm gesture. She stood up. "Will you be at the air show on Saturday?"

"Along with the rest of the town," he said. He saw them to the door. "I suppose you're going up?"

She grinned. "Yes. The boss wants me covering it from above, so to speak."

Nigel clapped Gideon on the shoulder. "Then I suppose you'll be going along for the ride?"

Gideon gave his infectious grin. "I've never been in a flying machine before. It'll be a new experience."

A slight bewilderment appeared in Nigel's smile, and Carin hurriedly made their goodbyes.

The drive back through town was quiet. Her wheel, scrabbled up the drive, and she pulled into the barn. Shag bounded out to greet them, and Gideon bent over to play with the dog. Having already determined that the man was a friend, the dog stood on his hind legs to lick Gideon's face.

Carin got them both into the house and locked the door. "Would you like something to drink?"

"Some of that decaffeinated coffee might taste good."

"Fine, I'll put some on." She was thankful to have something to do other than just contemplate Gideon, who strode about the house making sure all was secure.

She poured the coffee, then brought the mugs and set them down on the coffee table. She managed not to keep eye contact with him for long, but sat in a chair and lowered her gaze to sip from the mug. The awkwardness between them made her feel like a teenager on a first date. Gideon drained his mug and broke the silence.

"I don't know how I got here," he said slowly. "But there must have been a reason. More than one."

"Hmm. Meeting me gave you a chance to rewrite your history. Is that what you mean?"

"Maybe."

The long pause was deafening. Finally, he spoke again. "Carin?"

"Yes?"

"Why don't you come sit over here?"

"Because I—" her words were choked off. She didn't mind kissing a man she was attracted to, but she was afraid it would go farther than that.

And why not? If she lost Gideon to fate and time again, wouldn't it be better to have this much to remember him by? She was a modern woman, and she knew she would have the strength to go on if the thunder took him away.

even if her heart was broken. Why not hold him while she could?

"I know," he said as she got up to move to the sofa and he gathered her into his arms. "I know what you're thinking. I wish I could tell you it was different."

She settled her head on his shoulder. He touched her face and lifted her chin. Their lips joined as if they were meant to be together, and she knew in no uncertain terms that he wanted her.

"You're some woman," he murmured against the side of her head as he began to caress her. "I'd take you back with me if you'd come. I'd make you mine."

"Why don't you stay here instead?" Her voice sounded husky.

"With you?" He kissed the fingers that touched his face.

"If you wanted to."

"I want to be with you, Carin. I want to make you mine."

She was lost as she entwined herself with him. And even as passion flooded her, she laughed inwardly at the fact that she was falling in love with a man from another time. His caresses were gentle and slow, as if he didn't want to rush her. But her pulse pounded in her temples and tremors danced through her as he eased her down on the sofa and stretched his body alongside hers.

Somehow her shirt had come unbuttoned. Somehow his shirt opened to reveal his muscular chest. Then they touched each other and explored with small sounds of pleasure.

"Gideon," she breathed. "I want you to make love to me."

She felt the glow of his smile as he kissed her ear and lifted her to a sitting position.

"Then won't we be more comfortable in there?" He jerked his chin toward the bedroom.

She escaped for a few moments into the bathroom, where she rummaged in the cabinet for her diaphragm, an item that hadn't been used in more than a year. Even though passion was heating her, she took the time to make sure she was protected.

Leaving her jeans on the floor, she met him in the bedroom and trembling, she yanked back the covers. Gideon took time to undo her remaining shirt buttons while she undid his trousers. She barely heard his sigh of pleasure as he revealed her lacy bra and panties, so preoccupied was she with the gorgeous hunk of manliness she was revealing with every bit of clothing that came off.

Then he touched her, his desire full-blown in his golden eyes, his sensuous lips parted as he let his thumbs trail down to her breasts.

She crawled between the sheets. He came after her, taking his time exploring her curves. He pulled her against him, and she felt the thrill that came with flesh pressing against flesh. He managed to remove her panties, but turned all thumbs at her bra fastening. When it was released, he wasted no time in pressing his lips and tongue to her breasts.

He was strong and hard, and he was a match for her long limbs and voracious appetite once she clasped him to her. There was so much of him. The fire in her core burned with longing as her thighs came in contact with his long, male hardness. He finally satisfied the gulf of need and desire in her by inserting himself where he belonged. She took him in and joined in the age-old rhythm that sent her to a place where ecstasy overshadowed everything else. His mouth and tongue found hers as his whole body bent to the task of their shared loving. Then as pinwheels exploded within her, Gideon raised his head to cry out with pleasure. His thrusts reached their climax, and he gripped her shoulders as if to hold himself to the bed.

It felt as if they belonged together, and Carin made a silent vow as her spirit returned to earth that she would not let them part. If he wanted to stay with her as badly as she knew she wanted him, she wouldn't let time take him away.

Chapter Twelve

He held her against him as they lay enfolded by the night. The ecstasy turned to warmth and intimacy, but Carin didn't feel like sleeping yet. She sensed that Gideon was wide-awake as well.

"What will you do?" she finally asked, as her fingers traced patterns on his arm.

He inhaled a long breath and scooted upward on the pillow as if to position himself for better thinking. "We have to draw them out again. But on our own terms. We've got to get Allie to help us."

Carin shifted to lean on her elbow. She let her hand trail along his hard chest and stomach. "Yes. She seems to be the one on our side. If only she wouldn't run away every time strangers come around. I can't tell if she's crossed over to our time completely, or if she comes and goes."

She grasped his arm and squeezed the muscles. "But if she's as real as you, she must be here somewhere."

"Then we can find her."

"All right." She paused in her appreciation of his solid physique to think. "After the air show on Saturday, we'll try to set up a situation where she might find us. A safe place where we won't be interrupted by strangers, and she can speak freely."

Gideon gave her a thoughtful smile. "There's something else you can do."

"What's that?"

He put a hand on her shoulder and gave it an affectionate squeeze. "Print your stories about Wyatt in your paper. If he sees them, he'll get mad and show himself."

A throb of fear pounded through her. "You want a showdown."

His face took on that now familiar expression that meant he'd made up his mind. "Something tells me it's the only way."

She sat up, grasping the sheet to pull it over her lap. She was fully awake now, desperate to convince Gideon of the consequences of such a meeting.

"Don't you see, Gideon? If you do that, you'll be killed. History tells us that Wyatt lived until 1929. He was eighty-one years old. His brother Virgil lived until he was sixty-two. Doc Holliday died right here of lung disease in 1887. Morgan was shot and killed in Tombstone three months after you were jailed. That can only mean one thing."

Gideon glowered. "We're rewriting history, aren't we?"

She felt bewildered and frightened but hung onto her convictions. "It's not exactly the same. We're revising what people know of certain events. It's not like those events never happened. We're just bringing out the truth in them.

"We can't actually change events in the past. We can only publish the other side of the story, bring events to light that have been hidden before." She had to make him understand. "I know what I'm saying, Gideon."

"Then how do you explain the fact that I'm here? Did the newspapers say I escaped?"

She pushed the hair back from her face. His question

made her pause. "I don't know. We need to dig up the newspapers for the dates right after you remember being in jail. For that, we'll probably have to go to Arizona. It's a good idea. We can fly down after the air show."

She stretched out beside him again. "We'll cover the show Saturday, and then I'll take a week off from work. All my deadlines will be taken care of, so we can go do the research necessary to settle this."

He reached over and covered her hand with his. He didn't say anything, but the gesture was reassuring. Though he hadn't made any promises, Carin understood why. She knew he was a man of honor and wasn't going to make any promises he couldn't keep.

As long as she stayed beside him, she might be able to prevent Wyatt from killing him long enough to clear his name. Together, maybe they could find a way to confront the Earps and send them back to their own time.

Drowsiness began to draw over her, and she didn't fight it. She was too tired and satiated to do any more figuring. But there were some steps they could take to untangle the events they'd been drawn into. Gideon was right about one thing. Publishing the facts about his crooked trial was important. It would either draw Wyatt out, as Gideon suspected, or it would put him in his place. Maybe it would dissuade him from chasing them around anymore, if he was the one chasing them, and would send him back where he belonged. Time would tell.

FOR THE NEXT TWO DAYS, while Carin worked at the office, Gideon kept close by, not taking any unnecessary risks. He used the time to accustom himself to the still strange modern world.

Clear skies greeted them on Saturday morning, and Carin told him it would be a good day to fly.

The airport was located beside the Roaring Fork River

on a strip of land next to the rodeo grounds. This morning it was a hive of activity.

"Here it is," she said as they approached her flying machine. "A single-engine Citabria Explorer, approved for all basic aerobatic maneuvers." They were at the airport early, in plenty of time for Carin to get fueled up and check things out.

Besides the local pilots who would go up this morning, Carin pointed out stunt pilots who had flown in to put on an exhibition. Other pilots who were old friends came over to greet them and meet Gideon. A lot of local spectators wore Western dress, so Gideon wearing his gun didn't look so out of place at a show like this.

But he left Carin and the other pilots and mechanical people alone to speak a language he didn't comprehend. Suspiciously, he circled the small, spiffy, red-and-white flying machine. It was made of metal, and inside had a panel of instruments that he watched Carin examine carefully. He hadn't yet committed to going up with her in the rear seat, and while she checked the plane out, he wandered around, looking at the other planes.

None were much bigger than Carin's plane. They sat close to the ground on wheels and struts that she'd explained were landing gear. As the planes warmed up, their propellers whirred. One by one, they began to roll down the runway to get into position.

Gideon kept a careful eye on the crowd, too, but most of them were strangers or acquaintances he'd made while he was in town. Carin's friends, the deputies and Nigel Henshaw, were here and had exchanged good-mornings with him. But he minded his own business until Carin spotted him and came toward him from her plane.

He watched her approach him with pleasure. Her hair shone golden in this morning's sun, lifting to gust off her shoulders in the air that moved from the propellers. Her fitted jeans and blue-and-white striped shirt showed all her features to best advantage. He felt a surge of happiness as she smiled at him. And a sense of intimacy he liked. Something was growing between them that he didn't want to give up. The thought struck him just before she reached his side. He had more reasons than one now to settle this matter with the Earps. There was Carin to think of. In a few short days she'd become part of his life, strange as it might seem.

Before, he'd only had himself to think of. He could face danger and do the right thing when his job demanded it, because if he died no one would miss him. But he knew without her telling him that Carin kinda wanted to hang on to him. It warmed his heart with a nice fuzzy feeling that was new.

She reached his side and he automatically put his arm around her to give her a little hug. Then they walked back to the airplane together.

"Are you coming up?" she shouted above the noise of the engine.

He glanced at the interior of her plane and nodded. "I don't think you'd better be alone up there."

He climbed into the rear seat and looked around. Carin showed him how the straps worked then settled herself into the front, belting herself in and handling all the switches.

When it was her turn, she was waved on. The noise from her engine and all the others droned in his ears, but Gideon could see that Carin knew what she was doing.

Out the side windows, he could see the spectators in the bleachers at the rodeo grounds next to the airport. Many still milled about the airport and sat on the rodeo fence to watch. After all the local pilots flew by and did their maneuvers, there was supposed to be some sort of professional flyers who had come to do the show.

From his rear seat, Gideon watched as the other airplanes began to take off. They seemed to sail into the sky with little effort, and he stared out the window at the phenomenon. The planes banked and circled, keeping the same distance between them, and made a pretty sight as they began to form an oval in the sky above the long, narrow mountain valley.

It was finally their turn. As Carin unleashed the engine's power, the plane started to travel forward. Gideon watched the world rush past. He'd been on stagecoaches that had raced the wind across the prairie, but this flying machine was picking up more speed than that, and then they were leaving the ground.

He held on to his hat as the concrete runway departed from their wheels and Carin moved the large stick that seemed to make the plane lift off the ground. His heart took a leap at the unusual sensation, and he grasped the edge of the seat.

"I'll be damned," he muttered to himself, but the engine strained too loudly for him to carry on a real conversation with Carin. Then he had more of a surprise as she smoothly banked into a turn and he found himself tipped over to watch the ground become almost parallel with them. Blood pumped into his extremities. What if they fell out of the sky?

But the little plane hung in the air like a bird might, and he started to breathe again as Carin evened them out to fly in a straight line with the other planes. Below, miniature people waved their hats and bandannas. At least they were having a good time down there. Not that he didn't trust Carin to know what she was doing in this flying contraption. But he did have a moment when he'd rather be trying to bust a bronco than be up here.

He settled back, now that they were flying straight again, and tried to enjoy watching the scenery from this altitude. A wisp of a cloud passed beside them. The tops of the mountain ridges were just below them and he got a view of things that he never would have guessed at.

At the far end of the valley, he could see that the planes ahead of them seemed to disappear. Then he found them again, dots in the sky that had turned back and were coming toward them. Now the other planes were flying side by side, a little distance apart and at different altitudes. He shook his head. Pretty smart, all those instruments. His admiration for Carin's many talents bumped up another notch. He wondered for a minute how a woman like her could put up with a man like him who didn't even know how to drive one of the ground vehicles. Give him a horse and a gun and he could go anywhere and face anything. But some of these newfangled machines were a bit puzzling.

Carin crossed over a mountain plateau, and Gideon was admiring the scenery when she banked into another turn. This time he was ready for it, though he studied the ground just in case it was going to come up to meet them unexpectedly. But she eased the plane back into a level position and then he saw another plane beside them, presumably part of the formation. He gave a nod to the neighboring plane, a two-passenger affair painted bright yellow with black stripes on the tail and along the body. Then he saw his mistake.

The rear window opened, and the muzzle of a gun pointed their way before the blast took them. He ducked out of the way, but heard the gun roar and the bullet plunge into the metal. Carin's head jerked up and Gideon lurched forward, afraid she'd been hurt.

"Carin," he shouted, fear pumping through him as he grasped the back of her seat.

But she quickly handled the controls. Gideon hung on and their plane took a dive and banked away.

Another shot pinged off their wing. Gideon pushed open his window and returned fire.

The window behind his head shattered and he grabbed the seat again as Carin shouted for him to hang on and suddenly rolled the plane. His stomach was in his throat as he looked at the world upside down, unable to aim his gun or shout to see if Carin was all right.

The plane began to loop toward the ground, and Gideon had a moment when he thought it would be all over. But just as he thought he was about to meet his maker, leaving his body splatted with broken metal on the rocky plateau, Carin's little plane finished the loop, and suddenly they were right side up again, flying parallel to the ground. The needles on the instrument panel spun back to where they'd been before. Then she climbed again. Another shot blasted from behind, and he twisted to find the yellow plane. It was above them, just to the left. He fired back.

Carin grabbed the microphone and rattled off her position. "We're being shot at."

A voice crackled through the radio. "Are you declaring an emergency?"

"Negative," she replied. "I'm coming back. Requesting active runway and wind conditions. The plane that's after us is an Aztec N4647P."

Another shot pierced the skin of the airplane, and Gideon heard a crunching sound as if the engine had been hit. The little plane lurched, and Gideon pitched forward. But Carin got control, and they passed over the airport.

"Repeat, please," Carin spoke into the microphone. "We took another shot. I missed what you said."

The voice came out of the radio box. "We've had a wind shift. Wind is 180 degrees at 10 knots, gusting in the teens. The runway is cleared for you."

She acknowledged. He could tell from her stiffened shoulders that she'd bent her attention to steadying the plane and going into the turn. If the flying machine had been shot, Gideon considered it a miracle that they were still in the air. They tipped right and left as they descended. He felt the plane's power reduce, and out of the corner of his eyes he saw the flaps on the wings move. They hit an air bump and he felt the jolt. They wobbled a little, and then the ground came closer. He knew his life was in Carin's hands. He felt the bump as the wheels met the runway.

The fools standing beside the runway and over at the rodeo grounds were cheering as the plane fishtailed to a stop. They must have thought it was all part of the show. Carin's shoulders slouched as the plane came to a halt and Gideon reached around her gently.

"You all right?" he asked when the noise reduced so that they didn't have to shout at each other.

"Yeah, you?"

"Fine."

She twisted her body to reach for him, then they leaned their foreheads together. He felt the sweat on her brow and the trembling in her arms. He could tell she'd been scared, but she'd handled the plane.

"Good job," he said, cradling her head against his cheek and steadying her shoulders. "Cool-headed in a fight."

Others approached the plane, so they unstrapped themselves.

Nigel poked his head inside the cockpit looking concerned. His tanned face was pale, and worry lines etched his cheeks and forehead. "What was that all about?"

"The bullets weren't on the program." She gestured at the shattered window.

Outside, Hugh examined the bullet hole in the fuselage and then looked at the damage to the window. Nigel helped Carin out and Gideon followed.

"Are you two all right?" asked Nigel.

"We're fine," Carin said. "Although I'm afraid that was Gideon's first time in a small airplane."

She glanced up at him in concern. He was shaking his head as if to reorient himself on the ground, but he didn't seem to be injured.

"What's going on here, Carin?" said Nigel in a suspicious tone, once it was clear that neither she nor her passenger were hurt.

"Beats me." She shaded her face from the sun with her hand as she looked for the chairman of the air show. "But if that Aztec was registered in the show, we'll know who was up there with us."

Carin left Hugh to question Gideon about what had happened, while Nigel took her to the flight office where she could have a cup of coffee and collect herself. They located Matthew Higgins, the air show chairman, who asked if Carin or her passenger needed any medical attention. When she assured him that they were all right, he complimented her on good, safe flying in a crisis.

"Training pays off," she murmured.

She glanced out the glass front of the office and saw Gideon gesturing to Hugh about what had happened. Most passengers would have fainted after a flight like that, or gotten airsick. Gideon must truly be made of tougher stuff. In the air or on the ground, he seemed to be able to take whatever came. She pulled her attention back to Matthew, who was flipping papers on a clipboard and shaking his balding head.

"That Aztec isn't registered as part of the show," Matthew told her. "It's not hangared here. Flight service has already alerted nearby airports to watch for it and detain the pilot and passengers as soon as it lands. Based on the amount of fuel it carries, we can make a fair estimate of how far it can fly."

Carin's mind leapt ahead to possibilities. "We should also look in places they might land where there is no airport. Whoever was in that plane will know we've got an alert out on them. They won't land where police could be waiting for them."

She met Hugh on the tarmac and followed him to his car, where he radioed in the description of the plane and put out an all points bulletin. She listened while Hugh spoke into his microphone. Between phrases, he frowned in concentration.

"Did you see the pilot or the man who fired the gun?" he asked her.

She shook her head. "It was all I could do to fly while it was happening. Gideon got a better look."

Hugh gave her an odd look. He replaced the microphone in the car. "I've already talked to him."

She knew better than to ask what Gideon had said. "Okay. Look, I have a hunch that pilot is not going to land at any airport. I know a few places in the mountains that provide natural landing strips."

"If we're going to pursue them by air, I'd better come along this time, Carin."

"No, they would see us coming. If they've hidden their plane in the trees in a valley somewhere, we'll be better off going in by car and on foot."

"All right. Give me those locations, I'll have my men check it out."

"Let's go look at a map then."

Back in the office, a small group gathered around Carin at the laminated map on the wall. She saw Gideon come in and accept a cup of coffee, watching from where he leaned on a corner of a desk. Hugh, Matthew and Nigel peered at the map over Carin's shoulder.

She studied the diagram of the terrain she'd flown over so many times.

"Besides the airports, there are several long valleys nearby where a small plane might land on a natural landing strip. There's one here to the west of us." She pointed and then pondered. "And I remember this one, I've used it myself." But there were a couple of other possibilities.

Hugh took charge and issued orders to the deputies about who would go where. Then he used the flight service phone to call the surrounding counties' sheriff's departments to put them on alert. The others drifted away to answer questions as people began to come in.

"And I'll go here," Carin said to no one as she rested her finger on a spot on the map not very far away from where they were now. Gideon came to stand beside her and looked at the spot. Then he looked at her and nodded, but didn't say anything. He downed the rest of his coffee and then tossed the disposable cup in a wastebasket.

"Whenever you're ready," he said quietly.

She didn't argue, but it would also make sense to let Hugh know where she was going so they would have backup. When he got off the phone she approached him at the desk.

"I'm going to drive to Marble," she said. "I've seen planes that have used that long stretch beside that stream. And I saw a plane like the Aztec there about a year ago, though I can't be absolutely sure it was the same one. If they've gone there, we'll have to sneak up on them real quiet. If you follow in a marked car, it'll scare them off."

He frowned and rubbed the bridge of his nose. "This is police business, Carin. You let me handle it."

But she shook her head, her blond hair swinging in front of her face. "You need us to identify the culprits and the plane."

He sighed at her obstinacy, but gave in. "All right, but we'll take one of our unmarked cars. If they're your pursuers, they'll know your car and be watching for it." He gave a resigned glance toward Gideon. "Meet me at the gas station in five minutes. I'll have Pete meet us there with a car."

She crossed her arms stubbornly. "I'll drive my car, too. We'll park out of sight when we get there. If anything happens, we might need a second car for a getaway."

Carin didn't wait for an answer. She gestured for Gideon to follow her. Then they were out the door walking quickly to her car. They belted themselves in and Carin headed for the rendezvous at the gas station. Gideon checked his guns and ammunition. In a few seconds, Pete pulled up in an unmarked Chevrolet Caprice, and Hugh left his Chevy Blazer there to join the deputy. Carin pulled out, leading the way.

"It's only a hunch," she told Gideon, as they traveled down Highway 82. "I did see a plane like that before, but I can't be sure. There could be more than one yellow Aztec with those stripes."

"Well, whoever owns this one is in with some bad company."

"Did you recognize the Earps?"

"I'd be willin' to swear on a Bible in court that Wyatt was the one firing at me from that plane."

She gave him a sidelong glance. "Then they must have rented it and a pilot. We'll soon find out."

She clipped along at a lively pace. With the sheriff of the county following her on police business, she could hardly get a speeding ticket. The valley opened wider. The Roaring Fork, lined with cottonwoods, meandered through fertile pastures, and Mount Sopris loomed nearer. She slowed for the turn onto Highway 133 and in a few minutes they passed through the town of Carbondale. The two-lane highway leading directly south passed through rich farmland, and then the valley walls narrowed again as they approached the base of Mount Sopris.

Red sandstone cliffs lined the right side of the road, while the Crystal Creek tumbled along on the other side. To Carin's eye, this stretch south that went deep into the mountains was some of the most beautiful country in the world. Many others had found it so and had made homes here. It was a convenient place to get away from it all. Or to hide.

She sped along the twists and turns, intent on where she was going, leaving Gideon to gaze out the windows at the carved defiles in the red rocks that led off the side of the road to his right. They had to slow for traffic turning off to the village of Redstone, and then two minutes later the Cleveholm Manor peeked at the road from its exclusive setting on a woody green slope.

As she turned off the road for the hidden town of Marble, she had to think carefully. The stretch of meadow she remembered where planes could land by the stream was only a few turns of the road away. She pulled off into a gravel clearing where fishermen parked beside the Crystal Creek. The sheriff's car followed. They all got out and met between the cars. Hugh radioed their position to the dispatcher at the department.

"We can't drive any farther," Carin said. "The strip is another half mile. We'll have to cross the creek and go in that way."

Hugh eyed Gideon's guns and looked at Carin. But she brooked no argument. "Now is no time to argue, Hugh."

She reached for the revolver she'd kept in the back seat of her vehicle since all the trouble had started.

"All right," he said. "But don't use them unless you're firing in self-defense."

Gideon thrust his chin forward but kept his mouth shut. She watched him scan the territory they were in.

She knew what he must be thinking. It was a good place for culprits to hide. Trees lined the road and the stream.

A long narrow valley led between rising mountains, clothed in short green grass and aspen trees. A man could hightail it to the mountain and hide himself for a long time. But it wouldn't be that easy for a plane to hide.

"Let's go," Carin said.

She led the way back up the road to a bridge where they could cross the river. They were in the open here, and if their enemies had chosen this valley to hide in, and if they looked this way now, they would see the armed party crossing the bridge. But they were still some distance away from the natural airstrip, so if luck were on their side, they still had a chance to snoop without being spied upon.

Once across the bridge, they took off into the high grasses that grew near the stream. They would be on private property all the way, and she hoped no one would slow them down asking for explanations now. She turned to speak to the others.

"I think we should stay as close to the river as we can. The trees will give us some cover. We just have to hope our attackers haven't taken refuge in one of the cabins set back toward the slope."

The men gave no argument. They moved along single file while the creek rushed and jumbled beside them, midday sun glinting on the whitecaps. Though they weren't that close to the marble quarry, large chunks of the brilliant white stone were visible here and there beside the stream or at the edge of a field, cast-offs from the finer pieces mined four miles above, or pieces that had fallen off trucks carrying a load to its market.

As they got farther from the road, the sound of cars disappeared and they were surrounded by the hush of the mountains, only wind whispering in the trees and the bubbling of the stream creating soft, natural sounds. But Carin's senses were alert to any movement, watchful for signs of the plane they were looking for.

When they came to the edge of the long, grassy strip stretching ahead, she crouched. At that angle she could see the long marks pressed into the grass. Her hunch had been correct, and her spine tingled.

"A plane's landed here fairly recently."

She pondered for a moment and then pointed toward a stand of junipers they could reach by staying in the taller grass this side of the runway. Hugh nodded. Gideon moved forward, several steps ahead of them, half bent and heading for the trees.

When they had gathered at the base of a tall juniper, Carin squinted into the woods ahead. Patches of yellow were visible from here.

"Over there," she whispered. "We'll have to move closer to make sure."

The others nodded. Gideon drew his gun and stealthily slipped toward some trees that would give him cover. When Carin sprinted across and reached him, she was sure. The yellow tail of the aircraft showed bright between the junipers. Moving closer they could see the black stripes and the painted numbers that Carin had memorized in the middle of the fight. Somewhere in the woods, the pilot and the shooters lurked.

Chapter Thirteen

Gideon's fierce gaze pierced the surrounding trees. The quiet woods were hushed and eerie. A bird twittered above them, making an uncannily loud racket. Guns drawn, the party squatted behind rocks and trees, watching for any movement. If the plane had landed some time ago, the attackers could be anywhere.

"All right," said Hugh. "Pete and I will go in. You two stay here."

But Gideon had already begun to dart across a small clearing and behind a low blue spruce.

He paused only momentarily. On his next move, he got very close to the plane, his back against the base of a tall pine that stood at the edge of the small clearing used by the plane as a hangar. There was no one in the cockpit. Someone might be hiding within the plane, however, so they still had to be careful.

Nothing stirred but a chipmunk that raced across the pine needles and scurried up the tree, taking refuge in the branches. Gideon relaxed his stance, but kept his gun at his side. Carin came up behind him.

"They're not here," he said. His sixth sense told him no others from his time were in the vicinity.

But she didn't seem so sure. "They might not be here, but whoever flew that plane may be."

Deputy Pete had circled to the other side of the plane and had it covered. Gideon didn't see the sheriff, so assumed he might have continued in a wider circle to search the area.

"Cover me," Carin said to Gideon.

He took a stance and watched her bend low and run to the side of the plane, staying near its belly. She slid along to the door to the pilot's seat. Then he saw her reach up and grasp the door handle, flinging the door open and ducking with her gun pointed upward at the same time. Gideon aimed, but no one was there.

He followed closer as Carin crept upward, still angling her gun inside in case a perpetrator hid in the back. "I can see enough," she said over her shoulder. "No one's in the rear seat."

She stood up and breathed. "All clear," she said.

Still wary, Gideon searched the ground. He crouched and looked at the heel marks in the dirt.

"They've been here, that's for sure."

They had been shot at, that's for sure, Carin thought. But in the same manner that she felt about the car that had been traced to Julius Eberly, she found it easier to believe that a modern assailant had used the air show as a way to attack them.

Hugh joined them, being careful not to disturb any footprints that might be near the plane. "We'll trace this plane to its owner soon enough," he said.

Gideon followed the boot-heel marks into the trees.

"Looks like he's picked up a trail," Carin said. "Let's be careful of a trap."

"Doesn't he listen to anyone?" Hugh asked.

"He's not used to taking orders from anyone," she replied.

The ground was soft from recent moisture, and it wasn't hard for Carin to see that a number of persons had passed this way. The ground ascended and became more rocky. They picked up a footpath that was drier, but the boot heels had still left their impression. Then they came out on a grassy slope that curved around the base of the mountain. Farther on was a pristine mountain lake, and not far from that was a cabin. They all crouched near a rock outcropping that marked the edge of the woods.

"Any idea who lives there?" Carin asked Hugh, who had come up behind her.

He shook his head and looked around. Pete kept his gun at the ready as well. "No cover between here and there, either. I don't like this."

"It's frustrating to come so close every time and yet they still evade us."

"Not this time," said Gideon.

A tremor of fear raced through Carin's heart. She knew his determination to face his enemies squarely and was afraid he would shout a challenge and get killed in the process.

"Wait, Gideon. We have to think this through."

He was already gazing at the landscape, and she could see the wheels in his mind turning. They could surround the cabin and come in from different angles, but the short grass didn't provide enough cover. All they would succeed in doing would be to distract the attackers, who, given enough firepower, could hold out for some time and pick them off one by one.

"It isn't good," she had to agree with Hugh.

"Well, it's me they want," said Gideon, holstering his gun. His determined jaw jutted forward. "If they have any guts at all, they'll give me a fair fight."

"What do you think you're doing, Gideon?" Carin asked as he started to move forward.

He paused only long enough to grasp her shoulder and look into her eyes. Sadness and resignation resided in his own hazel depths, and her heart cried out silently. The earth seemed to move under her feet and she stifled the *no* that bounced around in her head.

"Wish me luck."

She swallowed a frightened sob, but she didn't hold him. She knew he'd been hoping for a showdown, and he wouldn't listen even if she grabbed his knees and clung to them as he tried to walk away. She stood paralyzed, her heart in her throat, as she watched him lift his hands in the air and walk forward toward the cabin.

"What does he think he's doing?" said Hugh. "He'll get himself killed."

For a second, she couldn't speak, waiting for an explosion to ring out. When nothing happened, she found her voice and swiveled in her crouched position.

"He's banking that the person who's after him will come out and give him a fair fight."

"He thinks the shooter is after him? Is he crazy or something?"

"No," she said coolly. It's the code of the West. There was no time to explain.

She didn't wait, but darted to the next outcropping of rocks and brush off the path, a little closer to the cabin. At least they could keep him covered. She tasted panic, but fought it down. The urge to run to his side warred with the rational part of her mind, telling her to stay where she was. The knowledge that in a split second Gideon could be blasted away from life was too terrible a consequence to contemplate.

She steadied her shaking gun hand, bracing her arms on the rock. She squinted at the cabin, searching for the glint of sunlight on metal that would tell her a gun was pointed at him. Then suddenly a consoling thought reassured her. If Gideon had managed to ride the thunder to the present century, surely the forces that had sent him here would not simply blast him away again. She'd always believed that people made their own fate, consciously or not. And she simply knew this was not the way Gideon was meant to end.

She pushed metaphysical thoughts aside and concentrated on the job she was doing, which was to fire at any sign of danger. Gideon was within earshot of the cabin. He called out in a strong voice, his hands still above his shoulders to show he wasn't reaching for his guns.

"Come on out and give me a fair fight," he yelled. "Let's even things up once and for all." His voice echoed over the slope.

Nothing moved at the cabin. He tried again. "Show yourself, Earp. Let's have it out here and now."

Carin steadied her nerves. She couldn't risk squeezing the trigger by accident. Still, nothing happened at the cabin. Maybe the culprits were waiting for Gideon to get closer and then would ambush him. But something told her that wasn't the Earp style. Wyatt Earp might be a showman and a con artist, twisting a situation so that he would look like the hero. But she'd never read anything that indicated he would stoop so low as to murder a man in cold blood.

However, she couldn't just sit here and risk Gideon getting killed. Maybe they were wrong and it wasn't the Earps inside the cabin. If their attackers were friends of Julius Eberly, she couldn't guess their frame of mind. She glanced to the side to see that Hugh and Pete were fanning out across the meadow in the other direction. It looked as if they meant to surround the cabin.

Gideon was walking closer to the closed cabin where nothing moved. It was time for a diversion. She stood up and raced across the slope for another rock outcropping. If she could get the attackers to fire at her, at least Gideon would know someone waited within. But nothing happened as she dove behind the rocks.

She peeked upward just in time to see Gideon make a dash for the corner of the cabin and press his back to the logs, while he drew his gun. She saw him glance to make sure no one was stalking him from the side, then slide near the window and duck under. Carin aimed for the side of the cabin in case someone showed. If she aimed for the door, she might hit Gideon by mistake.

Gideon kicked in the door and flattened himself against the other side. Still nothing. Carin couldn't contain herself any longer and sprinted down the slope to the north of the cabin, beside the corral. As she crouched behind a fence post, Gideon slid forward, his gun pointed inside. He disappeared within, and Carin bolted around the cabin, hoping to find a back door. She did, and it was open.

She sprang inside the small kitchen and crouched beneath a small four-legged table. But only the breeze pushing the checkered tablecloth in and out greeted her.

Then she heard voices from the other room and tensed again. She hurried to the door and squatted there, aiming her gun low. But when she saw Gideon untying a man who was stretched on the floor, she stood up. She checked the only other room, a small bathroom, and then lowered her gun and went to where the man being freed was talking excitedly and a little incoherently about being the pilot of the Aztec that had been hijacked. He looked to be of average height, dressed in blue denim shirt and jeans, with hair to his shoulders.

Gideon took out a pocketknife and sawed through the ropes tying his feet.

"Held a gun on me the whole time," the man was saying.

When Gideon got his feet free, he scrambled up and sat on the worn sofa. "Didn't sound like your average crook. The one telling me what to do had a gentlemanly southern drawl. The other two sat in the rear seat and shot out the window. Gave me a scare, all right.''

"I was flying the plane they were shooting at," Carin said, coming into the room.

The other pilot stared at her. "The Citabria?"

"That's right. I'm Carin Sage."

He stretched out his hand. "Harlan Foster," he said. His face appeared slightly drained of color. "I sure do apologize for the trouble. When those gents hired my plane to watch the air show from above, I sure didn't know they were armed, or that they meant any harm.''

"No, you couldn't know that," said Carin.

"Say, that was some flying you did. You all right?"

"Yes."

She stepped to the door to wave to Hugh and Pete, indicating they were out of danger. She knew they would still approach cautiously, checking out the scene for any signs of the attackers.

Back inside, Gideon was asking the pilot what the men looked like. She didn't even have to hear him finish to know he was describing the same men who had tied up the actors and joined the shoot-out at the O.K. Corral and who had fought Gideon in the alley. The question was, did these same men break into her cabin, leave a threatening note in her office, and try to run her off the road?

Only three men had gone up in the Aztec. Of course that was all the plane would hold. Gideon said he'd been followed here by three Earps and Doc Holliday. One of them hadn't gone up in the plane.

Gideon looked at Carin. "The one with the southern drawl would be Holliday."

"They told me to land somewhere away from airports," Harlan said. "This is the closest natural landing strip, so I brought them here. They ripped out my radio microphone to make sure I wouldn't contact anybody and marched me up here.''

''Do you know whose cabin this is?'' asked Carin.

He shook his head. ''Nope. Nobody was here when we got here. They just tied me up and left. That's all I know.''

Gideon stood by the sash window that looked out over the valley and the lake. ''Which way did they go?''

''Can't be sure. I was on the floor, tied up. Their voices seemed to go off in the direction of the road, though.''

Hugh reached the cabin, and Carin filled him in. He took charge of Harlan while Carin stepped outside. Gideon followed. For a few moments they stared at the peaceful mountain valley guarded by tall jagged peaks. They had pursued their pursuers, but as so many times before, the men they wanted had disappeared. Carin gave a little shiver.

She still found it incredible that time travelers had come here to threaten not only the man who had escaped their clutches, but also now herself. She knew how to fight modern-day criminals, but how could she fight beings who managed to do the impossible and come through time?

Gideon must have sensed some of what she was feeling and wrapped his arms around her from behind. She felt the support of his strong torso against her back and sighed shakily. That he was very much flesh and blood he had proved beyond doubt the last few nights. What had happened between them was no fantastic dream.

Gideon loosened his hold and came around beside her. ''Will you stay here while I track them?''

She gave him a little frown. ''No. You'll need backup.''

He glanced at the cabin and then at the deputy checking around the cabin for signs of intruders. She could almost read Gideon's thoughts.

"I know. You know how to track them because they're your kind. Not the common criminals the sheriff and his deputies think they're up against."

He let the air hiss out between his lips before he spoke. "You said that, not me."

Harlan emerged with Hugh. He'd agreed to go with Hugh to the plane so they could see if any evidence had been left behind. Carin and Gideon joined them and they followed the trail back toward where the plane sat among the junipers. But Gideon fell behind when they moved among the trees. Carin scanned the woods. The hairs on the back of her neck stood on end and she came alert, listening and watching for any signs of a presence.

"Do you think they came this way?" she asked Gideon.

He nodded. "They have. But they have too much of a lead on us."

She looked at the deep expanse of woods and the endless places in this wilderness for their enemies to hide. They could go in circles for days. Something told her they should stick to their original plan of locating the court transcript. Only when it was found would this end.

"Let's go, then." She had another task awaiting her in town. They headed back to where they'd left the car. The law would do their job now. Harlan would sign a statement. There was something else she could do for Gideon.

She notified Hugh before they made their departure. They drove back in silence. Carin couldn't help thinking how it might have turned out differently. The showdown Gideon was waiting for might have occurred. Why hadn't it? They'd been evenly matched. The Earp gang against Gideon and his backup, the sheriff, deputy and herself. The Earps could have waited and faced them all off. Gideon might have been killed.

She didn't like the iron knot in her stomach at that

thought and the way she was squeezing the steering wheel. She didn't like thinking of that kind of loss. But she forced herself to admit it might have occurred. Again, she told herself there was something she had to do.

As they wound up the road that led to her cabin, she finally broke the silence.

"We have work to do. You can help. It's time I wrote that article about the missing court transcript. Since we've traced it as far as the Hotel Colorado, I can publish the fact that we're looking for it. Anyone with any knowledge of it will come forward. I can tell your story, Gideon. It's time."

The Trooper scrabbled up the driveway, and she turned off the motor. Shag came bounding out to greet them. Gideon turned sideways to peel her hand off the steering wheel and warm it with his own.

"Wyatt won't like it. We'll have to be ready."

"I know it'll increase the danger. But I don't see how the anticipation can be any worse than it is now. We have to show our strength. Besides, it might drive him to do something careless. If he gets really desperate, he and his brothers and Doc Holliday might end up showing themselves in broad daylight."

She shook her head. "I know you don't think they can be taken by anyone not of their own time. I must admit I don't see how that could happen, either. I'm sort of out of my depth in dealing with time travelers."

Gideon tipped back his hat and pulled her closer. "I don't think you're out of your depth in dealing with me, madam."

Her spine tingled with erotic pleasure as he nibbled on her ear. Desire rocked her from the inside out and she reached around his neck automatically. After nearly losing him, there was nothing she wanted more than for him to make love to her again. But there wasn't time. She pressed her cheek against his and allowed the warmth to enfold them for only a moment. Outside, Shag was doing his best to distract them, leaping back and forth and barking his demand that they get out of the car and play with him.

"We have to clear your name, Gideon," she said, finding the strength to push herself away. "It's the least I can do."

His serious look still made her wobble as she got out of the car. But he didn't argue and came around to find a stick and give the dog the attention he wanted. Gideon and the dog played tug-of-war with the stick, Shag giving mock growls while Carin unlocked the cabin. Inside, she started a pot of coffee. While it was dripping, she unlocked the drawer where she'd put research material she could still use to back up the story she had in mind. She turned on the new computer hard drive and waited for it to boot up.

By the time Gideon came into the house, she was planted before the computer screen, deep in concentration, her fingers tapping out the story on the keys.

Gideon knew better than to interrupt her, so he poured himself and her a cup of coffee and didn't speak as he set her mug beside her. Then he found his way around in the kitchen to make sandwiches for them both. He munched his sandwich and watched out the back window until he no longer heard the clicking of the keys.

"I have to make a phone call," she said abruptly.

He only half paid attention while she paced in front of a low cabinet where her telephone sat. She was asking about the court records, and he presumed she was talking to someone about the missing court transcript. After a quarter of an hour, she thanked the party and hung up. Then she sat down slowly.

"That was the Arizona State Archives department. I'm lucky I reached anyone on a Saturday, but a gracious lady who must love her work was there catching up. I wanted to verify that we weren't on a wild-goose chase, that they actually don't have a copy of the court transcript from Judge Spicer's hearing.''

''Do they?''

She shook her head slowly. ''No.''

''Then Allie's telling us the truth.''

''Even if she isn't, there would still be no record of that hearing. The archivist just informed me that unfortunately the records of an inferior court in Arizona were kept for only fifteen years in those days. The Earp hearing was conducted before a local justice of the peace and was not considered a record of file. They don't know anything about the transcript being stolen at the time. All the woman could tell me was that they don't have it now, because it would have been thrown out before the turn of the century.''

She looked up at Gideon. ''Believe me, if we can locate it, we'll be doing history a favor as well as clearing your name.''

But her interest in history was nowhere near as great as her desire to flush out Gideon's enemies, and the only weapon she had at hand was her computer. After eating only one bite of her sandwich, she sat and glared at the machine. Then she placed her hands on the keyboard and spoke with determination.

''Okay, tell me from the beginning again. I want to write it all down this time.''

''Write what down?''

''Everything about the stage robbery and your trial. Every detail about the parts the Earps played. I'm going to publish it.''

Gideon made himself comfortable in one of her wing chairs, and prompted by Carin, he went over the last few months of his life working for Wells Fargo just before he broke jail. He talked about what he knew of the feuds in Tombstone, about the politics of the times. The men who ran Tombstone were split into two camps, each with a newspaper to tell their side of the story. Now that she had copies of the articles from both of those newspapers, the *Tombstone Epitaph* and the *Tombstone Daily Nugget,* she could verify that what Gideon told her was true.

The Earps ran for public office and lost, finding themselves up against the opposite faction. As Gideon talked, Carin lost herself in the story, typing what he said into the computer as the time sped by. They forgot about dinner, although she got up once to make a fresh pot of coffee.

When she was working on a story, time had no meaning. She began to feel as if it were she, and not Gideon, who had traveled to another century. She could feel the surroundings of Gideon's time, smell the sage, hear the sounds of an Old West town. Surely it was the dream of every historian to be able to go back and really see what it was like.

By the time he came to the stage robberies, she understood the complicated relationships among these ambitious, politically aggressive men. The loyalties and codes of the times had less to do with justice and more to do with advancing oneself and protecting one's friends.

When Carin returned to the room after making another plateful of sandwiches, Gideon described the robbers who held up the stage the night he was wounded.

"They wore masks, with long beards made of unraveled rope sewn to the edges. One of them wore a preacher's frock coat and collar. But I knew Doc Holliday behind all that disguise. Besides, I heard his voice. So did some of the passengers."

"So that's why they framed you. They thought you'd accuse Holliday."

He nodded. "He was Wyatt's friend. The Earps always stood together and that included protecting Doc."

Carin kept Gideon talking until the wee hours of the morning. When she finally had everything down she leaned back and stretched. "It's late. Why don't you go to bed?"

"What about you?"

"I suppose you're right. I'd do a better job of shaping this into something that will make a good article after a night's rest."

Gideon rubbed his eyes, but he wasn't too tired to grin at her. "What makes you think you'll get a night's rest in there?"

She felt the flush creep up her cheeks and hid the smile in her eyes by not looking at him. "What could possibly keep me awake at this hour?"

He got to his feet and pulled her out of her chair. "I can think of something."

She slid her hands up his iron-muscled arms and melted against him as he heated her throat with his lips. Words of protest that she was too tired fled as he guided her away from the computer and in toward the bedroom. He undressed her slowly and then turned down the bed for her. She gazed at him with pleasure as he got out of his own clothes and slid in beside her. Then he merely cradled her head in his hand.

"You're tired. You need to sleep. I'm not going to ask you to stay awake any longer."

"Mmm," she murmured and nestled against his warmth. Her affection grew with the care he showed for her well-being. But the soft caresses began to arouse her out of her stupor and she entangled her limbs with his and kissed his face.

She whispered into his ear. "I don't think I'm ready to sleep just yet."

He returned a growl. "Then I think I have a way of taking care of things."

He moved to cover her with his strong body and traced a line with lips and tongue from her throat to her breast. Her hands delighted in dancing over his skin. It could be this way forever, she mused, just before she lost herself in the comfort and excitement he provided with the slow movements that fused them. Forever had no end and no beginning. Forever was a long time.

Chapter Fourteen

"I don't know, Carin. The writing is good, as usual. But 'Wyatt Earp Con Man?' Why is that relevant to our audience? As far as I know, Wyatt Earp never set foot in Glenwood Springs."

Carin leaned forward, her elbows on her desk, her head propped in her hands, and sighed in frustration. She'd spent most of Sunday composing the article. She angled her gaze at her editor, Keith, as he waved her story in the air and paced in the small space in front of her desk. His hair was rumpled, and his glasses hung on the outside of his shirt pocket. His half-full coffee mug perched near the edge of her desk.

"I know that, Keith. But this town is Earp crazy because Doc Holliday died here. We just had a shoot-out like the one at the real O.K. Corral. You can't tell me people aren't going to want to read this."

"But the Earps were supposed to be the good guys."

"That's what the Hollywood legends say. But there's more to the story. They were cut from the same cloth as the members of the other side of that feud. It's a fascinating story, and my...our readers will eat it up."

He scratched his head, and the pencil fell from behind his ear to clatter to the floor. He didn't bother to pick it up.

"Okay, okay. I'll buy that there are two sides to every story. But why are you starting the series with a story about a stage robbery? You're saying that the Earps pinned the guilt on this Gideon Avarest, and that Doc Holliday was one of the robbers. You say your great-great-great-aunt's diary is your only source?"

"So?"

"That's biased, Carin. How do we know she's telling the truth?"

She glared at him as he frowned at the printout of her article.

"At the end of the article you have this interesting tid-bit about a court transcript that was allegedly brought here by Mrs. Virgil Earp and got lost at the hotel." He made a face. "What are you hoping for, a treasure hunt?"

"Something like that. Interest will still be high since we just had Doc Holliday Days."

"How are you so sure this transcript was brought here?" he asked. "Does she say that in her diary too?"

"Yes, she does."

Carin tilted her head upward and pushed the hair away from her face. She hoped Keith wouldn't ask to see that part of the diary because it was nonexistent. She certainly couldn't say that Allie had told her personally. Informants were usually the flesh-and-blood kind, and Carin still wasn't too sure about Allie's appearances.

He tossed the manuscript on her desk. "Maybe you'd better show me some of the research. I can't risk having you publish a story that isn't authenticated."

She opened her eyes wider and stared at him. "Keith, you know my research is always impeccable. You act as if you're afraid to besmirch the Earp and Holliday names. They're celebrities and they're dead. There's no risk of libel."

"I didn't say I wouldn't print it. I just said I want to see your research."

She held her temper in check, but just barely. The *Glenwood News* had published many a historical anecdote before without all this fuss. Why was he making her jump through hoops?

He picked up his pencil and replaced it behind his ear. "I suppose you're doing this because of your friend."

She had to remember that Keith thought it was Gideon's ancestor who was framed in the story, not Gideon himself.

"Uh, yes. I was already researching the Earps, and he gave me information passed down from his family. It checked out."

"Well, really, Carin. If you're going to defame the Earps, I think you should start with something earlier in their careers, like when Wyatt was in Wichita."

"Wichita? What's that got to do with anything?"

"You tell me. Wichita, Tombstone, what's the difference? The only connection is that Doc Holliday died here. As to your mythical court transcript, I have to see your source on that before you can put it in the paper. That's all I have to say about it."

He left her office and Carin had to consciously clamp her jaws shut. She couldn't believe he was being so picky. After a few minutes of fuming, she swiveled toward the computer and typed in a few lines, then printed them out. She marched over to Keith's desk and stuck the paper under his nose.

"Okay. I've changed what I want to print. But I want this in the issue that's going to press tomorrow. Any objections?"

He took his feet off his desk and rocked forward, taking the printout and reading it.

"WANTED: information leading to court transcript of

the Earp hearing taken in November 1881, Tombstone, Arizona. The transcript was allegedly brought to Glenwood Springs when Mr. and Mrs. Virgil Earp visited the Hotel Colorado in 1893. It is believed to have been misplaced or stolen and may still exist in this locale. Valuable historical evidence will come to light if the original document can be located. Contact Carin Sage at the *Glenwood News*."

"Is that all right? No speculation. Just an advertisement asking for information. I'll pay for advertising space in the classifieds."

He exhaled slowly. "Then you're going to hold off on your story?"

"Yes. All I want is help locating this document."

He sighed. "Okay. You win."

He got to his feet and went to the back office to hand the advertisement to the layout department. Back at her computer terminal, Carin added the codes needed to file the blurb for typesetting and sent it through the network to the typesetter. Then she leaned back in her chair and grasped the arms.

Keith's reaction had surprised her. He really hadn't wanted the story about Gideon to be published. The hemming and hawing about sources and authentic research were a blind. Not that he didn't like to see good and accurate journalism. But he usually trusted the writers after he got to know their work. Something about his reaction just didn't sit right.

She got up out of her chair and went to lean on the windowsill. She stared out into the same back alley at the same buildings and garages that had always been there. They hadn't discovered who had reached through this window and dropped a warning note onto her chair. The idea that Keith himself would do such a thing was preposterous. But neither had she expected such a violent reaction to the story about the Earps she'd hoped he would print. Could there be a connection she was missing?

The phone ringing on her desk distracted her.

"Hello."

It was Hugh. "I have news, Carin. We've booked Julius Eberly on a charge of fraud."

She sat down. "You have?"

"Handwriting on the deposit slips for the period he was overseeing the deposits shows that they were altered. Nigel has decided to file charges."

"My goodness."

"We found other evidence as well. It looks pretty definite."

She glanced out her door to where Keith had returned to his desk. "I don't suppose he's confessed to breaking into my cabin or trying to run me off the road?"

"Claims not to know what we're talking about when we asked him if he had any grudges against a certain newspaperwoman."

"I guess he wouldn't admit to anything."

"Let's hope the threats stop."

"Yeah, hope so." She thanked Hugh for calling and hung up.

Through the doorway she saw Gideon amble into the office, politely nodding to Carin's colleagues. She could see how the women followed him with their eyes. Most women couldn't help admiring a man of the West, a man used to dealing with the elements, but able to be moved by a beautiful sunset and a newborn calf. Little did they know that the charm they sensed in Gideon came not just from the West, but from the Old West.

He reached her doorway and leaned on the door frame, hat in hand. In the abrupt way she used, she ignored pleasantries and launched into the issue of the day.

"Keith refused to print the article."

His eyebrows went up in curiosity. "Why?"

"He doesn't trust my sources."

They exchanged glances, and she saw that Gideon understood what she meant. "However, he's letting me print a notice that I'm interested in any information about the court transcript allegedly brought to the Hotel Colorado in 1893."

Gideon entered the office and swung one leg over the corner of her desk and sat there. His new jeans stretched over his hard-muscled thigh. She swallowed, then continued.

"And Hugh called. Julius Eberly's been arrested for fraud."

"He has, has he?"

Gideon reached to her and ran his finger across her cheek, giving her a little shiver.

She clasped his hand in hers and leaned her head against it for a moment. Then she lowered it slowly, trying to concentrate on business. She knew that Gideon did not believe their threats had much to do with Julius Eberly at all. If so, then there was still much to find out.

"Keith's right, you know. I need some hard evidence to go with my articles. We need to find that transcript."

"What do you want to do?"

"For one thing, if Allie came through time like you did, she must have a room somewhere in town. We can make discreet inquiries as to where she might be staying."

"She might not use her real name."

"Maybe not. But we've both seen her. We can ask if a woman of her description is staying at any of the bed-and-breakfast places and check all the motels."

He nodded. "What do you want me to do?"

"I'll get a list of places to call. You can use my phone." Her lips lifted in a slight grin. "Can you use a telephone?"

He frowned as if offended. "'Course, I can. I've seen you do it."

She gave a little sigh. If the day came that they knew Gideon wouldn't have to return to the 1880s, she'd have a lot to teach him. But it would be a pleasure, she thought, instantly reminded of what he'd taught her in the intimacy of her bedroom. She pulled out a phone book and found the listing of bed-and-breakfast places.

"You can sit here. Go down this list. Just say you thought you recognized a friend of the family that you met years ago. You've forgotten her last name, but your family called her Aunt Allie. Then describe her. If you get any leads, don't leave a message. Just say you'll stop by to surprise her, that they shouldn't tell her you've called."

Gideon sat and looked at the list and the telephone. Then he gave Carin one of his dazzling smiles. "Yes, ma'am. I can do that."

His words and look warmed the cockles of her heart, but there was no time for sentimentality. If anything it spurred her to action. She would rather rip her own heart out than to lose him to pursuers, time travelers or no.

While Gideon was busy making the telephone calls, Carin pursued another line of inquiry. The Amtrak trains let passengers off opposite the Hotel Denver just as the trains had done a hundred years ago.

As she parked on the street and got out to walk along the sidewalk giving a view of the river and the five-hundred-foot hot springs pool on the other side, she envisioned Allie alighting here from a steam locomotive that would have chugged up the mountains from Denver in her day.

Carin stood for a moment and pondered how the luggage would have been removed from the luggage car and then taken to the hotel. Or would the Earps have claimed their luggage at the station and taken it to the Hotel Colorado themselves?

She didn't have an appointment with the station master at the railroad station, but he was in his small office behind the ticket booth and invited her to sit down. James Oster was middle-aged and slightly heavyset. Salt-and-pepper sideburns gave him the appearance of a man from another era. He was happy to answer her questions.

"The D&RG Railroad would have been the line that brought Mr. and Mrs. Earp here in 1893 on their visit."

Carin knew of the Denver and Rio Grande Western Railroad. It had battled with the Colorado Midland to get to Glenwood Springs and Aspen first in the late 1880s. He pointed out a photograph on the wall where many old railroading pictures decorated his office.

She went over to the picture and looked at the scene of Victorian travelers alighting at the station. She felt the tingle of excitement of being on the right trail.

"Does the D&RG office keep archives?"

"They probably do." He fingered his address file and came up with a card. "Here's the person you want to speak to. The headquarters are in Denver. If they have old records or archives, this man will know where they're kept and how you can best search them."

He copied down the name, address and phone number, and handed it to her.

"Thanks so much."

He smiled as he rose to see her out. "My pleasure. I'm an old railroader, myself, you know. Any facet of its history is interesting to me."

She shook his hand. "If I find what I'm looking for, I'll be sure and let you know."

It was a long shot, but it was just possible that while Allie's luggage was lost, someone went through it purposely. Or perhaps the contents just spilled out and the railroad personnel didn't know who it belonged to. Whether by intention or not, the transcript might have ended up in the railroad office. How easy it would have been for some clerk to set it aside, not knowing who to return it to. If only a later worker recognized it as an important document and at least saw that it was kept with the files.

Back at her office, she found Gideon leaning back in her chair, one booted foot on her desk, gazing out the window.

"No luck?" she asked.

He lifted a shoulder and let it drop.

"Well, never mind. Seems like when she has something to tell us, she finds us, not the other way around. But I have a lead."

She explained about the D&RG railroad and ended by saying that they should go to Denver tomorrow if they could get an appointment to consult the archives there.

She lifted a wry eyebrow. "Keith doesn't need me since I've filed my blurb for tomorrow's paper."

"How far is Denver?"

"About three hours east of here by car. Were you...ever there?"

He shook his head. "Do we have to go in your flying machine?"

"The plane is damaged. But I might be able to borrow Nigel's Piper Cherokee. It will save us time if we fly."

She hesitated to give the other reason for flying. That after looking in Denver, it might be time to go on to Arizona.

She thought he looked uncomfortable at her suggested means of transportation, but she hid her amusement. Of course his introduction to flying had included some unscheduled dives and rolls and being turned upside down. She didn't blame him if he didn't like being in a plane.

Once things were handled, if they ever got handled, she could show him the joys of flying on her own terms.

"I'm sure we can ask Nigel to look after your horse and Shag while we're gone."

Within the next half hour she had contacted the office manager at the D&RG headquarters on Stout Street in downtown Denver. They were all set. The historical documents were stored in a warehouse in lower downtown, but she was welcome to come and look. The office manager told her to wear old clothes and be prepared for a lot of dust. She hung up feeling hopeful.

"Maybe whoever rifled through Allie's luggage wasn't a thief," she told Gideon. "Maybe he or she was trying to establish who the luggage might belong to so it could be returned."

He was leaning against the window gazing out into the alley the way she had been earlier in the day. "Could be."

She swiveled around to look at him. Again the desire and warmth almost made her shake when she thought how tenuous their hold on each other was. Would he really stay here if he had the choice? Once the Earps were vanquished and he was free, did he really want to live here in this century and be with her?

She stood up and shoved the thought aside. She didn't want to confront the fact that he might not choose to be with her. Certainly his every action showed that he cared for her. But it was a lot to ask a man, and he was not an ordinary man.

"Let's go pack. We might be in Denver for a couple of days."

He turned his attention away from wherever it had wandered and grinned. Then he slid his arm around her shoulders and squeezed, kissing her hair as he did so. Her chest experienced a flip-flop feeling of weakness. But, since the office staff could see them through her door, she unwound herself after a quick squeeze around his waist and led the way out.

AT THE CABIN, they dined on barbecued ribs and pasta salad, procured from Carin's favorite deli, and opened a bottle of wine. The fuzzy feeling from the wine and sharing a cozy dinner with Gideon made her head buzz, and Gideon's looks from across the table gave her a promise of what was to come. As they ate, she pressed him for more details about his life in the Old West. The time ticked away, and she lost track of it altogether. Growing darkness outside finally nudged her to do something about the dishes before they turned in. And they still hadn't done anything about packing.

Carin was in the kitchen, her hands in soapy dishwater when a woman's voice startled her and she spun around.

"Your man's been lookin' for me."

"Oh, Allie, you scared me to death. Don't you ever knock?"

"I did. Your man let me in when he took the dog out."

Carin took a deep breath and reached for a dish towel to dry her hands. She was relieved to learn that Allie had not materialized through a locked back door. Here she was in a fresh yellow-checked dress and calico bonnet.

"Well, you have a way of appearing and disappearing that makes me wonder how you do it. We just want to talk to you."

"I don't like strangers, that's all."

Gideon came quietly into the room. Allie acknowledged him with a nod. "Here I am. What do you want to know?"

Carin exchanged a quick glance with Gideon. "We're going to Denver tomorrow. It's possible that the court transcript that got lost here in 1893 found its way to the railroad company that handled the luggage. They have records they'll let us look through.''

''I reckon it's possible.''

''Indeed.'' Carin pressed her lips together, unsure of how to phrase her next question. But she plunged ahead before the woman could decide to take herself off again.

''Aunt Allie, if Gideon wants to stay in the present, can he? I mean, do you know how he could do that? There's got to be a way to send your…um…Virgil and Wyatt and the others back. But…''

She flushed, hoping Gideon would come to her rescue.

He shifted his weight and found words. ''Seems right for your husband and the rest to return to their own time, ma'am. They're making a peck of trouble for us here.''

Allie moved her sharp eyes from one to the other. ''But you don't want to go back. Well, can't say as I blame you.''

Carin lowered her eyes in embarrassment, but Allie was straight-speaking, and she understood.

''You have to step through the window of time and face the Earps again,'' Allie said to Gideon. ''Send them back where they belong.''

''I'd like to, ma'am. But I'm not sure how. I'm ready to face them, but they don't seem to want a fair fight.''

''That's cause you're not on their turf. You got to go to Tombstone where this all happened.''

Carin looked up. She'd somehow known it would come to this.

''It makes sense, don't it?'' Allie gave a jerky little nod. ''They belong there. 'Course, we all left there for other parts later on, but not yet. Not till after the jailbreak and Gideon here got away.''

He scratched his chin. ''After I got away, how did people take it? Back then, I mean.''

Allie shrugged. ''Don't know much. I weren't there for

a few days." She rolled her eyes as if referring to being in the 1990s.

Carin shook her head thoughtfully. "I have copies of all the clippings from the *Nugget* and the *Epitaph* that relate to the Earp-Clanton feud leading up to the shoot-out. And I have copies of the accounts that covered the hearing. But I had no reason until now to want to see the issues that would have been printed in December of 1881, when Gideon was in jail."

She looked at Gideon. "She's right. After we go to Denver, we have to go to Tucson and look up those newspaper files. And then we'll go to Tombstone."

She looked back at Allie, who had walked toward the dining room. Carin followed.

"Would you, uh, like a cup of coffee or anything? Can we drive you back to wherever you're staying?"

"Not unless my horse can ride in that truck of yours."

"You came on horseback?"

"Well, a' course. Rented one to get around on."

"Oh, I see."

And with no more ado, Allie headed toward the front door. "I'll be getting along, now."

Carin had to hurry across the living room to follow her down the front steps. Sure enough, a small pinto was saddled and tied beside the driveway to her fence. Allie turned the horse to where she could easily mount. Her loose skirt covered her legs.

Carin stepped into the driveway. The summer night was still light enough for her to see Allie's features.

"Will we see you again?" she asked. "I wanted to talk about your diaries."

"They're in good hands. You'll know what to do with them." Allie clucked to the horse to head it toward the ridge behind the cabin. Of course, it made sense for her to come that way on horseback rather than by the blacktop road. She turned her head so they could hear her words.

"When you go to Tombstone, make sure it's during a storm. When everything's right, you'll know."

And she rode off, her bonnet soon hiding her face. They watched the pinto pick its way around the barn. Gideon came out to stand beside Carin. "Strange woman, isn't she?"

Carin put a hand to her forehead. "Strange is understating it. It's a good thing this is tourist season and there are so many people in costume for shows around town. Otherwise her appearance—and yours—might cause at least some comment."

She turned to lead Gideon back into the cabin, touching his solid arm to convince herself that at least he was real. Perhaps only now did she fully believe it had been the Earps after them all this time and not Julius Eberly in search of some sort of vengeance for her knowledge of his crimes.

"All right. Denver tomorrow since it's closest. Then Tucson to look up the news articles. You want to see what they wrote about you, don't you?"

"Guess so."

"Then we'll go on to Tombstone." She shivered as she said it and shut the door on a wind that hooted up from the valley. "I sure hope Allie is right."

More than ever she needed to see the articles Allie spoke of that described Gideon's jailbreak. She turned around and laid her hands on his shoulders as he studied her face.

"If the articles say you escaped from the jail and were never heard from again, then that might mean you never returned to your own time."

"Might."

"But if they found you again and brought you back..."

Her voice drifted off as she laid her head against his shoulder. If she took Gideon to Tombstone, how did she know she wasn't just handing him back to the time that had claimed him before?

Chapter Fifteen

The D&RG officials were only too happy to show Carin the warehouse where their archives were kept. After explaining to Hank Parsons, an old-time railroading man who knew more than anyone about the old records, they were taken to lower downtown Denver and led up a steep set of stairs in a turn-of-the-century building.

"This neighborhood's coming back to life," Hank commented as they proceeded down a wood-floored hallway that looked as if no one had been in it for half a century. Old railroading posters curled off green wainscoted walls. Office furniture from another era peered from under several layers of dust.

He stopped in front of a door with opaque glass in the top half that had the initials D&RG hand-lettered on it. He chose a key from a heavy key ring and unlocked the door. Carin peered into the room.

Boxes were stacked on top of each other, and several old oak filing cabinets were visible at one side of the room. But Hank didn't lose his cheerful tone.

"Not enough staff anymore to sort through this stuff. But if you're looking for something from the 1890s, I can show you where to start."

Carin shook her head, standing in a small aisle that led to a window they would surely need to open. She was feeling the heat already. Fortunately the overhead ceiling fan responded when Hank pulled the cord. The musty air began to move around. He propped the door open with a chair.

Gideon helped him move some boxes until the filing cabinets were clear.

Still, Carin had her doubts. "What if someone found the transcript, but didn't file it where they should have? After all, it would have been dated 1881."

Hank pursed his lips as he studied his keys to find the ones that would unlock the filing cabinets. "True. A clerk might have stumbled on it several years after your ancestor visited Glenwood. It might have gotten stored among papers from a later or earlier time. Guess all you can do is look."

Easy for him to say. He wouldn't be stuck here in this stuffy room going through musty files. But she tried to make her thoughts more charitable. She should be thankful that the D&RG, which only ran freight now that the great days of the passenger train were over, even had a place to store its old records.

"Bathroom's down the hall. Plumbing works fine. Plenty of places in the neighborhood to get a bite to eat. You need anything else?"

"I don't think so. Thank you, Mr. Parsons."

He left them to their task, and Carin could hear the floorboards in the hall creak as he returned to the stairs. Then the gloomy old building was silent.

She stared at the cartons and files. "Are you sure you want to do this, Gideon? I don't mind if you want to walk around the city and see some sights. I'll be okay for a while."

He was standing with hands on hips, an eyebrow raised at the boxes, but he shook his head. "We don't have time to waste."

She thought about Allie's instructions to get to Tombstone. "No, I guess not. Okay. I'll start here, you start there."

They hunched over their tasks, and Carin soon lost herself in old records and papers, many of which would have made enjoyable browsing. Some of the memos and account records were written in the fine handwriting style that mimicked copperplate engravings of the day. The faded ink on yellowed paper took her back to another time. It hardly seemed unusual anymore that Gideon actually came from that time.

The hours passed, and they dug through file after file, sustained by sandwiches and coffee from a deli downstairs. By five o'clock, Carin felt the first taste of discouragement. They'd gone over everything that seemed to be from the nineteenth century. Other cartons and drawers seemed to have records from a later time.

She bent backward, her hands on her waist. "I need a stretch. We'll eat some dinner and come back later if the light bulbs work in here."

Gideon unwound himself from a carton and leaned back on the folding wooden chair, raising his arms for a stretch. "Whatever you say."

They tested the lights and found them working. The summer evening in LoDo, as the locals called the old warehouse district in lower downtown, was pleasant. Just as Hank said, the area was now revived, with renovated buildings, restaurants and galleries. Union Station, a historic landmark itself, still dominated the bottom of Seventeenth Street.

At Wynkoop Brewery, a favorite local spot, they ate steak sandwiches and tried the ale. Feeling revived, Carin was willing to trudge back up to their workroom, trying to tell herself that if things worked out well, she could always bring Gideon back to Denver to enjoy what the place had to offer later. If things worked out.

With the single bulb illuminating the room, and a lamp giving a glow from the hall, Carin studied how far they'd gotten. "I think we should revise our approach."

"How so?"

"If the transcript is here, which we don't know for sure, it looks as if it might have been misfiled."

"Hmm. You mean someone put it in a carton at a later date."

She sighed. "Hank said a lot of these things were moved in here in the late sixties when the railroad gave up the offices on this floor and rented the space on Stout Street. If the transcript was stuffed in some clerk's desk and forgotten, it might not have found its way here until then."

Gideon sat on the wooden folding chair that creaked with his weight. He nudged a carton with the side of his boot. "So where are the files from the 1960s?"

The corner of her mouth moved upward in a grin. "I'm glad to see you take my meaning."

The drawers in an olive-colored metal filing cabinet revealed papers of all kinds from the 1960s. She pulled out a cardboard portfolio fastened with a string and handed it to Gideon, then she fingered slowly through the rest of the top drawer. Gideon finished looking through his batch and lifted another portfolio onto his knees to dig through.

She was concentrating so hard she was only half listening when Gideon finally spoke. "'Court Proceedings conducted before Justice of the Peace Wells Spicer, November 2nd, 1881.'"

"Yeah, that's what we're looking for."

Belatedly she realized that the tone of his voice had a quality of revelation about it. She'd been bent over for so long that she had to command her muscles to bring her back up straight.

"Gideon, you've found something?"

"Right here." She heard the grin in his voice and saw the light in his face.

He gingerly lifted a thick sheaf of paper out of the portfolio and held it toward her. It was handwritten, all right, neatly scrawled on lined paper as if it had been copied from earlier notes. She took it in shaking hands and eased back into her chair. She placed the pages on a space they'd made at the only desk in the room and began to turn them over.

"'Testimony of Sheriff John H. Behan, an eyewitness to the tragedy.'" She turned over several pages of questions and answers. "And there's his signature." Her heartbeat quickened with excitement.

She perused the next page of the historical document. "'Testimony of Joseph I. Clanton,' that's Ike Clanton. Gideon, I don't believe it. We've found it."

"Guess so."

Her heart hammered in her chest just as much as it had the first time Allie Earp had appeared in her backyard.

"We'll have to take it with us and read through it. Allie says there's testimony in here that points to the Earps' involvement with the stage robbery setup. Gideon, this could prove your innocence."

She saw the serious look in his hazel eyes and the straight line of his mouth. She knew he didn't dare feel hopeful until they verified that what Allie said was here.

He jerked his chin up. "Let's find it, then."

She carefully replaced the document in the portfolio and tied the threadbare fastening. She felt a little dizzy from leaning over for so long a time and her fingers were all thumbs. "Anything else in that carton we should see?"

He showed her where it had been stuffed beside old

magazines and correspondence of a much later time. She stood up straight and shut the drawer she'd been working in. "I guess that's it then. We'll take it with us to read over, then we'll put it in the hotel safe."

He nodded solemnly, then walked over to look out onto Wazee Street before shutting and locking the window. She knew what he was thinking. If the Earps had followed them here, they would stop at nothing to retrieve the document that pointed a finger at their guilt in the matter of conspiracy to rob a stage.

Downstairs, as she locked the front door and stepped into the dark street, she wished she'd let Gideon bring his guns. Instead, she had suggested he leave them at the hotel they'd checked into before they'd called at D&RG's offices. The galleries and storefronts on this block were dark, and she felt the hairs on the back of her neck rise as they hurried to the corner, where a streetlamp cast a pool of light and gave a feeling of more safety.

"This way."

She led Gideon across the brick street and down the other side. At least a restaurant at the end of this block invited clientele with its lighted signs and music pouring from the open doorway. Wandering downtown at night did not give a completely safe feeling until one was on the more populated streets offering evening entertainment.

She could see that Gideon too was keeping a wary eye out. Whether he was suspicious of modern city life or merely watching for any signs of the Earps, it kept him on his guard.

Carin didn't speak again until they had returned to their hotel and had taken the elevator to their floor. Gideon stood with his back to the wall, watching the hallway and stairwells while Carin got out the key.

Once they were inside and the door locked behind them, she sank onto the bed, still clutching the portfolio.

Gideon tossed his hat on a chair, checked the bathroom and closet, then examined the sash window to make sure no one could get in that way. Carin tried to make light of it.

"I guess we're jumpy, aren't we?"

"Can't be too careful."

She leaned back against the headboard, legs stretched out on the quilted floral coverlet and allowed herself to sigh. "I could use a nice bath. And then I'll delve into this." She patted the portfolio. "In the morning, we'll have t let Mr. Parsons know we found it and ask if we can make copies to take with us. I'm not sure what he'll want to do with the original."

Gideon raised an eyebrow from where he leaned on the bathroom doorjamb. "I think I can work the faucet handles if you'd like me to run you a bath."

A vision of Gideon sensuously soaping her back slipped across her mind, but she didn't let it lower her guard.

"Sounds delicious, but I'd better let you look at all this old handwriting and see if you find anything. I can run the bath myself."

He held up his hands in a gesture of surrender. "Whatever you say."

He removed his boots then stretched out on the bed while Carin disappeared into the bathroom. Though the bath was soothing and cleansed her of the dust in her hair and under her nails, she didn't dillydally. As soon as she was toweled dry, she wrapped herself in the terry cloth robe the hotel provided and joined Gideon on the bed, where he was following the transcription with one finger and muttering to himself. She sat sideways on the corner, facing him.

"Find anything?" She couldn't keep the excitement from her voice.

"Sure did. It's right here. Morgan Earp's the one who

rips up. He says that when he replaced Wyatt as a Wells
Fargo agent on the stages that carried bullion shipments
from Tombstone, he was well aware of the schedule of
treasure shipments in advance. He says that 'when an Earp
was riding shotgun on any stage, the outlaws knew to
keep away.'''

"That's interesting. He's implying that the outlaws
must have had a way to know when the Earps were riding
the stages and when they were not."

He turned back to some earlier testimony, scanned the
page and handed it to her. But the old-fashioned scrawl
was too difficult to read quickly. She would need some
time to get used to it. "What does it say?"

"It's Ike Clanton's statement about how Wyatt men-
tioned to him that neither he nor any of his brothers or
his friends were going on the stage the night it was held
up. It was the signal that a gang of Earps and friends of
the Clantons were going to disguise themselves and hold
up the stage."

She furrowed a brow over the tight handwriting on the
yellowed paper. "Wow. It really says that?"

"Sure does."

"Okay, so you put that with Morgan's statement that
the outlaws knew when to keep away, and it looks like
the Earps and the Clanton gang were in collusion at least
on some matters."

"I'm not sayin' they were friends. They weren't. But
sometimes it served their interests to act in common, like
when they wanted to rob a stage."

"And you got caught in the middle."

"Looks like."

She lowered the page carefully and put it back with the
rest. "I'm beginning to see why the Earps want this so
badly. It paints them in a bad light. And Wyatt was ob-

sessed with being thought of as a hero. He must not want
this testimony publicized.''

"That's right. He wouldn't be able to stand it if people
thought he robbed the stages he was said to protect.''

"Then he or one of his brothers left that note on my
chair in an attempt to try to get me off the scent.''

Carin was still excited, but her eyes were finally beginning to feel tired. "I won't rest until we make photocopies
of this and get the original into the right hands. Speaking
of which, we'd better take it down to the desk and put it
into the hotel safe right now. I'll make sure they sign a
receipt for it just to be sure.''

She looked up at Gideon, who was gazing at her in the
robe that had parted above one thigh. The towel she'd
turbaned around her head came unwrapped and she caught
it and dabbed at her still wet hair. She grinned at
him.

"'Course, we could leave it right here and sleep with
it under our pillows.''

"I don't think so. I've got other plans for what's going
to happen in this bed tonight.''

She didn't have to ask his meaning, but slipped into
fresh jeans and T-shirt. Then they escorted their precious
document to the desk and made sure it was secured in the
hotel safe.

HANK PARSONS shared their interest in their discovery,
though he couldn't know just how much it meant to Carin
and Gideon. There was no difficulty in making copies they
could take with them for Carin's research. He decided to
keep the original locked up in his office until he consulted
with the officers of the D&RG about donating it to the
Arizona State Historical Society.

After thanking him again for his help, Carin cautioned

him one last time. "I think you ought to keep that under guard if you decide to take it anywhere. It's a major historical document that's been missing for a century. There might be, uh, unscrupulous parties who would want to steal it."

He smiled in understanding. "Yes, it has historical value. And you're right. Someone might want to steal it and sell it for personal gain. Don't worry, I'll lock it right here in my desk drawer."

She chewed her lip for a second. She didn't know how to tell him that the parties interested in stealing it would rather see it destroyed, most likely, than sell it to anyone at all. But she felt some relief in the fact that they had at least made copies and she'd mailed one set to Nigel for safekeeping. Hank would mail another set to the historical society to see if they were interested in it.

She faced Gideon when they reached the sidewalk. The din of downtown traffic on a weekday and the high noon sun overhead made it seem like just another very ordinary day in the city. Not one in which they were changing history. He grinned down at her. "Well, that's one thing done."

"Yeah. Next stop is Tucson."

"You really think they kept copies of the papers about my jailbreak in Tombstone?"

She shrugged and they began to walk back toward the hotel where they had checked out earlier and their luggage waited for them. "It's what Allie said. And so far, she hasn't led us wrong."

They took a cab to Centennial Airport, where Nigel's plane was fueled and ready. Being the responsible pilot she was, Carin put all else out of her mind except for the pre-flight checklist. She got weather conditions before they climbed in for takeoff.

Nigel's plane was a sleek-looking, low-winged craft with a wide instrument panel, and it was easy to fly. Unlike Carin's Citabria, which was so small that Gideon had to sit in the rear, the ample Cherokee allowed the passenger to ride beside the pilot. The controls still befuddled him, but Carin could tell that he had gotten over the first horrible experience and was now beginning to enjoy the phenomenon of flight.

As they lifted off the runway and sailed into the clear blue sky, Carin felt a sense of excitement. They'd come away from Denver with exactly what they'd gone there to find. Would they have similar luck in Tucson? She scanned the horizon. The sight of the majestic Rocky Mountains to their left sent a thrill up her spine. She was excited for Gideon to be able to see the West this way.

Still careful not to become careless, she searched the area for other planes, focusing her vision in the recommended ten-degree segments for one second each. There were no other aircraft nearby. If they were still being followed, their pursuers had not commandeered another plane to attack them in these skies.

They talked little. Instead, they watched the changing landscape below. Flying over the Rocky Mountains was a sight she would never get tired of and one that had made her want to get her own pilot's license years ago.

After a smooth landing in Durango to refuel and stretch their legs, they were up again. And they were treated to a breathtaking sunset in the Arizona skies as she radioed her approach and checked her position to make sure she would avoid the airspace around Tucson's main airport. When she spotted the smaller landing strip she was to use, she radioed the flight service station for wind speed and direction.

In a few more moments she set the Cherokee on the landing strip with only a slight bump. They were down. Only after they'd taxied in and the engines had died did she turn to Gideon to see if he'd enjoyed the ride.

"Well, what do you think?"

"It made me recall the stories my mother used to read to me when I was a tyke."

"What were the stories about?"

"Fairy tales with dragons and princesses. The hero always had to rescue the fair lady and fight the dragon. But there were swans and geese that a boy could get on and fly to the moon. I feel like we just flew to the moon."

THE OLD ISSUES of the *Tombstone Epitaph* and the *Daily Nugget* were kept on microfilm at the Arizona Pioneers' Historical Society. After explaining to Gideon how a microfilm machine worked, Carin quickly located the issue of the *Epitaph* published two days after Gideon's jailbreak.

She was glad that her forehead was pressed against the machine and Gideon couldn't see her face as she began to move the levers to scan the columns of old type. She was almost afraid of what she might find. Gideon was at the machine next to her, and from his mutterings and the sounds of the film slapping against the metal casing as it came out of its roll, she could tell that he was all thumbs with this type of equipment.

But her distraction was forgotten as she came to the elongated letters announcing the headline, "Wells Fargo Agent Breaks Jail." She was afraid to breathe as her eyes flew across the words.

The sheriff's office suffered an embarrassment last evening around nine o'clock when Deputy Billy

Breakenridge was on duty. A woman purporting to be cousin to prisoner Gideon Avarest visited the jail.

The article told of the jailbreak in the exaggerated, flowery language of the day in which the reporter did not hesitate to state his opinion as he wrote the story. The end of the tale at the bottom of the page was much as Gideon had told it.

It was ascertained that the culprit had stolen the deputy's horse. The ever alert former city marshal, Virgil Earp, just now recovered from wounds received at the O.K. Corral fight, and his brothers, accompanied by Doc Holliday, took to their horses to give chase. Those who followed reported that a confrontation did indeed occur some ways out of town. But due to the storm, the prisoner was not apprehended.

As is their habit, the Earps and Holliday have continued on the trail as an unofficial posse and have not returned to town.

She scanned the rest of the page, but that was all it said. She was still too tense to mention anything to Gideon. The posse hadn't come back that night, but what about on future days?

She fast-forwarded to the next day's issue, but there was nothing reported. Impatience gnawed at her stomach.

When she didn't pause to help Gideon with his machine, a librarian came to his rescue. But she barely heard their words. She had to know if the posse or the prisoner got back to town.

She checked the issues of the *Epitaph* for the next week. There were only small articles at the bottoms of some of the pages saying that the posse was heard to be hunting the prisoner as far north as Prescott, then again that they'd crossed into Mexico and were looking for him there. It was too good to be true.

But how far should she look? A thorough researcher, she didn't like to leave any stone unturned. And if the posse kept on the trail for several months, they would have several days of looking at microfilm.

She finished her roll of film and rewound it on high speed. She was about to tell Gideon what she'd found when he made his own discovery.

"Well, I'll be darned." He was staring on his own screen at the fuzzy reproduction of an article from the *Daily Nugget* about the jailbreak.

She gave him a moment to figure out how he could move the page around and read the article that was enlarged on the backlit screen. She watched his reaction when he reached the bottom of the column he was reading. Then a slow smile spread over his face along with some pride that he'd outwitted the posse. He turned to find her staring at him.

He pointed to the article. "Just like I said."

She nodded slowly. "Just like you said."

"Well, now what?"

She reached out to touch his hand. "I looked in all the rest of the issues of the *Epitaph* for the next two weeks. All it says is the posse is still on the trail."

He focused his golden eyes on her, understanding her meaning. He gave a slow nod. "Still on the trail."

"After coming all this way, we'd better be sure. I'll search through another few weeks' worth of issues."

She returned to her task, but found little else. Either interest in the posse had dropped as other events in the life of Tombstone captured the readers' interest, or there was nothing conclusive to report about Gideon's whereabouts at the time.

She replaced the last microfilm roll in its cardboard box and switched off her machine. She didn't need to read anymore. She spoke quietly. "It's time to go to Tombstone, like Allie said to do, and send that posse home."

Chapter Sixteen

Gideon had a hard time recognizing Tombstone as the place he'd once known. He gazed at the two rows of buildings that Carin explained had been reconstructed for tourists. It took a while to figure how things had been rearranged. At least the courthouse was still standing.

The houses that remained on the back streets were so few as to be nearly unrecognizable as the booming mining camp he'd known. It gave him a weird feeling to come back to a place where he'd spent some time and see that it was dead. Just like he would be if he hadn't jumped in time.

A tumbleweed rolled up the street from the desert and caught on the boardwalk where he was leaning against a post.

Carin stood silently beside him, her hair mussed from the wind gusts that had come up. The weather was blustery, all right. Gray clouds puffed across the sky, hiding the sun intermittently. She was looking over what was left of the town. He decided to fill her in.

He pointed to an ice-cream parlor, all dressed up to look a little like it might have in the old days. People wearing clothes from his time added to the flavor, except you could tell they were playacting.

"That's where the Wells Fargo office was."

"You mean where that ice-cream place is now?"

"That's right."

"Hmm. What about the saloon over there?" A second floor wooden storefront bore the sign Alhambra Saloon.

He glanced up and down the street. "That's in the right place."

"And the hotel?" She nodded toward a restored brick building.

He gave a nod. "Nellie Cashman's old boarding-house."

As Gideon described the other changes to Allen Street, Carin began to visualize Tombstone as it used to be.

A pharmacy and gift shop once housed the Oriental Saloon. A museum selling souvenirs had held the Bird Cage Theater. A gas station had replaced Billy King's blacksmith shop. The name "Can Can" was barely visible on the front of an old wooden building that was just now being rejuvenated.

Gideon stepped off the boardwalk and into the street. Carin followed as they continued to look. A larger-than-life mural painted on the wall of the Pioneer Clothing Store showed Wyatt Earp with frock coat pulled aside to reveal the gun on his hip. He was still keeping vigil over a town now reduced to fifteen hundred souls.

They trudged on to the site of the O.K. Corral. Cardboard figures were positioned in poses of the infamous gunfight, and signs everywhere advertised a reenactment. A loudspeaker with a button to push played a recording that was supposed to tell what had happened here. Gideon strode around, scuffing his boots in the dirt, studying the wooden buildings on three sides. He finally shook his head.

"Nope. The butcher shop was here. That vacant lot over there next to that house. That's where the fight took place."

She nodded silently. A ghost town. Laughter and music came from the saloons and the shops where present-day tourists were entertained. But over here in the corral and staring at the vacant lots, she could feel the ghosts. It was their town. It always would be now.

One block over was Fremont Street. They walked toward First Street, and Gideon located the house where Allie and Virgil had lived. A freshly painted picket fence surrounded a little yard. A curtain moved inside. Carin wondered who lived there now.

She glanced up at the blustery sky. She had watched the weather channel and had known they had to get to Tombstone before tonight. Rain had been predicted for the evening. Allie said to come when it rained. Sure enough, storm clouds continued to move in from the west. Wind gusted off the desert, bringing more tumbleweeds. Her hair flew across her face.

"C'mon. Let's go back to the hotel."

He nodded. He'd seen enough. He had things to do to get ready.

They had been able to rent horses from a stable at the edge of town. One was a piebald gelding. The horses would be saddled and ready for an after-dinner ride.

Upstairs in their hotel room, Carin sat in a tapestry-upholstered wing chair and watched out the window as the clouds moved in. It was near night in the street below, darker than usual because of the oncoming storm.

Gideon polished his guns. He checked his cartridge belt. Then he slipped an extra box of ammunition for his Winchester .44 rifle into the pocket of the duster he'd worn. He checked his silver-cased pocket watch, which was ticking again, then he tied the leather scabbard sheathing his bone-handled knife to his belt.

Carin got up, checked the ammunition in her own Winchester and then put on a long duster she'd brought for the occasion. With a hat pulled low over her brow, it would be hard to tell just who she was.

A jagged Y lit the gray sky in the distance. It was far away and the crack of thunder a long time in coming. She looked at Gideon, who was setting his hat onto his head. "It's time."

Before they left the room, Carin stuck a Peacemaker .45 in the holster strapped to her hips, then covered it with the duster.

They hurried along the boardwalk as other people unfastened goods they'd been selling on their porches and carried things indoors. They reached the corral where their horses waited. Gideon tied their rifle scabbards to the saddles.

By the time they untied the reins and mounted up, drops were coming down, only a few at first. But the lightning was traveling across the sky in long, jagged streaks, sometimes touching the ground out in the desert. The wind blew through the town as people fastened doors and shut windows, lighting lamps inside early tonight. Gideon and Carin began the ride down Allen Street.

Rain started to come down steady now and trickled off their hat brims. Folks made a dash across the wide street in front of them, getting in out of the rain. Piano music drifted from the restaurants, the saloon and the hotel. It was darker now, and the horses' hooves plodded in the dirt road. Kerosene lamps shone from the street corner, blurred by the rain in front of her face.

She turned her head as boisterous laughter erupted from the Oriental Saloon and Gambling Palace. The words were painted in an arch across the glass window. A group of men staggered out onto the boardwalk. They wore high-peaked black Stetsons, long black frock coats with string ties dangling down white shirtfronts. Black trousers were drawn outside black, high-heeled boots. She knew those men.

She turned her face away, but she heard their carousing on the boardwalk under the overhanging awning, out of the rain. They were almost to Fifth Street when behind them footsteps pounded along the boardwalk from the direction of the jail.

A voice yelled out. "Prisoner's loose. Avarest broke jail."

Thunder cracked overhead as the past was momentarily recreated.

"There he goes. That's the deputy's piebald."

"Now." Gideon's voice was raised above the rain.

He and Carin slammed their heels into the horses and bent into the rain to gallop out of town. Allie had said they had to step through the window of time and face the Earps. Her words echoed in Carin's mind as she rode almost blindly beside Gideon.

"Send them back where they belong." It was as if Allie were calling to her, but she didn't have time to look around and see.

Lightning lit up the road in front of them. She trusted Gideon to know where he was going. The time had come.

Voices raised behind them, and men clambered onto horses to give chase. She rode for her life. Lightning and thunder were only split seconds apart now, followed by gunfire behind them. When another flash of lightning showed them where they were going, Gideon called out to her to follow him. He left the road.

She clung for dear life as the horses bolted across the open prairie. She prayed her horse wouldn't stumble in a prairie dog hole. Then she saw the rock outcropping just ahead and felt the ground rise beneath them as the horses took the incline. Bullets whizzed passed. The posse was following in hot pursuit.

Her heart thundered in her chest as loudly as the storm all around them. She'd never had such heightened senses. Not only was her life at stake but Gideon's as well. And some sort of time warp they had to beat. If they took Gideon, he'd stay in the past or he'd die right here. Her love for Gideon had to separate the past from the present. Allie had said they would know what to do.

They dismounted and dragged the rifles from their scabbards, taking position behind the rocks. Gideon yelled his challenge into the wind.

"Come on, you bastards. I'll pick you off one by one if that's what you want."

From the distance guns blasted. They could hear the riders getting closer.

In a second, lightning showed them four riders coming abreast across the sagebrush desert. Now she could hear their words.

"There he is," shouted Wyatt from the far left. "Shoot to kill."

Doc Holliday's shotgun blasted from the far right.

She ducked as the shot sprayed over the rocks. Gideon got off a shot in the clap of thunder that followed. In the next flash of lightning she saw the riders get off their horses and take positions down the slope, behind the rocks. Suddenly she knew exactly what she had to do. She'd be damned if they were going to get the man she loved.

"Cover me," she shouted to Gideon.

She came out from behind cover and ran toward the enemies, right into the middle of the gunfire. Her arm was extended and she fired at Wyatt, then at Doc Holliday. She was unafraid of the bullets. Her love for Gideon made her unafraid of anything. It was up to her to send them back to their own time and keep Gideon in the present.

She faced them all, determined to see justice done. Gideon would not hang for their crimes.

"Go back," she shouted in a voice that carried across the desert. "Leave him be."

She stepped sideways and ducked just before the rifles blasted again.

"Carin, get back." It was Gideon calling to her. Then he was beside her, pulling her down to her knees as bullets flew overhead.

"I love you, Gideon," she yelled to him. "You're mine from now on. I won't let you go back. Not now, not ever."

Lightning flashed. It was enough to show her the Earps' positions.

She ran forward, confronting them all.

"Let him go," she yelled, heading straight for Wyatt. "He's innocent."

It was a thrilling moment. She knew that even if she died it would be worth it. She was prepared to stake her life on her love for Gideon, and love was more powerful than the greed and politics that had made the Earps pursue him.

The wind coursed through her hair, she had a moment when she knew without question that she was a spiritual being and would live for all time, not just in this body. But for now her will was to stay in the present with Gideon beside her. All the forces of nature and eternity joined with her as she felt larger than life and faced the small men who cowered behind the rocks.

"Go back," she said and ran forward again. "Go." And she fired again in Wyatt's direction.

Their rifles blasted again, but from a greater distance.

The Earp gang was enshrouded in mist, the gunfire came from farther away. She pursued them, Gideon on her heels.

They reached the rocks where the gang had taken their positions. For a moment she saw them, translucent, as they retreated to their horses. And then they were gone.

The rain slackened. Gideon stood beside her, peering into the darkness. The lightning moved off toward the horizon, the thunder muting in its wake.

They were dripping wet, her heart pounded in her ears, but they were alone.

She threw her arms around Gideon's neck.

The Earps had gone back to their own time and Gideon had stayed with her, all hers. Justice and right would be served at last.

He squeezed her, sloshing her wet hair against him, looking over her shoulder into the distance as the rain finally stopped. A final glow from the western horizon was all that was left of the day.

Neither of them dared speak for a moment, but he held her tight. It was her cry for them to go back that had changed things. Her love had sent his enemies back in time and kept him out of their reach. In the end, she gave him his second chance at life. He'd be a fool not to take it.

"I love you, Carin," he murmured against her. "You are my twentieth-century woman, and I want to make you mine forever. Say you'll marry me."

Carin cried then from joy and a release of tension, from the exhilaration of being in love in the rain. She sobbed and laughed at the same time, wiping her eyes with her sleeve. "I love you, Gideon. You're going to stay, aren't you?"

She sobbed some more as he held her, laughing and wiping the moisture out of his own eyes at the same time.

They rode back to town as the rain quit. Without having to exchange a word, they turned down the street where Allie's house was. From the road, they saw that her porch was lit with a lantern, and she came out. In the glow from the lamp, they saw her lift her head. She smiled and nodded in approval.

Carin got down off her horse and handed the reins to Gideon. "I want to thank her."

She hurried up to the gate in the picket fence. But as she struggled with the latch, Allie called out.

"I have to go in now. I have to go back with Virgil. We got a lot of years left to live, some in California, some in other places. I gotta make sure we get away from that Wyatt."

Carin grunted as she finally succeeded in getting the gate open, but she heard hinges squeak on the screen door. Allie retreated into the dark house. Gideon got down and followed Carin up the walk. The house was dark except for the lantern Allie had left on the porch.

"Well, will you look at that." Gideon pointed out the small sign beside the door. It had been put there by the Tombstone Restoration Committee. The house was part of the historical museum. No one lived there.

Carin put a hand to the whitewashed wood and knocked. What had happened to Allie?

No one answered. Then she dropped her hand and stepped back, shaking her head slowly. "She's gone. I can't believe it. I'll miss her."

Gideon slid an arm across her shoulders. "So will I. So will I."

Allie Earp had disappeared inside a house she'd lived in more than a hundred years ago. There was nothing else they could do here.

"Come on." Gideon eased Carin off the porch and back through the swinging gate. "We have to get the horses back to their owners. Then there's a hot bath waiting at that hotel."

She smiled at him, moisture in her eyes once more, as

the horses whickered, anxious to be home to their feed bags.

"I hope there's something else waiting at that hotel." She knew her expression conveyed emotion she was free to indulge in now that Gideon was hers and hers alone.

"I think your every wish can be accommodated, madam. After all, I don't have anything else to do for the next hundred years."

They walked their horses slowly along the rain-freshened street. Tourists came out again to enjoy the summer night, passing from one building to another in search of entertainment.

All Carin wanted to do was relax in Gideon's arms. As for excitement, she'd had more than enough to last her a lifetime. She would bask in Gideon's love and spend every moment from now on looking only toward a future they could truly share together. For finally, she knew without a doubt, there was no more reason to look back.

EVER HAD ONE OF THOSE DAYS?

TO DO:

☑ at the supermarket buying two dozen muffins that your son just remembered to tell you he needed for the school treat, you realize you left your wallet at home

☑ at work just as you're going into the big meeting, you discover your son took your presentation to school, and you have his hand-drawn superhero comic book

☑ your mother-in-law calls to say she's coming for a month-long visit

☑ finally at the end of a long and exasperating day, you escape from it all with an entertaining, humorous and always romantic Love & Laughter book!

ENJOY
Love & Laughter™
EVERY DAY!

For a preview, turn the page....

Here's a sneak peek at
Carrie Alexander's THE AMOROUS HEIRESS
Available September 1997...

———————————

"YOU'RE A VERY popular lady," Jed Kelley observed as Augustina closed the door on her suitors.

She waved a hand. "Just two of a dozen." Technically true since her grandmother had put her on the open market. "You're not afraid of a little competition, are you?"

"Competition?" He looked puzzled. "I thought the position was mine."

Augustina shook her head, smiling coyly. "You didn't think Grandmother was the final arbiter of the decision, did you? I say a trial period is in order." No matter that Jed Kelley had miraculously passed Grandmother's muster, Augustina felt the need for a little propriety. But, on the other hand, she could be married before the summer was out and be free as a bird, with the added bonus of a husband it wouldn't be all that difficult to learn to love.

She got up the courage to reach for his hand, and then just like that, she—Miss Gussy Gutless Fairchild—was holding Jed Kelley's hand. He looked down at their linked hands. "Of course, you don't really know what sort of work I can do, do you?"

A funny way to put it, she thought absently, cradling his callused hand between both of her own. "We can get to know each other, and then, if that works out..." she murmured. *Wow.* If she'd known what this arranged marriage thing was all about, she'd have been a supporter of Grandmother's campaign from the start!

"Are you a palm reader?" Jed asked gruffly. His voice was as raspy as sandpaper and it was rubbing her all the right ways, but the question flustered her. She dropped his hand.

"I'm sorry."

"No problem," he said, "as long as I'm hired."

"Hired!" she scoffed. "What a way of putting it!"

Jed folded his arms across his chest. "So we're back to the trial period."

"Yes." Augustina frowned and her gaze dropped to his work boots. Okay, so he wasn't as well off as the majority of her suitors, but really, did he think she was going to *pay* him to marry her?

"Fine, then." He flipped her a wave and, speechless, she watched him leave. She was trembling all over like a malaria victim in a snowstorm, shot with hot charges and cold shivers until her brain was numb. This couldn't be true. Fantasy men didn't happen to nice girls like her.

"Augustina?"

Her grandmother's voice intruded on Gussy's privacy. "Ahh. There you are. I see you met the new gardener?"

*A woman alone—
What can she do...?
Whom can she trust...?
Where can she run...?
Straight into the arms of*

HER PROTECTOR

By popular demand we bring you the exciting reprise of the women-in-jeopardy theme you loved. Don't miss

#430 *THE SECOND MRS. MALONE*
by Amanda Stevens (August)

#433 *STORM WARNINGS*
by Judi Lind (September)

#438 *LITTLE GIRL LOST*
by Adrianne Lee (October)

When danger lurks around every corner, there's only one place you're safe...in the strong, sheltering arms of the man who loves you.

**Look for all the books in the
HER PROTECTOR miniseries!**

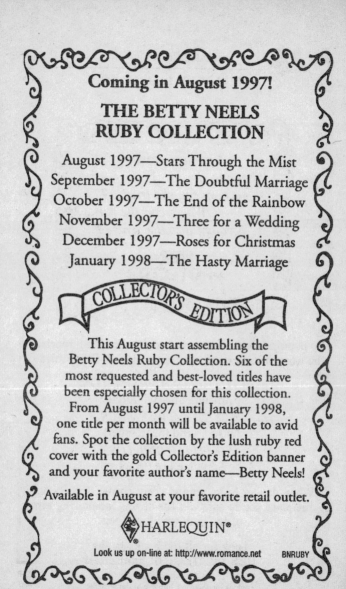

Coming in August 1997!

THE BETTY NEELS RUBY COLLECTION

August 1997—Stars Through the Mist
September 1997—The Doubtful Marriage
October 1997—The End of the Rainbow
November 1997—Three for a Wedding
December 1997—Roses for Christmas
January 1998—The Hasty Marriage

COLLECTOR'S EDITION

This August start assembling the
Betty Neels Ruby Collection. Six of the
most requested and best-loved titles have
been especially chosen for this collection.
From August 1997 until January 1998,
one title per month will be available to avid
fans. Spot the collection by the lush ruby red
cover with the gold Collector's Edition banner
and your favorite author's name—Betty Neels!

Available in August at your favorite retail outlet.

HARLEQUIN®

Let's Celebrate!

LOVE & LAUGHTER™

invites you to
the party of the season!

Grab your popcorn and be prepared to laugh
as we celebrate with **LOVE & LAUGHTER**.

Harlequin's newest series is going Hollywood!

Let us make you laugh with three months of terrific
books, authors and romance, plus a chance to win a
FREE 15-copy video collection of the best romantic
comedies ever made.

For more details look in the back pages of any
Love & Laughter title, from July to September,
at your favorite retail outlet.

Don't forget the popcorn!

Available wherever
Harlequin books are sold.

 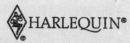 

◈ HARLEQUIN®

Look us up on-line at: http://www.romance.net

LLCELEB

HARLEQUIN WOMEN KNOW ROMANCE WHEN THEY SEE IT.

And they'll see it on **ROMANCE CLASSICS**, the new 24-hour TV channel devoted to romantic movies and original programs like the special **Harlequin® Showcase of Authors & Stories.**

The **Harlequin® Showcase of Authors & Stories** introduces you to many of your favorite romance authors in a program developed exclusively for Harlequin® readers.

Watch for the **Harlequin® Showcase of Authors & Stories** series beginning in the summer of 1997.

If you're not receiving ROMANCE CLASSICS, call your local cable operator or satellite provider and ask for it today!

Escape to the network of your dreams.

ROMANCE CLASSICS

RMCLS

HARLEQUIN AND SILHOUETTE
ARE PLEASED TO PRESENT

Love, marriage—and the pursuit of family!

Check your retail shelves for these upcoming titles:

July 1997
Last Chance Cafe by Curtiss Ann Matlock
The most determined bachelor in Oklahoma is in trouble! A
lovely widow with three daughters has moved next door—and
the girls want a dad! But he wants to know if their mom needs
a husband....

August 1997
Thorne's Wife by Joan Hohl
Pennsylvania. It was only to be a marriage of convenience—
until they fell in love! Now, three years later, tragedy
threatens to separate them forever and Valerie wants only to
be in the strength of her husband's arms. For she has some
very special news for the expectant father...

September 1997
Desperate Measures by Paula Detmer Riggs
New Mexico judge Amanda Wainwright's daughter has been
kidnapped, and the price of her freedom is a verdict in
favor of a notorious crime boss. So enters ex-FBI agent
Devlin Buchanan—ruthless, unstoppable—and soon there is
no risk he will not take for her.

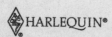